Falling

A WALKER SECURITY NOVEL

UNDER

New York Times Bestselling Author

LISA RENEE JONES

ISBN: 978-1682303948

www.lisareneejones.com

Playlist

"In My Head" by Brantley Gilbert

"You Could Be That Girl" by Brantley Gilbert

"Gone Away" by Five Finger Death Punch

"Believer" by Imagine Dragons

"i hate you, I love u" by gnash

"Make You Miss Me" by Sam Hunt

"Tequila" by Dan + Shay

Prologue

Jewel

The New York City afternoon air is cold and wet. The fog patchy and eerie. The casket black. I stand next to my father, the high-pitched sound of bagpipes cranking up my already hyped emotions. The wind gusts lifting my blonde hair, that is for once not in a neat braid at my neck, and I pull up the collar of my black trench coat, seeking shelter from the weather, though there is no escape from the grief clawing at my mind and body. In that moment, I have a renewed sense of my father standing next to me and the heaviness of his grief. He reaches for me and pulls me under his arm, sheltering me with his substantial six-foot-two frame, as if he's afraid I will die next. No. Not *as if.* That's what he fears and how can he not? We're surrounded by men and women in badges, all honoring the death of my uncle, his brother, and one of New York's finest homicide detectives. There's no way around the fact that I'm one of those badges, a newly-knighted detective, and even in the wake of my uncle's death, an eager protégée to his legendary skill. That's a hard pill for my father to swallow on a day like this one, especially when I'd once found my father's pharmaceutical empire the inspiration for a medical degree, now long abandoned.

1

My gaze lifts and I scan the thick crowd of uniforms and suits, some heads bowed, some heads lifted to the sky as if looking for answers. Many with tissues in hand and to their eyes. A sudden, strange pull has my attention lifting beyond the casket and to the right, far in the distance. I squint and bring a man in a hat and trench coat into focus. He's a good twenty-feet from the service, and yet, he's focused on us. He is too far away for me to decipher his features, and surely the scene, complete with flags, trumpets, bagpipes and uniforms, is a spectacle to see, but every instinct I own tells me he's here for my uncle. While that could be about respect, my gut says otherwise. Perhaps he's here to celebrate the death of a man who brought many a killer to justice. I do not like this man, nor the new chill that chases a path up and down my spine and has nothing to do with the weather.

The trumpets begin to play Taps and I suck in air at what feels like the beginning of the end. My father's arm falls away from me and he clutches his fist at his chest. All thought of the man in the distance fades. I take his arm, holding onto him, never wanting to let go. Too soon, the song fades into gunfire: one, two, three, four shots, and my father and I are suddenly holding each other, holding on so very tight because a killer, one who my uncle was closing in on, decided to end his life. The way a random criminal in a convenience store had ended my mother's life two years go. Just as a monster had raped and murdered my best friend in college.

The rest of the presentation drags on eternally. It could be five minutes, but it feels like an hour of emotional torture. I'm handed a flag. I shake hands, so many hands. I say: "thank you" over and over. Finally, and yet too soon, it's over. Those who've come to honor Jonathan "Big C"

Carpenter fade away and for a long time my father and I simply stand at the casket. We don't speak, but we do cry.

A long time later, I think, we walk toward the car. A single droplet of cold rain splashes down on my nose, but there is none that follows. I crave the next for some reason, perhaps because when there is nothing more to follow, there is nothing but death.

Three days later...

It's after seven in the evening on a Friday night, and word from my father's assistant is that he's worked fifteen-hour days since the funeral and has yet to offer one of his brilliant, now famous, quips and smiles. Concerned for him, my shift drags on forever until I can finally head to his office, a fancy high-rise building in the financial district that is a ghost town this time of evening. I enter the building by way of a glass door etched with "Carpenter Pharmaceuticals" to find the lobby quiet and empty. I head through the sparkling lobby, with its shiny black floors and silver-steel accents, to the security post where I greet Joe, the sixty-something guard I've known since I was a kid.

"I brought him some of his favorite cookies," I say, holding up a bag. "I want to surprise him."

He indicates the coffee shop on the opposite side of the lobby. "He's in the back corner. Been there for hours."

The grim look on his face matches his tone and stirs my concern. "He's not good," I say, and it's both a statement and a question.

His lips thin. "I have nothing but instinct and twenty years working here to go on, but no. He's not good."

Instinct and observation is golden, I think, or so my uncle used to say. "Thank you, Joe."

I turn away and waste no time finding my father in his little corner of the now-deserted coffee shop. The minute I round the corner his head lifts, his handsome face rather gaunt, while I swear his brown hair is washed in more gray than it was yesterday. The lines around his pale blue eyes are perhaps a smidge deeper. He watches me walk down the narrow aisle, his expression unreadable, lacking the normal gleeful joy he'd otherwise exude from my surprise visit.

I sit down and indicate the bag. "I brought you the macaroons you love from Aaron's Place."

"You have to quit the force. Go to medical school. Save lives that way. You're twenty-five. You can be practicing by thirty-one."

"Dad—"

He slams his hand on the table, shocking me with the display of temper. "I mean it. You have to quit."

"Now is not the time for me to quit," I say. "Now is the time for me to fight harder. I have to make up the gap that is left behind now that—"

"My brother and your uncle is dead?" he demands sharply.

"Yes," I say. "Exactly. Now is the time that I fight monsters like the one that took him from us."

"I lost my wife. I lost my brother. I cannot lose my daughter."

His voice trembles, his voice *never* trembles. He runs an empire. He's powerful. He's strong. "I know you're grieving," I say. "I'm grieving, too."

"You *will quit*. The end." His gaze lifts over my head and I turn to find his corporate attorney, Nick Rogers, approaching.

4

"We have a problem to deal with," my father says as I turn back to him. "I don't know how long it will be. Let's have dinner at the house tomorrow night and talk about your future. Yes?"

I want to argue, but now is not the time. "Yes," I say, standing up while he does the same. "I'll see you—"

He pulls me close and whispers in my ears. "Thank you for the cookies. I love you."

"I love you too," I say, tears forming in my eyes.

He pulls back and there are tears in his eyes, too. Damn it, this is killing me. I turn away from him and do the cordial thing with Nick before I exit the building to the street. I start walking toward my apartment eight blocks away, and while the night is cold, I reject the idea of wearing a coat over my pantsuit. Now more than ever, I want that easy access to the gun at my belt. I replay the conversation with my father in my head, more so the look in his eyes that was gut-wrenching even in memory. I turn right onto my street which is lined with street lamps as well as gated private walkways leading to concrete steps and private doors. I stop at my apartment, my hand on my gate, when a sense of being watched has me pausing.

My gaze lifts and reaches down the street and to my left where I find a man in a hat and trench coat. The man from the cemetery. I feel his energy. Obviously, he's here to talk to me, perhaps about my uncle, or about a case my uncle was handling. I start walking in his direction, and he holds his ground, seeming to wait for me, but just when I might make out his features, he disappears around a corner. An instant sense of urgency and loss overcomes me and I start running.

Pushing forward, I am across the street in rapid speed. Rounding the same corner that he disappeared around, I halt as I bring a cookie-cutter street into view, and find no one that resembles the man anywhere in sight. Actually, I find no one at all, but there is no way the stranger made it the full length of the street to disappear. He's here, sheltering in one of the gated entrances to the apartment buildings. The problem is that there are about a dozen buildings on either side of the street, and ten tenants in each building, and he could have slipped into a doorway easily. Or he could be hiding against a wall, hoping I won't follow. He's playing a game with me and I don't like games. I start forward, checking each building and its mini-courtyard. I cover the entire street, and then back down the other side. He's not here. He's inside a building, and probably out the back door. Finally, I have no choice but to accept that he's outsmarted me.

I don't know who he is. Maybe he's a confidential informant my uncle used, of which he had many, and he's trying to decide if he can trust me, too. Maybe it's the asshole who walked into a restaurant and shot him dead that has yet to be caught. Or maybe it's one of the assholes at the precinct who hate women cops, and see this murder as a good time to spook me. "Sick bastard," I murmur, "whoever you are," but for now, I let him think he's won when no one on my list of probable offenders gets to win. Especially my uncle's killer, who I plan to hunt down and make pay.

I return to my apartment and open the gate, walking into the courtyard, then up the stairs. I'm about to key in my code into the panel by the entrance only to find a note taped across the keypad that reads: *You're not ready yet.*

I frown and grab the note, keying in my code and then scanning the street before entering the building. I head up two flights of steps to my level, which I share with no one, and enter my apartment. I lock up and I'm about to crumple the note to toss it, but I think better. Instead, I walk through my living room to my kitchen and flip on the light before sticking that note on my fridge, and I read the words all over again: *You're not ready yet.*

I stare at the handwriting and remember the day I earned my detective's badge. I'd hurried to share the news with my uncle, finding him in his office in the basement of the department behind records, because well, he'd earned his privacy and he hated most people. Except me, my father, and his job. I'd rushed through rows of files, and found him sitting behind his old wooden desk, a cigar in his mouth. Suddenly I am right there, reliving that moment.

I hold up my shiny new badge. "I made it."

He scowls at me. "You're not ready, kid."

Those words punch me in the chest. "I'm ready. I'm been working hard and—"

"You will never be ready for the shit this job will throw at you and the minute you think you are, you've let your guard down, and then you know what happens? You die. And dying sucks."

I jerk back to the present and the cold hard memory of his casket. "Yes," I whisper. "Dying sucks." *Which,* I add silently, *is exactly why I don't intend to die any time soon.* To which my uncle would say, *"No one plans to die, little girl."*

"And yet they do," I answer as if he's here. "Which is why I have a job."

FALLING UNDER

Chapter One

Jewel

Two years later...

Hurrying down the New York City sidewalk toward my daily coffee destination, I mentally recite what has become my morning mantra since my uncle's death: *I'm not ready. I will always have a weakness, or two or ten, that I must know and battle every single moment of every day. I will never get overly confident.*

I believe those words. I will never stop believing them or living with the constant need to improve myself. Exactly why I was in karate class until late last night, despite the need to finish online homework for a medical pathology class when I got home. And despite the fact that I knew today was Valentine's Day, because while yes, it's the day of love and romance, there's a fine line between love and hate, which makes it a busy day in homicide. It's also the last day to get my favorite kind of love: the heart-shaped sugar cookies my favorite coffee shop sells, with little droplets of chocolate icing on top.

Reaching the coffeehouse, I open the door and enter the quaint little place with bookshelves filled with books and baubles on the walls, to find the line eight deep, but I am not deterred. I really need my caffeinated cup of "ready" and my dose of sugar love. Besides, I'm excused from the morning briefing since I'm celebrating a fresh arrest on my last case, and there is wrap-up I'm to attend.

The line moves quickly and I reach the halfway mark when Bethany, the sweet young college girl studying criminal justice at the counter, waves at me. "I got you," she calls out, lifting a cup and pointing at the case of food. "Cookie?"

"Yes please," I call out, my stomach growling with the very idea of that cookie, but then, I can't seem to remember what I ate for dinner. Oh yes, I can. A cherry pop tart, which means I really need to eat something for lunch that isn't sugar and caffeine.

I move two spots up the line when my cellphone rings. Digging it from my fold-over briefcase, I eye the caller ID to find my father's number. Frowning, I answer the line. "Aren't you on some European trip?"

"I took a private jet back early this morning. I need to see you."

The strain and urgency in his tone straightens my spine. "What's wrong?"

"Let's talk in person," he says, dodging the question again.

"In other words," I say, "there's something wrong."

"I'm in my office. Can you meet me there?"

"Now?"

"Yes," he confirms. "*Now.*"

The emphasis on the word "now" is all I need to hear. "I'll be there." I disconnect the call, with three people still ahead of me before I reach the counter. Too worried about my father to worry about cookies and coffee, I step out of the line and walk to the counter. "Excuse me," I say to the man at the counter before glancing at Bethany. "I have to run," I say. "Charge my account." I don't wait for a reply, turning away and heading toward the door.

Once I've exited to the street, I glance at my watch to confirm the early eight am hour, with only one other thing in my mind: my father is either in the middle of some sort of legal issue or he's sick. He's not sick. I reject that as an option. He's only fifty-five and in tip-top shape. That means he needs my professional expertise, which is only mildly comforting, considering my expertise is murder.

Since I'm only four blocks from my father's office, I take off on foot, and in barely ten minutes, I'm claiming a spot in a packed elevator in his building, and counting every floor that passes. Once the car arrives at the corporate level, I exit and hang a right to the open doors of the lobby.

Kendra, a sweetheart of a receptionist, sits behind the fancy, white built-in desk that reads "Carpenter" across the front in the same gray as the carpet. "He's waiting on you," she says as her phone rings.

"Thank you," I mouth as she answers her call, and walk around the wall behind her to the executive offices. Hurrying down a hallway, it's not long before I'm in yet another lobby, where Shelly, my father's secretary, who is probably as gray as him, but colors her hair blonde instead, sits behind a heavy mahogany desk. "Hey sweetheart," she greets, because she's been with my father his entire career, which means she's known me since before the police force made me not-so-sweet. "He's waiting on you."

"Thanks," I say, ignoring the seating area to the left to head right where double doors are now closed. I open one of them and step inside.

My father and the man sitting in front of his desk stand up. My father is my first focus and I find him to be his impeccable self. His suit is blue with a pinstripe and pressed

11

to perfection. His brownish gray hair wavy, thick, and neatly styled. His jaw clean shaven. "Come in, honey," he says. "Meet Royce Walker of Walker Security."

It's then that I size up the tall, dark, and good-looking stranger with him, who is also impeccably dressed. His suit is gray. His shoulders wide. His hair long enough to be tied at his nape. His features hard and handsome. "Nice to meet you, Detective Carpenter," Royce says, extending his hand.

I step to the visitor seat opposite him and accept his hand for a quick, firm connection that ends with me folding my arms in front of me. "What's going on?" I ask, looking between them.

"Let's sit," my father says.

I want to stand, but doing the opposite of what you want to do requires the kind of discipline that catches criminals, which is why I sit. Once I'm firmly planted in my seat, my father and Royce follow. They share a look, and when it lasts too long, I focus on my father. "What is going on?"

"I'm navigating a merger for the company with a competitor. Tensions are high. Protests have been frequent. Royce's company is taking over the security for the company, and for that reason, I felt you should get to know him. His firm is highly respected. In fact, they're impressively in charge of every positive change to airport security in the past three years."

"It's a constant battle to get the right people to listen," Royce comments, "and a battle we fight daily. Additionally," he adds, "I'm a former FBI agent and my entire team is made up of highly skilled, highly educated individuals. My youngest brother is ex-ATF and married to a former FBI agent. My middle brother is a former member of SEAL Team Six."

12

"You're making your case to me," I say, and then look at my father. "*You're* making his case to me and you don't justify your actions ever. Translation: You deal with threats all the time, but there's a new one and this one is different. You hired Walker Security for personal protection."

"Yes," my father confirms. "I did."

The firmness of his voice, the lack of inflection, tells a story. This is serious. "Have you contacted the police?"

"I felt I should talk to you before I made that particular call," he states. "The threat is against you, Jewel."

I blanch, but recover quickly. I get threats. It's part of my job. "What kind of threat?"

"There are a series of notes that fixate on you as the target," he replies.

"Can I see them?"

"They're with my team," Royce states. "I wasn't expecting your father or this impromptu meeting this morning, or I would have brought them to you."

"An explanation that indicates knowledge of the notes for an extended period of time," I comment. "How long?"

"Four days," Royce replies.

I look between him and my father. "We'll circle back to that timeline. The general tone of these notes is what?"

My father responds. "One example that sticks out: She's a chip off the old block, so it has to be her."

"You've gotten letters before," I say. "Why are these different?"

"I've never gotten letters focused on you," my father states. "That's what's different."

"I'm a detective," I say. "I'm sure this fool knows that. Don't let them get to you."

"We aren't simply dismissing this," my father replies, dismissing my statement instead. "Royce is putting a man on you."

"His name is Jacob King," Royce adds. "He's one of our best and—"

"No," I say in instant rejection. "I do not need a man on me." I laugh without humor. "Believe me, I really do not need a man at all. Have him protect my father."

My father leans forward, jabbing a finger at the desk. "You will do this," he orders. "You will take this protection."

My lips thin with his tone, which takes me back two years, to his demand that I quit my job. It had taken me two weeks to calm him down then, but I try to reason with him now anyway. "I have a job to do. I can't babysit a security guard. It could put lives in danger."

The intercom buzzes. "Jacob is here," Shelly announces.

"Meet him," my father says.

"He's one of our best," Royce reiterates. "He's quiet. He doesn't interject himself into conversation or activity unless it's critical, which is why I felt he was a good match for you."

"I'm a detective," I say. "I'm surrounded by detectives and members of law enforcement. I'm safe."

"You're surrounded by people who have jobs to do that don't include protecting you," my father says.

"Actually," I argue, "we all protect each other."

"Just meet him," my father presses, his tone and body language dogmatic, his fear for me palpable. "What harm is there in meeting him?"

"Fine," I concede, certain he will have no peace until I agree, no matter how illogical his request. "I'll meet him."

My father wastes no time hitting the buzzer. "Send him in," he orders, standing up with myself and Royce following.

"Work it out with him," my father urges. "Do this for me. Please."

The deep burn in his voice, and the look of desperation in his eyes, which I haven't seen since right after my uncle died, is what guts me. "Fine. I'll figure it out with him."

"He can shadow you," Royce suggests. "You'll never know he's there."

I whirl on him. "Of course, I'll know he's there," I say, "and it'll distract me from my work."

"You won't know he's there," Royce repeats as the door behind me opens.

"I'll know he's there," I insist, turning to find a GI Joe version of Royce Walker with short military-style brown hair. He's also sporting an abundance of brawny muscles which are impossible to miss considering he's wearing a snug black T-shirt and jeans that hug every single damn inch of him. Not know he's shadowing me? Seriously? How can any woman not know this man is shadowing her?

He lifts his hands to indicate the coffee and bag he's holding. "White mocha and sugar cookies. You left your order back at the coffee shop."

Realization hits me, and I do an angry, slow rotation to face Royce. "You had him following me this morning?"

"For the past four days," my father says. "I didn't want to tell you any of this on the phone and I flew back the minute I got a break in Europe which came last night, right along with another threat."

My jaw goes slack and I look at my father. "Four days?"

"Yes," he confirms. "Because I love you. And I need you to make this work *for me*."

My cellphone buzzes with a message and I grab it from my bag, to find my boss asking for my presence. I stick my phone back in my bag. "I have to go."

"And you'll do this for me?" my father asks.

He is rarely unreasonable, but when he is, it's usually about me and my safety. He's fucked up over the loss of people he loves, and I get it. I am, too. I hang photos of dead people around my house. And so, I give him peace of mind. "I'll work it out with Jacob," I say, but I don't leave room for more questions or clarification. I turn away and walk straight for Jacob, but I don't stop. He reads the message to back up and he does just that. He backs up and allows my departure, and damn it, he smells way better than I want him to smell. Why am I even noticing how he smells?

Frustrated, I don't wait on him. I make my way back to the main lobby and then the elevators. I feel him at my back, pressing forward, all macho alpha expectancy, but then, I'm used to his kind. Mr. Thinks-He-Can-Save-The-World-Better-Than-Anyone-Else and look better than most doing it.

I punch the call button to the elevator and the doors open. Wasting no time, I enter the car, and when Jacob, predictably at this point, joins me inside I hit the lobby button. After all, he can't. His hands are filled with my coffee and cookie, which he got after I left the coffeeshop. And I didn't know he was there. That idea burns inside me and the minute we're sealed inside alone, we face each other, and if he expects me to fade to the other side of the small space, I do not. I step up to him. "You followed a detective?" I demand.

"Yes," he says, offering no apology or explanation, his expression hard, unreadable.

"That's what I call illegal in about ten ways I can recite if needed to, starting with stalking. Do it again and I will have you arrested."

"I take it that this means that you have no intention of keeping your promise to your father back there?"

Promise.

I want to hit him for using that word.

"I said I'd work it out with you and I am. You get a free ride. Say you're with me and then go to the gym and pump up your already pumped-up muscles some more. Or go see a movie. Just go do it all without me." The elevator stops, and I step away from him as several people join us. He doesn't let me get away though. He moves in my direction, and before I know it, his shoulder is pressed to my shoulder. Damn it, I'm oddly, intensely aware of this man. Okay, it's not odd. He's gorgeous and big and I managed to have this specimen of man follow me and I never saw him. My uncle's voice plays in my head: *You're not ready yet, kid.*

Damn it, I'm so obviously not ready.

Then the doors open. I exit and leave him behind again, only he's still on my heels. I am midway across the lobby and I stop to find him right behind me. "Stop following me," I say.

"I was a Green Beret."

"And?"

"And I'm not what any detective expects. I could fuck you and make you beg for more and then have you beg me to kill you afterward. That's how good we are."

"Did you really just say that with a straight face?" I challenge.

"I got your attention," he states. "And that's what I was after to make a point. I'm not what you're used to knowing. That's why you didn't know I was following you. And we both know that's why you're upset right now."

He's arrogant. And worse, he's right. That is what's bothering me. And now, I really am pissed off at him or me.

Or both of us. I take the coffee and bag from him and when our hands touch, heat darts up my arm. I'm definitely pissed at him. "If I was any other woman," I say, "your arrogant good looks, along with this coffee and cookie might make my panties wet. But I'm not any other woman. I'm not what you're used to knowing. *Goodbye*, Jacob 'Green Beret' King."

I turn and leave. A few steps into my departure, I know that he isn't on my heels, but that means nothing. There's no question in my mind that I haven't seen the last of Jacob King.

Chapter Two

Jewel

I enter the subway car with no signs of my new knight in shining armor anywhere in sight, but that means nothing. He's been following me for four days, and I never knew he was there. The man is gorgeous and the size of a treehouse, and I *never* knew he was there. I'm furious with him over this. No. No. It's easy to be furious at him. That's why it was my first reaction. My anger belongs to me. I mean, the man brought me a cookie and coffee. I just hate that I didn't know he was following me. And the thing is that I'm *always* aware of my surroundings. I'm not foolish enough to do otherwise, which means that good-looking arrogant asshole of a man, is just that damn good.

Which means I'm not that damn good.

A prospect that I contemplate as the car starts moving and I stuff my cookie bag in my briefcase, because anyone who eats on the germ fest that is the subway is taking their lives in their own hands. I might be stupid enough to miss a Green Beret, but I'm not that stupid. But cookies are good. You walk or run a little extra and get rid of the damage. The wrong man is another story. He sticks around. He makes you awkward and uncomfortable, even if you try to pretend you aren't awkward and uncomfortable, because it shows. It always shows, which is how you catch bad guys. Jacob King doesn't make me awkward and uncomfortable. But he does have my attention. What would happen if I was up against a criminal that was an ex-Green Beret? I'd lose and I can't lose. I fight for those who can no longer fight for themselves. I fight for their loved ones.

Reaching the door of the precinct, I toss my now empty coffee cup in the trash and pass through the mandatory security before heading up several flights of stairs that I could have avoided by using an elevator. I plan to enjoy that cookie. Gotta do my walking now. I quickly reach the third level, where the detective bullpen is located and head to my desk, which is one of about a dozen in the open room. Random crap is going on all around me, of course, which is the norm. DJ, one of the greener detectives, is interviewing a pretty blonde who is crying. Kasey, a more seasoned detective than DJ by way of age and experience, is on the phone, and makes kiss-kiss lips in my direction as I walk by. I shoot him the finger, because I've learned to set aside my mother's insistence on proper manners, and speak the language of detectives.

I keep moving through the row of desks and Dennis Wylie, who most of us think isn't right in the head, shouts out, "I love you, Little C."

I like that nickname. Little C reminds me, and those around me, that I'm the Big C's niece. "I love you too, Little D," jesting about his man part, which earns me laughter and a snappy crude remark from Dennis.

With a smile on my lips, I just can't help, I sit down at my desk across from David Rodriquez, who's a seasoned detective at thirty-six, and single because despite his hotness, he's an asshole to everyone but me. And it only took me three and a half of my four years with him to achieve that sweet spot. "I saved you a chocolate donut," he says, indicating said donut on my desk. "I thought it might keep you from being a bitch today."

I grab the donut and take a bite. "Sorry. I still feel like a bitch today." I pick up the stack of love notes on my desk that the guys write me every year, most of which are naughty. They think they're funny.

I grab a folded red heart and read: *Roses are red, violets are blue, my gun is bigger than your gun, Little C.* I smirk and toss it in the trash. "Real adult, guys," I murmur as my gaze catches on the big red envelope that reads: *Jewel* across the front.

No one here calls me Jewel, so whoever wanted to stand out, has won. I'm curious and I reach for it, finish my donut, and pull out a card with a simple heart on the front. Flipping it open, I read: *Finally, it's our time.*

It's kind of a creepy statement, but that doesn't say much, considering this crowd, but something about it still manages to hit an uncomfortable chord in me. I turn the card over and study the handwritten "Jewel" there, confirming there is no address anywhere on the paper, which means this is for sure an in-house delivery. And the neat printed handwriting looks familiar, too, but I can't place it. "Who wrote this?" I call out, holding up the card.

"Carpenter!"

At that shout by my boss, Norman Ross, I set the card down and stand up. I'm already walking when Rodriquez yells, "For the record, Little C. You still *look* like a bitch, too."

I shoot him the finger around my back without even turning, and bring the corner office into view, where Lieutenant Ross stands in the doorway, his suit well-starched, a streak of gray touching his dark hair at each of his temples. "'Bout damn time you got here," he grumbles just to grumble since I don't work a set schedule. He's grumpy like my uncle, but then, it fits. They were best friends who shared a birthday, both fifty-one a week before my uncle died.

My boss disappears into his office, with the obvious expectation that I follow. By the time I clear the entrance, he's rounded his desk and is standing behind it with a key dangling from two fingers. "What's that?" I ask, leaving the door open, because you don't shut his door unless he tells you to shut his door.

"Your reward for your fortieth closed case," he replies. "The key to Big C's old office and your pick of the cold cases you obsess over from this point forward."

My heart jumps in my chest. "You're letting me have his office and the cold cases?"

"You stay in rotation," he says. "You work fresh cases, but if you can fit in the cold cases, I'm going to give you the same confidence I gave your uncle, and I know one won't hurt the other." I reach for the key and he closes his hand around it. "Don't make a fool of me."

"I won't. Fresh cases still come first of course."

"Your uncle was a good detective. A cranky old man, but the best of the best. He could have had my job ten years before *I* had my job. He chose not to take it. Do you know why?"

"No. He never said."

"Because he didn't want to deal with wet behind the ears babies like you unless it was you."

I laugh. "Sometimes he didn't want to deal with me."

"Neither do I," he replies. "But I'll do it for him."

He studies me a moment and then opens his hand to allow me to take the key. "Go. Make him and me proud."

"I will," I say, palming the key and I'm out of the office, and headed through the bullpen in an instant. I don't stop at my desk. I'll grab my junk later. I don't answer any shout-outs either. I'm through the bullpen and at the narrow stairwell leading to the basement in no time flat. I travel four flights of winding steps to enter the windowless basement some would call a cold, dingy hell and that I call success. I hurry down the hallway to the steel door and open it, entering a massive room lined with rows of files. In front of it all is a desk. Behind that desk is Becca, a fifty-something black woman who is more stunning than most twenty-year-olds, despite the severe way she pulls her hair back and her hard expression.

I show her the key. "I'm with you now."

"I heard," she says dryly. "Don't get loud. Don't get in my way."

She also has a bad attitude and can level even the hardest of men with a few words. I love her, which is why I give her a hard look and say, "Don't get in my way."

We both burst out laughing because we're the bad bitches of this place that is far too male, and I start walking past her desk. Once I'm in the center of two rows of files that are long and high, my fingers drag over the files, which represent a history of crime and law enforcement so deep and broad, that even I cannot fully conceive of its meaning. But I respect the history, and the answers that can be found in the history that tends to repeat itself, even though the names, shapes, and times, vary. At the end of the row, I cut right and stop at the only door in the room. I stick the key inside and open the door.

Stepping inside, dust tickles my nose but so does the hint of sandalwood that reminds me of my uncle. I flip on the light to find the old steel desk and stacks of boxes here and there. I shut myself inside and there is a pinch in my chest and eyes. God, I miss him, and as I flash back to the funeral, and the sound of the rifles going off, I'm reminded that my father's actions are driven by fear. Fear that I can't wholly dismiss. It's a part of loving someone with a badge.

I round the desk and sit down, pulling my bag's strap over my head and setting it on the desk. It's then that my cellphone rings from inside it. I dig it out and note the unknown number that as a detective I can never ignore. I hit the answer button. "Detective Carpenter."

"You didn't eat the cookie."

"Well if it isn't Mr. Green Beret himself," I say at the sound of Jacob's voice. "I hope watching me ignore food is interesting. And how are you calling me? I didn't give you my number."

"I'm resourceful," he says.

"You asked my father."

"If I'd done that, he'd know that you've attempted to reject me."

"Attempted?"

"Are you still trying?"

"I already did. Because you deny my rejection does not make it obsolete. And how did you know I didn't eat the cookie? You weren't on the subway car with me."

"I didn't until you just confirmed it, but it was an easy guess since only a stupid person eats on the subway. And we both know you're not stupid. Which is why I know that you'll come around and use me for the resource that I am."

"You really do think a lot of yourself."

"I have no choice," he says. "The minute I doubt myself is the minute someone dies on my watch."

"The minute you think too much of yourself is the minute you think too little of your opponent. That's when you, and/or someone, dies."

"According to you, I already do think too much of myself, and so far, I'm not dead. Nor do I intend to die or let anyone under my care die."

"I'm not under your care. Take a vacation."

"I can't do that," he says. "If something happened to you on my watch, I'd have to live with that. And I've seen and lived with a lot of bad shit. You getting hurt won't be on that list."

"It's a few notes from a protestor trying to rattle my father over his merger," I say. "I'm a detective. You have to see the insanity of me needing protection over this." I frown. "Unless there's more to this than I know."

"Nothing I'm aware of at this time, but if that changes I'd certainly inform you immediately."

"Then we're back to my point," I say. "Involving Walker Security in this matter is an overreaction by my father. If you follow me—"

"You'll cuff me?"

"Was there a sexual undertone to that question, Sergeant?"

"Major," he corrects. "And no, ma'am. I'm always completely professional. Just letting you know that I'll go where you lead."

I smile despite myself. "If only it were that easy."

"Easier than you might think."

"Easier than *you* might think," I say. "Because I've never cuffed a man that I didn't shoot first. You've been warned."

"Sounds dangerous," he says. "But if I scared that easily, I wouldn't be the one assigned to protect you. Look, Jewel—"

"Detective."

"Jewel," he says firmly. "Because I'm talking to the part of you that isn't bulletproof right now. Loving people like us is not easy. I know you know that."

"Of course I know that."

"Your father loves you."

"I know that, too."

"Then you know that he's why I have you now and more importantly, you have me. And while it's not the ideal situation, despite that fact, I'll stay out of sight, unless necessity deems that impossible. You won't know that I'm there unless you need me."

And with that highly inaccurate statement, he actually hangs up, but I don't call back to point out the obvious, which is that, he's wrong. After meeting Jacob King, even if I don't see him, I'll know he's there.

Chapter Three

Jewel

My phone buzzes with a text message and I glance down to read: *Call me if you need me —Jacob*

Great. I'm officially in the most committed relationship of my adult life with a hot ex-Green Beret that I just met and probably don't like. I grab my phone and dial Kendra. "How soon will the merger be done?" I ask after our greeting.

"Two months at the most, if we're all lucky."

Her line rings. "I need to grab that, but did you need to talk to your father?"

I could talk to my father and insist he fire Walker Security, but to what end? Jacob was right. Loving someone like us isn't easy, and if my father needs this right now, he needs it. "I'll call him later," I say. "Take your call."

We disconnect, and I accept the inevitable. Jacob King is here to stay, at least for a month or two. Fortunately, and unfortunately, I deal with pushy, ego-inflated men every single day of my life. I might not know how he managed to stay off my radar while following me, *yet*, though I will before this is over, but I do know how to set boundaries. And I will.

I open my uncle's top drawer, and the realization that it's mine now punches me in the gut. Setting aside the emotion that would appall my uncle, I start digging for any inspiration for a cold case that merits my attention. One drawer leads to another and I end up on the floor, digging through boxes, but nothing really grabs my attention.

I skip lunch to keep working right up until I head to the DA's office to discuss the recent arrest of a man who killed his pregnant wife and really needs to burn in hell. With the growl in my stomach, I dig into the bag with my cookie in it from my briefcase to discover there are three cookies, not one. I approve. Jacob might be single and hard to love like me, but he knows how to make-up with a woman. I take a bite of my sugary delight and as always, memories of the ones my mom used to make flood my mind, and with that memory is motivation to do my job and do it well.

That leads me back to Jacob, and those boundaries I need to set. I don't like how he taunted me this morning, which to me indicates a need to showboat. Showboating could place him in the center of my work, and that could jeopardize the integrity of my investigations, which would be unacceptable. Not only that, he pushed my buttons. I need to understand this man before I agree to let him shadow me for what could be two months.

I pull my MacBook from my briefcase and pull up Walker Security, which has nothing about Jacob on the site. Just lots of impressive data on their services, including a contract with the local police department. It doesn't say in what capacity, therefore I can't assume that means they'll respect the integrity of my investigations, but it's a small vote of confidence.

Trying another tactic, I shut my MacBook and pull the keyboard connected to the monster computer sitting in front of me closer, and search the database for Jacob King. He's not in the criminal database. Of course. I knew he wouldn't be, but it's just automatic that I check. A few phone calls and I determine he is indeed a Major, thirty-five, and well-decorated, but most of his file is top secret. I'm not going to learn much about this man that I don't learn from him. But maybe I can learn about men like him. I pull up the cold case records and type "Green Beret" and get one hit. I grab a pen and paper and write down the case number. A few minutes later I have that file in my hand and I'm intrigued. Jesse Marks killed his family and then disappeared.

The alarm on my phone goes off and I shut the file, stick it in my briefcase and grab another stack of files from my uncle's desk—no. My desk. I hurry out of the file room, wave to my new co-inhabitant and when I would normally head upstairs, I smile and change my mind. Let's see how good my new Green Beret shadow really is when he has a real opponent. If he's good, he'll anticipate my next move. I head to the garage, and walk through rows of cars, to exit to the street. I start the eight-block walk, and I've made it three when I feel him. I do. I feel Jacob nearby. I need to know how he does it. I pull my phone from my pocket and dial his number.

"Do you know where I am right now?"

"Yes."

"Tell me," I press.

"The corner of Fifth and Broadway."

"How do you know that?" I ask.

"It's my job to know," he replies. "But then we both knew you were going to take the rear exit. We both knew you were going to test me."

I don't confirm nor deny that statement. "What if I'd gone out either the front or side door?"

"I'd have known," he says without hesitation.

"How did you watch every door?"

"Cameras."

Suddenly, I wonder how many people are watching me. People I don't know, who will be following my case work. I can't let that happen and not go to my boss and I'm not going to make a fool of myself over something this ridiculous. It's time to set some rules. I end the call and walk toward the massive church to my right that draws tourists and me right now, I climb the steps, then turn to scan the streets but I don't have to scan long. Jacob appears on the steps, wearing a thin, black leather jacket, and heads my direction, all loose-legged swagger, and hot, lethal man. Professional observations, of course, I tell myself.

He stops one step below me, and I still have to look up to look into his eyes, which are steely-gray and intelligent. "How many of you are following me?" I ask.

"There's a rotating team."

"How many?" I press.

"Two to four at any given time."

"Oh no," I say in instant rejection. "This set-up doesn't work for me, or the integrity of my investigations, or those investigations that are being conducted near me. You have to see that. Walker is contracted with the NYPD."

"We are," he says. "And I hope that gives you confidence that you can trust our team."

"I don't even trust everyone who works for the NYPD. I don't know you. I can't begin to trust you. I can't even check you out fully. Your military file is top secret."

"Yes," he says. "It is."

"That's it? 'Yes. It is.'"

"Yes. That's it."

"Then how am I supposed to get to know you?"

"Aside from the obvious premise of actually talking to me, I have references, which were provided to your father. I'll ensure you get a copy. I can have them to your email within the hour."

"Personal references?"

"Yes. People who have worked directly with me, one of whom is the owner of Riptide."

I don't have to ask what Riptide is. Everyone knows that they are one step up from Christie's auction house these days.

"Do you have a card with an email?"

I slip my hand inside my jacket pocket, where I always keep a supply of business cards, snag one and offer it to Jacob. He reaches for it and our fingers brush, something that probably happens ten times a week to me, but this time is not one of those times. This time, heat rushes up my arm and my eyes jerk to his, the awareness between us instant, jolting.

I pull my hand back and cut my gaze just long enough to recover before I look at him, composed and focused again. "The cookies and the coffee," I say.

"What about them?" he asks, sliding the card into his pocket.

"That was a cocky show-off move, meant to prove you're better than me. Don't do that again or we won't find common ground. Without common ground, I'll have no choice but to go to my father, and end this over-reaction." I walk around him and start down the stairs.

"Your mother's bakery that was sold when she died makes those cookies," he says.

At those words, emotions I don't let myself feel or even name slam into me and he successfully stops me dead in my tracks. I stand there for two beats before I turn to find him facing me. I don't like anyone to occupy this private place he's taken me, and I close the few steps between us. "What are you trying to prove?"

"I'm not big on proving myself with anything but knowledge and actions, which was my intent. I knew today was the last day they make those cookies until Easter. And since I understand more than most what that might mean to you, I didn't want to start our relationship off by denying you something you have left of her."

"Words on paper do not make you understand anything I feel or think."

"Nor would I presume to understand the aftermath of death, if I didn't know death quite intimately."

Just like that, he's torn down the wall that I've spent years building. And just like that, he's seen to the other side, stirring emotions in me in the process that I don't want to feel. That I quickly smash, right along with every question he's made me want to ask him, about him, about death. "If you're lying about your motives to bring me those cookies," I say, my voice low, tight, "if you're using this to manipulate me, I really will cuff you and I will shoot you."

His eyes narrow ever so slightly, before he takes my bait, and asks, "You mean shoot me and then cuff me, right?"

"No," I say, "because if I shoot you first, it's over for you. You won't have to wait, and anticipate, the pain of the bullet."

"And I'd deserve that and more," he says, with just a hint of lift at the corner of his mouth, that quickly fades as he adds, "but I'm not that guy, detective. I wouldn't do that to you or anyone."

I study him, the way I do everyone who tells me that they're innocent. I read him the way I read everyone, the way I see beneath the surface of people others do not, and thus prosecute bad people that others would not. And I decide that he isn't one of those bad people. I decide that I actually believe him. "I don't like that you know this about me," I say.

"If I don't know you, I can't protect you."

"You don't get to know me at all. I didn't sign up for this and I didn't invite you into my private space. You just barged into it."

"I didn't understand your motives to buy those cookies because it's my job to understand you. I understood because of who life, or rather death, has made me."

"But you only had that opportunity, because you researched me for a job that I didn't ask you to do."

"And I get that. I do. I understand that this isn't what you signed up for, and that you don't believe that you're in danger."

"Do you? And be honest. Don't answer because it's how Walker Security wants you to answer to keep this job."

"We are the best at what we do. In many cases, the skill sets of our team allow us to do what no one else can, or will, do. In other words, as an asset, I could be making the company far more money than I am by following you around."

"But yet here we are. Why?"

"Royce thinks a great deal of your father. He's a good man in a sea of corporate monsters."

"He is a good man, but you've talked circles around my question. *Do you believe that I'm in danger?*"

"I believe the Carpenter operation needed a major security update years ago and the very fact that it hasn't been done leaves us with inadequate data to fully evaluate any threat to you, your father, or the staff and operations. So, in the context of caution, here's my proposal to you.

Work with me. You won't have to think about the notes or look over your shoulder. You catch a killer. Let me cover your back."

It's more a question than a demand, and yet, everything about this man is a demand that I'm not used to experiencing. And I know a lot of demanding men. "We'll talk later," I say, leaving out any commitment of when and where. I start to turn and hesitate on unfinished business. "I don't usually make assumptions. They cloud reality and investigations, but I made an assumption about you. For that, I'm sorry."

"You weren't completely wrong about me. If I have to be to be an asshole to protect you, I will be and I won't be apologetic like you are now."

"That statement assumes my stupidity at some point and that doesn't say partnership at all."

"That statement prefaces any action I might take by necessity, not choice."

"If that necessity means that your team stakes out a police facility, that's unacceptable and we have to talk about that and more. Just not now."

"When?"

"I'll be in touch. Until then, stay in the shadows and away from the precinct. I don't need questions inside my department that lead to problems and neither do you and Walker Security." I turn and actually start to walk this time, but damn it, I can't leave yet. I rotate and face him. "Thank you for the cookies and the coffee. And I think I sound angry as I say that but I'm not. It's sincere."

"You're welcome and they're damn good cookies. I greedily kept one for myself."

"They were better when my mother made them," I say, and damn it, my voice hitches, and my response confirms he was right. The cookies matter to me. I turn away from him and this time I don't stop walking. I have a meeting to get to, and damn it, what is this man doing to me? He just saw more of me than I've let any man see in years. And I let him, I opened the door he had only cracked, and I did so despite the fact that I still don't even know if I like the man.

FALLING UNDER

Chapter Four

JACOB

I fall into step a short distance behind her, my blood pumping, adrenaline punching through my veins. I let the damn cookie thing get personal. What the fuck was that? I don't do personal on the job. And yet, at multiple times today, I've damn sure been thinking about pulling her hair free from the prim and proper braid she wears to work and kissing the fuck out of her. And I damn sure have my eyes on both our surroundings and her tight little heart-shaped ass.

One block. Two. Three. She weaves in out of the clusters of bodies that thicken as we near the DA's office. I keep pace, ensuring that she is never out of sight, but then, I have back-up. Finn, a new guy, and an ex-Chicago detective himself, is in the surveillance van and I have Adam, king of disguises, and ex-Navy SEAL on foot. Both are connected to me with the earpiece in my ear that I turned off when talking to "the detective" as she wants to be called, and turned back on when we'd started walking. I told myself I'd done that to protect her privacy, but I'm not one to fool myself long. I'd done it to protect both of our privacy.

Jewel, Detective-Fucking-Carpenter, I mentally correct, crosses the street, and I'm not far behind her. She's just reached the other side, stepped over the curb, and is now in the last block of her walk as I step into the road, when a homeless man lunges at her. I move quickly, doubling my pace to save her, but then she's no damsel in distress. She uses a judo move I know she learned from her pre-karate college days and with a kick of her leg, the man is on the ground. She then reaches into the bag at her hip, tosses money down to him, and then moves along. As if it never fucking happened, which reminds me that she was a beat cop for two years before moving into a detective training program.

I head toward the homeless man, but a gut feeling, and the certainty that Adam is watching Detective Carpenter, has me pretending to throw something in a trash can, and then tie my shoe to watch him. He lifts to his elbows, grimaces at the money, and looks in Detective Carpenter's direction. He then stands up and begins to follow her, pulling a phone from his pocket and placing it to his ear. He's on that call all of thirty seconds when the phone is back in his pocket and he cuts right into an alleyway. Agile, comfortable, not a homeless person who is malnourished and weathered in ten different ways at all.

Suddenly, my gut feeling that there was more to that man and to the threat against the detective than meets the eye that I've had from the beginning is feeling pretty damn validated. "Did you see that?" I ask, speaking to my team through my mic.

"I'm on him," Finn assures me.

I double-step and catch up to Jewel just as she reaches the door of the DA's office building. I stop walking and step to a wall beside a bank to give her room to enter and head to the elevator. A man exits as she intends to enter, tall, dark, good-looking enough for a guy I decide, one I place around forty-ish, and he's impeccably dressed. He greets Jewel, and it's clear in the way his expression lights that he knows her, but she doesn't react with recognition, but rather the kind of obvious hesitation she didn't show with me. But then, anger drove her reaction to me and damn she's sexy when she's angry.

Fuck.

Where did that come from?

I refocus. The man offers her a well-manicured hand, the kind that has never seen a hard day beyond a golf club and a bar in a fancy fluffed-up gym. I have an overwhelming desire to stop her from taking that hand. Maybe it's that gut feeling about danger that I've had all week, or maybe it's me having a thing for this woman that I shouldn't have, but the result is the same: I don't want her to touch him.

But she does.

Jewel shakes his damn hand and he holds onto her longer than he has to, giving her a smile. She doesn't smile back, but rather tugs her hand free. She disappears into the building and the man grimaces, his expression almost angry. Adam sounds off in my mic. "I'll find out who he is, but that leaves you the detective's only coverage."

"I've got her," I say, pushing off the wall, reminded of telling her the same damn thing, when even that phrasing wasn't as professional as I'd expect from myself.

I walk toward the building and I intentionally head straight for Mr. Manicured Hands. Once he's almost directly in my path, with people are on either side of us, I knock the fuck out of his shoulder. He curses at me, and my lips curve with a satisfied smile. I cross the short space to the building and open the door. I walk inside the compact lobby that isn't much but walls and an elevator, since security is on the upper level. I find the front and rear exit and until I have my team on board, I'm staying right here. I claim the only bench in the place and have a seat.

"Jacob."

"Yeah, Finn," I say.

"Our homeless guy walked into a restaurant. I followed and he's not here. I checked the bathrooms and even the kitchen."

"Did he exit a back door?"

"He could have exited the kitchen, but I have a hard time believing the joint would allow that. There's only two options. I missed him and that didn't happen. Or—"

"He changed clothes and is unrecognizable."

"Exactly," he says.

And just like that, my gut feeling is validated. I'm not ready to say that Detective Carpenter is under imminent threat, but I'm not willing to say she's not at this point, either. Which means I'm not pulling my team back and I'm keeping her real damn close.

Chapter Five

Jewel

I'd much rather be obsessing over why Jacob King makes me hot all over when he touches me than living in the aftermath of Davis York's handshake, I'd wanted to refuse. I step onto the elevator in the DA's building and grimace, rubbing my palm on my pants to wipe away the touch. It's symbolic, of course, but it feels good, because despite his good looks and charm, the man is one of the top criminal defense attorneys in this country. He makes a living getting the same bad guys off that I work my ass off to get arrested. He's slime just like them. And the man is defending Bruce Norton, the bastard I just arrested for killing his pregnant wife. Unfortunately, the bodies haven't been recovered, which is why the DA needs me to come across strong on this case in a big way.

The good news, I think, punching my destination floor, is that we're in an election year so the pressure for the DA to convict is high. I like election years. They deliver results and while they won't make the bastard who killed his wife and unborn child burn in hell as I'd prefer, I'll settle for him rotting in a jail cell. The doors shut and my cellphone buzzes in my pocket. I dig it out and read a text message from Jacob: *Judo move approved*

I smile and type a response: Now you know how easily I can cuff you before I shoot you.

What if I know judo, too? he replies.

Of course, you do, I type. You're a big, bad Green Beret.

Yes, he responds. *I really am.*

I laugh, aware that his over-the-top arrogance is now for my amusement and, in fact, he's mocking his own announcement of his credentials. He can laugh at himself and I'm officially finding it harder and harder to believe he's the asshole I thought he was this morning. The elevator stops on my destination floor and I exit to greet a security guard who puts me through the typical bag search and metal detector before I'm walking down a hallway to the appropriate meeting room I know well.

I reach my proper doorway, which is open, and enter to find Evelyn Chris, the assistant DA that I'm working with on this case, sitting on the opposite side of a scuffed up wooden table facing me. "Come in, Detective," she greets, managing as always to be as welcoming as she is beautiful and tough in a courtroom.

I claim the seat in front of her and she shoves her long brown hair behind her ears and fixes me in a hard, steady, green-eyed stare. "The defense council was just here."

"I saw him downstairs. Pretty boy asshole. Something about him bugs me. He's too perfect. No one is that perfect."

"His track record is pretty damn perfect. This case is one hundred percent circumstantial. You know that, right?"

I set my bag down and settle my hands on the table, and give her my hard, steady, blue-eyed stare. "It's an election year."

Her lips thin. "I hate that fucking answer. That wasn't: We got him. We have proof. We have this or that. It was pressure on me to work a miracle."

"We do have him. We do have proof. And yeah. I believe you can work a miracle. Get a confession. I'm going to give you what you need to get it."

Her phone buzzes and she grabs it off the table where it sits next to her perfectly manicured nails. She glances at the message. "A witness on another case is here, claiming mind-blowing information. I have to deal with this. But we have to get through this bail hearing tomorrow, so you can't leave."

"I brought work and my computer with me. I'm fine."

She stands up. "For the record, I believe this bastard is guilty as sin and should burn in hell. I want to give you, his wife, and that baby, ten miracles."

She rounds the table and leaves me with validation as to why I like her so damn much. We think alike. We fight alike. We are alike in all the important, ethical ways, we just play on slightly different fields and thus package our attacks accordingly. I open my briefcase and pull out my MacBook, files, and the bag with my cookies. My cellphone buzzes again. I grab it and read the message from Jacob: *Who was the guy in the suit at the door?*

I could respond any number of ways, but Jacob and his "I'm professional" self just invites a little baiting. Thus why I can't help myself when I type: *My lover. He's very good. Did you feel the chemistry between us?*

I'd hate to see how you respond to a guy you hate, he replies. You were as stiff as a corpse.

I grimace and type: I was not as stiff as a damn corpse. And you already saw how I warm up to someone I hate this morning. How did that work for you?

My phone rings and I answer it to hear, "You don't hate me," Jacob says. "You were confused about that."

"Are you sure about that?"

"I am even if you aren't, just yet."

"Just yet?"

"I grow on people. Who was he?"

"Davis York. The defense attorney defending a slime-bag I arrested who I know killed his wife and unborn child."

"And your relationship with Davis York?"

"If I could fuck him, I would, and I don't mean in a bedroom or with my clothes off."

"Understood," he says, quite formally. "On a scale of one to ten, how likely are you to text me as you head to the elevator?"

"A five and that's only because I am, at this very moment, holding a cookie in my hand that you bought me."

"Stalking isn't easy, Detective Carpenter. I'll buy you dinner to go with the cookies if you'll just make my life a little easier here."

"As in you and me alone?"

"Yes," he confirms.

"No."

"We can talk through a working relationship."

"We will most definitely talk about that relationship but not right now, and not tonight. You and the stalking Detective Carpenter theme for the day is distracting and I have to be in court tomorrow morning."

"All the more reason to talk tonight and start tomorrow on a different note."

"Not tonight," I repeat, "but—and this is a big but—since I'm about to enjoy this cookie *you* got me, I'll text you when I'm leaving, but don't get used to it and don't expect that to foreshadow future negotiations on our working relationship. I'm just not that agreeable."

"We'll see about that."

My brow furrows. "We'll see about that?"

"Yes. We'll see about that."

"There are no more cookies until April."

"We'll find another common ground. I'm sure of it."

He hangs up and I take a bite of my cookie, the first common ground. The common ground that let him see behind my wall, which is why I turned down dinner. The cookies will be gone by morning, my wall restored, and my weird reaction to Jacob King gone. I'm sure of it. On that note, I grab the cold case files, and find the one that's piqued my interest, flipping it open to stare at a photo of a Green Beret named Jesse Marks. Thirty minutes later, I'm still waiting on Evelyn and I've hit the same roadblock I did with Jesse that I did with Jacob. Jesse's military record is top secret.

I thrum the table and think about Jacob and my declaration to Royce Walker that I'd know if I was being followed. Right before Jacob walked in with my coffee and cookie. Because I didn't know I was being followed. But Jacob King is on my side, hired to protect me, which is a waste of him as a resource. Which is why I need to put him to use helping me solve this cold case, and in the process, teach me how to face someone in the elite armed forces and win. Jesse Marks, the Green Beret, who killed his family, is officially my new cold case target and Jacob King is going to help me catch him. In fact, the one thing that defeats my own personal demons and inhibitions every single time, is a good challenge that can lead to catching a killer. My wall and Jacob King's ability to pull it down, no longer matter. Dinner is on.

FALLING UNDER

Chapter Six

JACOB

Sitting in a surveillance van with Finn is not for the weak of mind or body. The man is an ex-detective, who's a sharpshooter with MacGyver skills to match that of an uncatchable convict. He also has habits. Lots of habits. He thrums his fingers, runs his fingers through his longish brown hair, and taps his foot. Not to mention the eating. He eats and eats and eats, mostly M&M's and Doritos, like they're different brands of cigarettes and he's got a ten-pack-a-day habit. And I'm stuck in a small space with him for hours.

Come sunset, I'm ready to get Detective Carpenter out of that DA's office and I'm not afraid to push. I text her. *You still alive up there?*

Her reply is instant: Yes. Kudos to you. I'm not dead yet.

I can think of about five ways to reply and none of them are professional. None of them are what I would say in this same situation with someone else, because what I would say with someone else would be: *Yes, ma'am.* That's the thing about this woman. I had the luxury of watching her for days when she didn't know I was watching, and just as I said to her, I get her in a way no one else would. She's like me, carved in blood and loss. And while our response is

47

reserved, mine is quiet and defensive, hers is fresher, more offensive.

I set the phone down and with that gut feeling of trouble nagging me, I refocus on the MacBook in front of me, where I'm going through the past few weeks of footage at the Carpenter building, despite our team doing so already. Beside me, Finn taps his foot a good twenty times before I look at him and say, "The detective won't have to look far to solve your murder. I'll be right here, waiting on her, standing over your body."

He winks. "I love it when you talk dirty."

I give him a silent snarl and he offers me an M&M. I take the whole bag. I'm fucking starving. I eat the entire thing, or what's left, and forty-five minutes later, there's no word from Detective Carpenter when Finn taps his computer screen. "I'm talking to Blake on messenger."

Blake being Blake Walker, one of the founding three brothers of Walker Security. "Isn't he on another job?"

"Yes, and tied up until morning, but I've been looking for cameras to catch our homeless man for hours with no luck. But I'm no hacker and there are a few I can't seem to access. I need a master hacker like Blake."

My phone buzzes with a text and I grab it where it rests next to the MacBook. *I'm leaving. That's my last text message of the night.*

Good, I think. One-on-one conversation works best, and since I have no intention of doing this one foot in and one foot out routine again tomorrow, we're having one tonight. "We're on the move," I announce to Finn and Adam, who is still on live mic and covering the surrounding areas.

I exit the van, and start walking toward the building at the same time that Detective Carpenter exits. For the next fifteen minutes, I follow her, and she doesn't take the subway. She walks, as if she's letting me keep her in sight, which would be odd, since as she said, she's just not that damn agreeable, if I didn't get her all over again. She wants to figure out how I followed her and how she didn't know I was there. She wants to learn and I have to say, I'm a willing teacher to Detective Carpenter. Perhaps a little too willing, but I won't let this go anyplace that isn't professional.

That's a guarantee. Because I'm a professional and Detective Jewel Carpenter is my assignment.

FALLING UNDER

Chapter Seven

Jewel

I know Jacob is following me, but damn it, I can't spot him. I feel him. God, I feel that man way too easily. I spy a subway station and I decide to throw him for a loop. I head down into the next subway tunnel and I am quick on the draw with my pass card. In short jog, I'm through the gates, down the stairs and jumping on the next train. I'm smiling when me and a horde of twenty people step onto a train. There is no way, Green Beret or not, that man kept up with me.

The price I've paid however, is being squashed between bodies and forced to grab the overhead grip that I'm barely tall enough to snag. The train starts to move and sway when I have that awareness of Jacob I've had all day. No. Impossible. I scan over the top of heads, and my gaze collides with a set of gray, intense eyes looking right at me, a punch of awareness hitting me that is all about the man he is, not about the incredulousness of his presence. Jacob is here, that rat bastard. He arches a damn arrogant brow, and I gape at him and mouth, "How?"

He doesn't smile but he mouths back, "Green Beret."

I laugh. I can't help it. He's joking. I know that, but yet this man doesn't laugh or smile. He's stone-faced. And while

51

I'd never admit this to him, it's an endearing reminder of my uncle, who was Mr. Stone Face, who seemed so damn cold, but everything he did was to protect the innocent. And Mr. Green Beret didn't join the army to protect himself. He's one of the good guys, and I know this by instinct, history, and actions. I offered him a vacation. He declined. As much as I wanted him to back off at the time, he didn't, and no man of honor would have.

Nevertheless, despite his honor thus far, macho, alpha guys like Jacob, of which the department has many, push hard when they have a pushover in front of them, I consider giving him my back. But then, I can't see him either. I miss any chance of reading emotion in those stoic handsome features and can't know what he's thinking, if that's even possible. But more so, I can't see where he is and with about twenty bodies between us, and another twenty on either side of us, it would be easy to lose him. And so, I school my features to be as stone cold as his, and we stare at each other, in what is the most intimate moment I've shared with a man in years. Okay, technically not the most intimate. I've had sex. Once. But I didn't look into his eyes.

The train stops, and I don't immediately move. Jacob is on the other side of the train, which was a misstep in my book. He can't get to the door or me in anywhere near enough time to keep up. I watch him. I wait to see the moment he moves. The doors open and the rush to the door erupts. I slide into the center of the crowd, and just as they rush out, I do the same. I'm out of the train long before Jacob and hurrying up the stairs, only to have him step to my side.

He looks over at me and I look at him, and damn it, I smile and shake my head. Damn it, because I'm encouraging him, which isn't the idea here. We hurry up the remaining steps and then through the station to the next set of steps that leads to the quiet street above, not far from my apartment. Once we are there and past the exit, I turn to him, my hands in the air. "How? How can someone as big as you get around like you do?"

"I lived in a jungle for six months at one point," he says. "The city is only slightly more challenging."

"But I can't lose you and I don't see you when you follow. How do you do it?"

"I'll tell you over that dinner."

"Dinner is already planned," I say, a chilly breeze teasing my exposed neck, my braided hair and unlike Jacob, who is properly attired, no coat for shelter. But I don't shiver. I don't show weakness. I've learned that any little blink could get me pushed around, or worse, dead. Instead, I start walking, looking forward to a warm indoor location and food.

"I thought you had court tomorrow?" Jacob asks, falling into step with me.

"I do," I respond. "But this meeting is business and it's only a few blocks from my apartment to Nino's Pizza, my dinner destination, which is amazing by the way. I think you'll like it, if you give it a shot."

"You do know that the best way to keep this low key and off everyone else's radar is for you to communicate with me, right?" he asks, missing my hint that he's my dinner date.

"The best way to keep this off everyone's radar, is for you to take a vacation, but I get it. You won't." We turn a corner, onto a quiet street that has apartments sprinkled in between random gift shops and bakeries, among other businesses.

"I told you why I won't walk away from this," he replies.

"Yes," I say, giving him a look. "You did."

"And?" he prods.

53

"I didn't say 'and.'"

"There was an 'and,'" he insists as we stop in front of Nino's Pizza, which is more an Italian sit-down restaurant than just a pizza joint.

"And I actually respect you for your obvious morals. It's inconvenient for me, but you were right earlier. I might not hate you."

He gives me a deadpan look. No reaction. Just, "Is that right?"

"Yes, but that doesn't mean I trust you. Not when your military file is top secret. That leads me to questions you won't answer. But at this very moment, those questions are not on my mind. Food is on my mind. I'm going inside."

"Are you going to text me when you're done?"

"There is a zero chance of that happening," I say, and giving him no chance to argue, I cross to the restaurant door, open it, and enter the dimly lit, and amazingly cozy restaurant.

One of the owners, Rosie, a plump, wonderfully warm Italian woman in her sixties, with white-gray hair she wears to her shoulders, greets me. "Twice this week," she says. "I love it."

"I love it too," I assure her. "All of it. Everything about this place."

She smiles. "You make me a happy old woman," she says. "And your regular table is open."

"Terrific," I say. "Thank you."

She leads me to my spot on the opposite side of the restaurant in a back, private corner nook, where the table barely fits four. I settle into the seat with my back to the wall and Rosie chats with me a few minutes before departing. My waiter, Sebastian, Rosie's good-looking thirty-something son, arrives to greet me. "The lovely detective is back," he says, his dark hair curling at his temples. "Do you want your usual?"

"Make it an extra-large tonight," I say. "And I'll take two Coronas."

"Two?" he asks holding up fingers.

"Yes. And two plates."

He wrinkles a brow. "Is it a date and I no longer have a shot at being your one and only?"

I laugh. "You are already my one and only. You make me pizza. I'm easy like that."

He laughs and hurries away, while I open my briefcase and pull out the Marks file and hang the strap on the seat next to me. I then set the file on the seat. Already, Sebastian is returning with the plates and the two beers. "Should I tell my mother to be on the lookout for your guest?"

"No," I say. "He's an expert at finding me."

"I sense a story behind that."

"Not a good one," I assure him.

"Now I'm curious, but I'll ask questions the next time you're alone with a full belly." He turns and departs.

My phone buzzes with a text from my father. I'm stuck in a meeting. Are you okay with everything?

I want to say no. No, it's not okay. You've turned a seasoned detective into a college kid with a babysitter, but Jacob's words "we're hard to love" play in my head and I bite back the words. Besides, I'm making this work already. Jacob is going to help me close a cold case. With all this in mind, I type: *I'm great. Love you Dad.* But I don't hit send. I really *am not* that agreeable. I backspace and clear my words to amend my reply to: *I don't like this but I'm working out a livable situation with Jacob for one reason and one reason only. I love you.*

He replies with: Thank you, daughter of mine, who I adore and cannot lose. I love you, too.

I can almost feel his relief in that typed message and I am suddenly, incredibly glad that I didn't say no to this Walker Security intrusion.

Refocusing on my plan for now, I set the beers side-by-side, pull my phone from my pocket, and snap a photo. I then snap a second photo of the empty chair in front of me. I text both to Jacob. I send no caption. He's smart. He'll get it. I move his beer to the side of his plate and take a drink of mine. I've just wet my tongue when Jacob appears in front of the table, almost too fast, as if he was already headed to me before I sent those photos.

I set my beer down and tilt my chin up, my gaze admiring the journey upward and over the perfect, hard length of his body, by accident of course. Eventually, too soon really, since his body is the least complicated part of this man, I meet that intense gray stare of his. Eyes that are sharp even in the dim lighting of the cozy restaurant, which in hindsight might have made this a bad choice. This isn't a date. It's a business meeting with a man who just happens to be looking at me with the kind of intensity I don't invite from any man, especially one who is now my personal bodyguard. And yet I'm looking at him just as intensely as he's looking at me, and I find that I want to know what's behind *his* wall and I won't pretend it's all business. The truth is, that *I want* is not a statement I have made in a very long time.

Chapter Eight

JACOB

Still standing on the opposite side of the table from Jewel, there is no mistaking the charge between us. "Was your meeting cancelled?" I ask, weighing exactly where that photo invitation she sent me came from.

"It was you," she says. "It was always you, Jacob King."

She says *Jacob King* in a low, raspy voice that has me looking at her mouth, wondering when the last time she was kissed good enough and well enough to forget her badge and just be a woman. A thought I've had a half-dozen times just today, but I don't let her see my reaction. I never let anyone see my reactions, but unlike most, who take my stone face as an invitation to be silent, Jewel, Detective Carpenter I remind myself—not sure why I keep fucking forgetting that—seems to see that as an invitation to push my buttons. And so, it seems, I enjoy pushing hers.

Which is exactly why I lean forward, my hands settling on the back on my intended chair, and ask, "Are you flirting with me, *detective*?" reversing her question to me from earlier today.

"Of course not," she says, and then, proving she can give as good as she gets, she turns my earlier statement on me. "Flirting with you, major, would be unprofessional." She pauses for affect and adds, "And I'm *always* professional."

I don't smile on the outside, but I damn sure am on the inside. I do, however, pull out the chair and sit down across from her. "We have that 'always professional' thing in common, then," I say. Only we both know, whatever this is happening between us isn't professional at all, nor does it seem to be stoppable.

"That and being hard to love," she says, which I assume to be a reference to how I'd convinced her to stick this out with me. That is, until she surprises me by adding, "Me more so me than you, I think."

"Why would you say that?"

"You can choose your assignments, I assume. My job will always be a collection of revolving dead bodies."

"You can move out of homicide."

"No. I can't. This job is who, and what, I am. That won't change. Which means that I will always have at least one photo of a dead body in my briefcase. And most likely another pinned to my fridge or sitting on my kitchen counter so I can study it over my morning coffee. Or afternoon coffee if I'm at a murder scene all night. Those things are not easy for a civilian."

"And I'm to believe that's easy for you? Because I saw more damn bodies some single days in the army, than you will see in your career. I don't remember ever thinking that was easy."

"It's not supposed to be easy," she says, "nor do people like us take our jobs, thinking otherwise. Our peace is in the peace we give others."

"Nothing about what I did, is like what you do," I say, thinking of the thankless job that took me all kinds of wrong places. Too many wrong places. Places I'm not going with her, or anyone else, which is exactly why I pick up my beer, tilt it back, and take a long, deep drink, with one intent:

shutting her out. She knows it too. I can feel her watching me, trying to figure me out. She'll fail, but she's a detective. She has to try.

I set the bottle down to find that sure enough, she's unapologetically staring at me. "What do you want to ask me, detective?"

"Is every Green Beret's file top secret?"

"Missions are top secret. Anything that ties to those missions is also top secret."

"Is that a yes?"

"No," I say.

"Why'd you get out?"

"It was my time."

She slides her plate to the left and flattens her hands on the table. "Tell me again how talking to you helps me get to know and trust you?"

I slide my plate to my right and rest my arms on the table, fingers laced together. I lean forward, so close to her now that I can smell the sweet, floral scent of her that softens her, and defies her tough exterior. "You're asking the wrong questions," I say.

"The wrong questions," she repeats, narrowing her eyes on me.

"Yes," I confirm. "The wrong questions. Ask me something I can answer."

"In other words," she says, following my lead, "your time in the service, and your reasons for getting out, are top secret."

"Exactly."

"Okay then," she says, never missing a beat. "Why'd you enlist?"

"My father and brother were both Green Berets."

"Why did *you* enlist?"

"Enlisting is what the men of my family do," I say, unsurprised that she's seen past my standard answer. It's my wall and she's damn sure got experience with that, with one of her own.

"That's not a real answer, *major*," she says. "Especially since you went to college to be an engineer."

"I told you I'm not a major anymore."

"That's still not an answer, but you know what? That's okay. I get it. You barely know me and there are just things we don't like to talk about ever. Or with anyone."

Any other person who pushed me for more anything would get more nothing, but every pass I take with this woman, offers her a pass. I don't want to give her a pass. And so I give her more. "I was raised by my grandmother," I say. "She needed me. I stayed for her."

"And when she died, you enlisted," she assumes.

"No," I correct. "I enlisted six months before she died."

She frowns. "But you said—"

The pizza is set down on our table in that moment, saving me from the rest of the question. Hand delivered by the owner's son, which I know because this is Detective Carpenter's regular spot. "Can I get you anything else?" he asks us both.

The detective—Jewel, I think—because she's more than the damn detective shield she wears, looks at me. "Pepperoni okay?" she asks.

"My favorite," I say, glancing at Sebastian. "Thanks, man."

He gives me a nod and looks across the table. "All is well, detective?" he asks.

"It's perfect," she assures him, and he hurries away, while she points at the pizza.

"I normally get a large" she says, "but this time, I got an extra-large, so you can have like two slices." She pulls her plate in front of her and reaches for a slice.

"I think I need at least three," I say quite seriously.

She considers me a moment. "Right. Because you're so damn big."

"You keep saying that."

"It keeps becoming relevant." Her lips that I still fucking want against mine, curve ever-so-slightly. "You can have more. I can't eat this whole pizza anyway, but my eyes always want more than my belly."

"You eat like shit," I comment, picking up a slice and taking a bite that's so damn good I swallow and add, "And I now see why. This is damn good."

"The best," she says, "and you're wrong about my eating habits."

"I'm always wrong, right?"

"*Finally,* we agree on something."

"You do remember that I've been watching you for four days, right?"

"To the point that I can't stop thinking about it," she says, and she doesn't give me a chance to clarify the meaning of that statement, as she quickly, intentionally I'm certain, refocuses on the initial topic. "I do a once a month clean-up diet week which means eating egg whites, salads, and protein. It works for me. I suppose an ex-Green Beret, who obviously is in good condition, eats only egg whites because you're just that kind of disciplined."

"Depends on the job," I say, indicating the pizza in my hand. "Sometimes it's impossible."

"Now I'm a bad influence?" she challenges.

"You are *most definitely* a bad influence," I say, reaching for another slice, and thinking about my damn obsession with her mouth.

She thankfully changes the subject. "How long have you been with Walker?" she asks, downing a swallow of beer.

"Two years," I say, sprinkling red pepper over my food and then offering it to her.

She accepts it, our fingers brushing in the process, the charge between us sending her gaze to mine, the impact a punch of awareness. She fights it the way I should be fighting it, her gaze quickly cutting sharply to her plate. She hyper focuses on that shaker, and not until she sets it down again does she look at me. "How long since you got out of the army?"

"Three years. I went back home, and the owners of a high-end apartment complex recruited me to help out."

"You were over qualified."

"Very, but Blake Walker was working with one of the tenants. I met him, helped him with that job, and one thing led to another. And here I am."

She slides her plate to the side, and once again, she's unapologetically staring at me. I, too, slide my plate aside. "What do you want to ask me this time?"

"You said that you stayed with your grandmother," she says. "That she needed you, but you left long before she died."

"And the detective in you can't stand the contradiction."

"I want to trust you, Jacob, and to let you into my world, which is a law enforcement world, I also *need* to trust you."

"And I too, *need* your trust but there is no big secret here. My father was killed on a mission. My oldest brother was still enlisted. I had this burning need to enlist, and find my way to the Berets and protect him, despite him being the seasoned soldier."

Realization slides over her face. "He's dead."

"Yes. Two years after I entered the army he was killed in combat, and on our first mission together. He died in my arms a year to the day my grandmother died of cancer without ever telling me she was sick." I intend to stop there, but I don't. For some damn reason I add, "It's pie for me, detective, not cookies. Coconut pie at Christmas. No one makes a coconut pie, like she did."

She studies me for several long beats, holding her breath I think, her expression as unreadable as most would say mine is on any given day. One second passes. Two. Three. And then she leans forward, her hand next to mine, but not touching it. "I know you know this," she says. "I know you've told yourself this a million times over, but I'm going to say it again for you. Sometimes there just isn't a right choice."

"How many times a day do you tell yourself that?"

She sits back. "Twice. When I wake up and when I go to sleep, but we aren't talking about me. How long has it been?"

"Twelve years for my grandmother," I say, taking a swig of beer, before I add, "eleven for my brother, and thirteen for my father."

"Three years in a row."

"Yes. Three times are not a charm for me."

"Seven, four, and two for me. Best friend, mother, uncle, in that order. All murdered. All victims of crimes."

"You joined the police force after your best friend died," I supply, knowing her history well. "Detouring from medical school to the police academy."

"I knew I had to make a difference," she says.

"A doctor makes a difference," I point out.

"It wasn't the way I was supposed to make a difference."
Her jaw sets, her mood shifting in fierce immediacy. "And
that's why you're here. I'm doing this thing with you for my
father, but the integrity of my job is critical. So that brings
us to rules."

"Yes, detective," I say. "Let's talk about rules."

"My rules," she says.

"I was thinking more of mine."

"Good luck with that," she says. "You don't get to set the
rules."

"I'm protecting you."

"From what? A *soft threat* from a note writer?"

"I've seen people die with less warning." I don't give her
time to reply. "This doesn't work unless you cooperate and
communicate. If you can't do that, I'll go to your father and
excuse myself from this job, and tell him why."

Her eyes sharpen, right along with her tone. "Did you
really just say that to me?"

"I'm doing my job here."

"Right. Your job. I can't forget that."

"Don't take that to places I didn't intend it to go."

"I'm your job. It's all professional, all business. I get it.
But I too, have a job to do."

"Then let's negotiate terms we both can both live with."

"Is that even possible?"

"We don't know if we don't try. You go first. What can I
do to make this work for you?"

"I work with you and you alone. No one else follows me."

"Then I'm your personal protection," I say. "I'm with
you twenty-four seven."

"That's not even possible. You can't go to work with me.
You damn sure aren't sleeping with me."

"I'll escort you to and from without chasing you in the shadows," I say, offering her the compromise that keeps me out of her workplace and her home, the latter of which, where we'd end up naked. "You give me your schedule," I add. "You text me before you leave any location."

"This is nuts, and don't say I won't know you're there because I'll just say what I've been saying. I'll know, damn it."

"I'm glad you'll know, detective," I say. "That means you also know that you're protected. Because I can promise you this. No one will hurt you with me on the job. Use me while you can. I'll help you take down the bad guys, whoever they are for you right now."

"Is that an official offer?" she challenges.

"Yes. It is."

"Then let's get started." She reaches to her seat and sets a file in front of me.

"What is this?"

"You'll know when you open it."

Curious now, I tear my gaze from hers and glance down at the file. Flipping it open, I find myself looking at a photo, and I don't have to look at the name. I know who Jesse Marks is, the details of which I will never tell her. I shut the file. "What is this?" I ask, my tone hard, unemotional, anything personal we've shared tonight shut down, gone.

"I'm in charge of cold cases now," she explains. "I'm now hunting Jesse Marks and I chose him for an obvious reason, beyond the fact that he killed his family and disappeared. He's a Green Beret and you can help me get that family justice."

"You will not touch this case."

"You can't tell me that."

65

"I can, and *I did*." I reach in my pocket, grab cash and drop it on the table. "You will not touch this case," I repeat.

"I can, and *I will*."

"If you do," I say, leaning forward, "you'll really need me to keep you alive."

"I can take care of myself."

"You have no idea what would come at you," I bite out.

"Tell me," she says. "Explain."

"No." I stand up and take the file with me.

She stands up. "You can't take my file."

"I already did." I start walking and I don't stop. I exit the restaurant, round the corner to a quiet alleyway and pull out a lighter, which I always keep with me for just such an occasion. I hold out the file and I set it on fire with my mind racing. She must have made calls about Marks. She dug where she shouldn't have dug and that is a problem.

Detective Carpenter rounds the corner. "What the hell are you doing?" she demands, rushing towards me and my bonfire.

I reply by setting the other end of the file on fire and dropping it to the paved ground.

She double-steps and stops in front of it and me, but it's too late for her file. It's all but ash and she's not pleased. "I'm just going to pull the computerized records," she says, "but I think I'll do that after I arrest you for interfering in a criminal investigation."

I step around the fire and offer her my hands. "Cuff me, detective. Or maybe I should call you Jewel since we're getting kinky and shit now. But wait. Detectives don't carry cuffs, now do they?"

She reaches under her jacket and pulls out zip ties. "I do."

"Zip ties?" Now I laugh. "Really?"

She slides them around my wrists and pulls them tight. "Really," she says, her hands on mine.

"Are you arresting me?"

"No," she says. "I'm just leaving you the fuck here." She turns and starts walking.

"You know I can get out of these," I call after her.

"Have fun," she calls out.

I lift my arms and shove my fists against my waist and the zip ties bust open. The file is complete ash now, but I stomp on it to be certain the fire is out, and then I'm on the detective's heels. She's a block ahead of me by the time I catch her, and I don't even try to hide. She knows I'm here. We cover another block and we arrive at her building. She opens her gate, and never looks in my direction. She enters her courtyard and walks up the steps, pausing at the security panel but instead of reaching for the panel, she kneels down as if she's dropped something. Only I didn't see her drop anything.

She stands again, studying something in her hand and then keys in her code. I'm at her gate at the same moment she disappears into her building, but this doesn't end here. Not after she showed me that file. It's a game changer. Any distance that I thought was the way to keep this professional is no longer an option.

I give her a sixty-second lead and walk to the security panel where I key in her code that I know thanks to Blake's hacking. Once I'm inside the tiny foyer, I wait until her door opens on the second level and shuts before I head up the stairs. At her door, I ring the bell. Smart girl looks through the peep hole and then opens the door. "How are you even up here?"

"How can I protect you if I can't get to you?" I step closer and force her to back up or let me walk right into her, which would be my preference: her body against my body. She backs up just enough that we're toe-to-toe.

"What are you doing?" she demands.

"We had a deal. I'm your one-on-one protection. That means I stay with you. That means I sleep here with you."

Chapter Nine

JACOB

I expect her to push back after my announcement that I'm staying the night with her, and she does. "Turn around," she says, blocking my entry into her apartment, "and walk right back down those stairs behind you. You aren't staying the night with me."

"This isn't a negotiation, detective," I say. "I'm staying."

"Detective is the key word in that statement," she says. "So, *I repeat.* Turn around, and walk back down the stairs. And do it now."

"*This isn't a negotiation,*" I repeat, and then add, "Jewel," before backing up those words.

I step forward, crowding her with the intent of forcing her to retreat. She doesn't budge, which leaves me no option but to make her budge. My hands settle on her slender waist, and I'm also walking her backward, until we're inside her apartment and I'm kicking the door shut behind me as I do.

Her hands go to mine, an obvious attempt to control me, but all she does is make me hot and hard, when I have no business being hot and hard. She's my client. "You're out of line, major," she snaps and right when her knee would land painfully in my groin, I catch her leg, turn her to press her against the door, and capture her legs with mine.

"Jacob is the name," I say, flipping the lock by her head into place while she reaches for her weapon. I catch her hand.

"You don't want to do that," I say.

"I don't like being manhandled," she says. "Back off."

"That's not going to happen," I say. "I'll do what I have to, to protect you. Because that's my job."

Her eyes sharpen. "Your job, is it? Well sleeping here with me isn't your job."

"Around the clock protection is my job. If I sleep with you, it would not be part of my job. It would not be with our clothes on. But it would most definitely be because we both wanted it."

"You arrogantly say that like it's ever going to be an option."

"It won't be. Not as long as you're my duty, but I am staying here tonight. You need me. We both know that's no longer in question, but if you want to shoot me, do it. Let's just get it over with or don't do it at all." I release her and push off the door, stepping backward to give her just enough space to pull that gun.

She steps right back up to me, and twists my shirt in her hand. "You talk to me. You don't manhandle me. You don't shove your way into my apartment. And that's non-negotiable."

There is a sudden whiplash effect of energy between us, sexual tension that can't be ignored. I don't move. I don't speak. I just stand there, with that mouth of hers tilted in my direction, tempting me to kiss her, and I'm not the only one thinking about it. She looks at my mouth, and fuck, I want to pull that braid of hers free, and dive my fingers in her hair.

But I can't.

70

I won't.

Her fingers ease from my shirt and then fall away. She steps back but doesn't look away. "Non-negotiable," she says before she rotates and starts walking.

I don't stand around like a scolded puppy. I pursue her past a living area, vaguely noting the stone walls and modern gray seating area, my attention focused on her as she rounds the gray wood-framed island. She presses her hands to the surface and watches me, waits on me. Obviously readying for battle, and I'm up for whatever battle is before me. I step to the island across from her, my hands also planted on the smooth surface.

We stare at each other again, a push and pull between us that is damn near combustible, and since we can't fuck, I prepare for the fight to follow. But when I expect her to head down the Jesse Marks rabbit hole, that's not where she travels.

"Do you have men on my father the way you do on me?" she asks, instead.

I narrow my eyes on her, certain that Royce had to have covered this. "We have a full detail on your father, and we're revamping the company procedures as well."

"Who's watching him and how closely?"

"There were no threats against your father," I say. "If that wasn't clear this morning with Royce, I'll make it clear now."

"But he *is* he being protected?"

"Yes," I confirm. "Rick Savage, also a former Green Beret, is in charge of his detail. And Rick is a crazy insane killer that would take a bullet for your father and makes me look small."

"Did you serve with him?" she asks.

"No."

"Do you trust him?"

"He's good at his job," I assure her.

"That's not a declaration of trust."

"I *trust* him," I say, her interest in my trust telling me she knows I'm competent. "Do you want to meet him?"

"Yes. Please."

I don't miss the polite request that tells me she's in a completely new zone, one that I haven't seen to this point. "Done," I say. "I'll arrange it. Now tell me what changed between the restaurant and now. And don't tell me that I distracted you, and you are circling back to your father. We both know it's more than that."

She tilts her face upward and looks to the ceiling, her actions tell me something happened in the last twenty minutes, which leads me to the only place it can lead me. "Why did you squat down by the door?"

She lowers her head and looks at me. "You don't miss much, do you?"

"I would have been dead years ago if I did."

She opens the drawer next to her and sets a plastic baggy with a dead orange and black Monarch butterfly on the counter. "That's what I bent down and picked up. It's butterfly mating season, which I know because it became relevant to the forensic evidence in a murder I solved last year."

It could be symbolic to her. A reminder of the murder that changed her life. But I don't think that is where this is headed. "What does that mean to you?" I ask, watching her closely.

"Before I answer that. You studied me. You watched me without me knowing, thus why you now have your stalker nickname."

"I'd prefer protector, just an FYI."

"How about asshole?" she challenges.

"I'll be whatever it takes to keep you alive."

I expect a snap back and once again I don't get what I expect. Her lips thin and a two-second beat passes before she asks, "Did you know that my best friend in college, the one that was murdered, was obsessed with butterflies? Jewelry, clothes, figurines... you name it, she collected it."

"No, I did not," I say, and then I go where she is leading. "You think someone left this for you."

"My gut says that's exactly what happened, and if that's the case, this person knows where I live. This person found out more about me than you and your Walker team of experts. This person is dangerous. Which is exactly why I tried to send you away."

"Explain."

"We don't know who this person is or how they might react to you, or Walker being involved."

"My being involved tells them that I'm protecting you. It tells them to back the fuck off."

"Or it tells them to find a way around you, and that leads to the precinct, where this person might attack others. Or a public place. Or a redirect to my father."

"We have your father well covered."

"What about the entire precinct? Or innocent people around me? We don't know who this person is or what they are capable of. But we do know that if they really did leave that butterfly, they're steps ahead of us."

"Something we can agree on."

"And at this point," she adds. "I'm not sure you being here makes a difference. We had dinner. We were seen together. Anyone who figured out the butterfly connection will figure out my connection to you already. Whatever nerve we might have hit, we've hit. Whatever set of actions we've set into play, are already in play."

She's right. I feel it. Trouble is coming and it's not gentle. It's fierce. It's angry. It's deadly. And it's definitely two steps ahead of us.

Chapter Ten

Jewel

"Pack a bag," Jacob orders. "We're going to my place, which is in the Walker-owned, and secure, building. You'll be safe there."

"That's not going to happen," I say in instant rejection.

"You just told me that you had a gift left on your doorstep. We aren't staying here where that doorstep exists."

"An improbable gift."

His jaw sets hard. "Let's recap. You yourself said that if that improbable gift was a real gift, we have a problem. And as a point of considerable reference, that living butterfly is now *dead.*"

"If the butterfly was alive," I say, "it wouldn't be of much interest, because it would have flown away. If it were alive, it wouldn't potentially represent yet another person in my life who ended up dead. Furthermore, what you leave out of your brilliant summarization of my own words, while using *my own words* against me, is the part about you being a trigger that could get my father killed."

"Your father's well-protected. And if this person we're dealing with is as smart as these actions indicate, your father choosing to hire protection was anticipated."

"And most likely expect me to reject it."

His brow furrows. "Based on what?"

"Based on my job and studying my behaviors. No male detective on the force would accept a bodyguard, which means if I do, I look weak."

"Being predictable is a good way to end up dead."

"*Appearing* predictable while we work behind the scenes to be otherwise, keeps the focus on me with the idea being that *no one else* ends up dead."

"My job," he says, "is to keep you alive first, and everyone else second."

"You can't protect someone first who protects others first."

"And how will you protect anyone else if you're dead?" he challenges. "I'm not leaving."

"Keep your field people in place," I say. "But you can't stay."

"Call the police and have me hauled out of here," he says. "That's the only way I'm leaving and for all we know this 'butterfly slayer' thinks we're fuck buddies, detective."

"How does that help us? You're still unexpected. You're still working for Walker Security."

"I'm not leaving," he replies stubbornly.

"Just tonight," I negotiate. "Until we can analyze this problem more closely."

"We can analyze it more closely together, here, tonight."

"You're making me crazy," I bite out this time.

"Ditto, detective," he assures me, before he perches on the edge of the barstool to his left and pulls his phone from his pocket. "Right now," he says. "I'm going to get us the security footage for the apartment we setup so we can look for our butterfly's arrival." He places the phone to his ear.

I stare at him for several anger-charged beats and consider my options. I really could arrest him. I could get him out of here, and maybe that would please what might be my real stalker. Even keep my real stalker away from my father and other innocent people. Or not. There really isn't a good option right now, other than information gathering, that either brings me to his position or him to mine. That decides if he stays or goes.

"Hey Ash," Jacob says, while I find myself staring at the broken wing of the butterfly, which is too precise to be accidental. "I need all the security footage for Jewel Carpenter's residence," Jacob continues on his call. "Also, my overnight bag and my MacBook." There is a pause before he adds, "*Tonight,*" and I have no idea why but that one word, "tonight" shoots my gaze to his, and his to mine, a punch of awareness rises between us, followed by a charge that screams with possibilities. Possibilities that will distract us both from catching the butterfly slayer, therefore I rejected them and him.

I rotate and present him with my back, closing the space between me and the counter, next to the gray wooden finished fridge, where I grip the counter and will any attraction to Mr. Green Beret to go away. While I fail, he continues his conversation. "The clothes can wait, if necessary," he says, which has me wondering what he plans to sleep in, if anything at all. "But," he adds, "the sooner the better on that MacBook and the footage." He must disconnect the call because the next thing I hear is, "Thirty minutes, detective."

I let out a heavy breath and grab two wine glasses from the mounted shelf under the kitchen cabinet, along with the bottle of red wine I keep ready in the way I hope to always be ready. Turning, I set the glasses and the bottle on the island. "Because I don't have whiskey," I say, "which at this point, I'm considering a misstep despite the fact that I hate the stuff."

"Then why is it a misstep?" he asks, shrugging out of his leather jacket, and in the process, subjecting me to ripped, powerful arms, and a broad chest.

A view of which frames my reply. "It's as good a night as it is a bad idea to drink myself silly," I say.

"You're too much of a control freak to drink yourself silly," he comments, settling his jacket on the empty barstool beside him.

I uncork the bottle. "Sounds like you're talking about you, not me," I say, indicating the bottle in my hand. "Do you drink wine?"

"I was stationed in Italy for six months and yes, I learned to love the grape."

"Well then," I say, filling our glasses. "You should love this. It's Italian and expensive, compliments of my father." I set the bottle down and claim the stool directly across from his.

He lifts his glass, while his lashes lower, and he smells the ruby red liquid, and then sips. "Excellent," he says, offering me an approving stare. "Your father knows how to pick, because price alone does not make a drinkable wine."

"Agreed," I say, resealing the bottle, surprised by the knowledge behind that comment, while wondering why the hell I'm noticing that he has wine on his bottom lip.

"I do like control," he says, jerking my gaze upward to the smoldering heat of his stare. "In all things. It's power. It's protection. It's necessary."

Suddenly I don't know if we're talking about work anymore. "Is that supposed to surprise me?"

"Simply laying the groundwork," he comments.

"The groundwork for what?"

"My decisions," he says. "My actions. My motivations."

"We may have problems then," I say, suddenly hyper-aware of him. Of his size. Of his scent that I now believe to be dashed with cinnamon. His piercing gray eyes that tell so little but say so much. "Control is like a bag of chocolate to me. I can't get enough."

"And yet you want to drink yourself silly?"

"Want and do are two different things."

"Sometimes you have to let it go," he says.

"Never going to happen," I reply. "Not where you're concerned."

His lips don't give me the smile I watch for, but his eyes light with mischief. "Nice apartment, by the way," he says, lifting his glass to indicate the space behind him, changing the subject.

"If that was a question," I reply, the air softening, the mood shifting, a degree of formality returning, "the answer is yes," I add. "It belongs to my father and I rent it out for a ridiculously low price tag that would be zero if I left it up to him. Actually, if I left it up to him, I'd be in a high-rise, and living in luxury."

"Most people wouldn't turn that down," he comments, studying me with those gray eyes of his that always appear cool when he looks elsewhere, and hot when he looks at me. Like now.

"I'm not most people," I say, "much to my father's chagrin half the time. But I also wasn't foolish enough to turn this place down, when I'm living on a skimpy detective's salary."

"Then why not upgrade to the mansion in the high-rise?"

"I can't stay in touch with a detective's world while living in my father's. And my father didn't earn his money to make it my money. I chose this life. I make my own money."

"But he obviously supports your decisions, or you wouldn't have this apartment."

I snort. "He hates my job. He'd lock me away in a safe house if I'd let him, a detail of which I'm certain to regret, as it's certain to fuel your caveman nature."

"I came by the caveman thing naturally," he says. "Inherited from the likes of my own father, just like my insistence on control. *Your* father told me to keep you safe, but all methods and actions are my own. And speaking of your father." He sets his glass down and grabs his phone from where it rests beside it. "We need to give Savage a heads up on your little gift." He hits auto-dial and then places the phone between us. "Ask whatever questions you want." He hits the speaker button.

The line connects almost instantly. "What's up, asshole?" a man I assume to be Rick Savage answers.

"Way to make an impression, Savage," Jacob says. "I'm here with Detective Carpenter."

"Oh fuck," Savage murmurs, and then quickly adds, "I mean—my apologies, detective. Nice to meet you."

"Nice to fucking meet you," I say, because I hate being treated like a delicate flower. "I'm a detective, Savage. If the word 'fuck' offended me I couldn't have half the conversations I have in any twelve-hour window. Speak how you speak, just take care of my father."

"Nothing is going to happen to your father, detective," Savage vows, proving he knows when to set aside all his bullshit yack, of which, he has plenty. "You have my word."

"What we have," Jacob says, "is reason to believe that a gift from our note writer may have been left here at

Detective Carpenter's apartment. One that took significant planning and that means we're dealing with someone with a degree of skill and intelligence. Tighten the reins on Carpenter Senior."

"What kind of gift?" he asks, just as I would in his shoes.

"Nothing we're going to talk about right now," Jacob replies, his eyes warm when they meet mine, his actions honorable, loyal in fact, when I didn't expect loyalty from him. "Just tighten the reins," he adds.

"The gift was a dead butterfly," I supply, letting Jacob know he has a thumbs-up. "My best friend in college, who was murdered, loved butterflies."

"Are we dealing with her killer?" he asks.

"It can't be," I say. "He's in jail. I know this because I keep tabs on him."

"Then a connection to him, perhaps?" Savage suggests.

"Maybe," I say. "It's worth exploring."

"And we will," Jacob offers. "And quickly."

"Does your father know yet?" Savage asks.

"No," I say, "and there is no 'yet' to this. In fact, if he finds out, I will personally come and emasculate you, ex-Green Beret or not. He worries enough. We're doing what we need to do without him knowing more than he has to know."

Jacob gives me a deadpan look, because that's what's carved on his handsome face, I decide. There's nothing more. "Well then," he says. "I'm not sure you got the point across. Savage? How'd she do?"

"Emasculate," he says. "I'm pretty sure I learned that word in 'Don't Piss Off A Woman 101.' We're clear here. And as for the security levels, we're as tight on your father as a skin on a banana, but I'm going to alert my team to give it an extra squeeze."

Jacob glances at me and asks, "Anything else?"

"Are you with him around the clock, Savage?" she asks. "And if not, who is?"

"Durk Keifer is with him," he says. "He's ex-FBI and damn good. He's also about half my size and looks mighty fine in a suit, like that pretty boy daddy of yours. Must be why your father likes him and announced him as his personal bodyguard. Blake, ex-ATF and hacker extraordinaire, is setting up the company security. There's four more on the team."

"I have an outline of the team I can give her," Jacob offers and motions to the phone. "Last call. What else?"

"I want to see the letters sent to my father."

"I can get those for you," Jacob replies, picking up the phone. "We'll be in touch, Savage."

"One last thing," he says. "Detective?"

"Yes?"

"No one dies on my watch. You can take that to the bank."

That vow, obviously meant to comfort me, isn't comforting at all. It's that reality check that the only person in my life that hasn't been murdered is now quite possibly in danger of being murdered. I see a lot of things in this job, but this...I don't really even know what to do with this.

Jacob notices my reaction. I see it in the sharpness of his eyes. I don't want him to see it and I pick up my wine glass and walk out of the kitchen. "We'll be in touch, Savage," Jacob repeats, and I can feel him turn and follow my progress to the living room where I sit down on the cushy gray couch. The one thing that I'd bought with my annual payment from my mother's estate, before investing the rest with my father's investment banker because as my father has said, "One day you'll be glad you did it, even if you decide to donate it all. The more to be generous with."

Jacob picks up his wine glass and walks in my direction, and I'm once again struck by his grace coupled with a lethal quality. I've called him arrogant and it's true, but I'm comforted by my growing impression that he can back it up. By the fact that I believe him to be a skilled killer in his own right, and as my uncle told me many times, when you chase a killer, you have to be willing to become one yourself. I *am* willing, but in all things, practice makes perfect, and Jacob King has had practice.

He stops at the chair with the fluffy blanket, and picks it up to sit. One look at the small, sunken center and he drops the blanket while I laugh. "I really want to see you in that chair with the blanket over you."

"That's not happening," he says, stepping to the other side of the table. "I'm joining you."

"Okay," I say, scooting over. "Join me."

He rounds the stone coffee table and sits down on the opposite end of the sofa. Both of us face forward, sipping our wine for a good three minutes, before he says, "I don't tell anyone about my family."

I glance over at him and the minute our gaze collides, the air thickens. "You said that," I say.

"It seemed worthy of repeating," he replies. "I need you to trust me."

"Then don't burn my files."

He sets his wine down. "You need me."

"I need you?" I set my wine down and face him. "Because you don't want me to touch the Jesse Marks case?"

"Because you need me."

"That's not an answer."

"There's a dead butterfly on your kitchen counter. That's your answer." There's a knock on my door. "And so is that," he adds.

"Because I didn't buzz anyone up," I say. "But you know that's your man."

"That's right. Because anyone who wants to get to you, can, and you know it." He stands up and walks toward the door, where he'll be given an overnight bag. In other words, he's staying here tonight unless I forcibly kick him out. And I could, but he's right. Anyone who can get to me, will, and just because that butterfly didn't make it to my front door doesn't mean the person who delivered it won't.

Chapter Eleven

Jewel

Jacob crosses my living room, opens my front door, and in about thirty seconds shuts it again. Just that fast, his sexy, arrogant, big-ass self, is closing the space between me and him again, all loose-legged swagger with his overnight bag in his hand. The bag that says he's not leaving because he doesn't believe the butterfly slayer is going away. I wish I could argue. I wish I could say that he's wrong. I wish I could send him away or keep him here for the right reasons—he's hot and we're hot together—because it's been a long time since I've been hot with anyone.

He stops on the other side of the coffee table and pats his bag. "We should have everything we need now."

"Including your overnight boxers?" I ask, because I just want the man to blush, or smile, or react in some human way.

"I'm a tighty-whitey kind of guy," he says, which might seem like a joke from someone else, but from Jacob, it sounds like a fact check.

But I'm not ready to give up. "I think you should know," I say, as he rounds the coffee table to join me on the couch again, "that our conversation about your tighty-whitey underwear means that I'm officially in the most committed relationship of my adult life. With a man I still haven't decided if I like."

"We already covered this," he says, pulling his MacBook from his bag. "You like me. You said so."

"I don't hate you. I've committed to nothing else."

"And *this* is the most committed relationship you've ever had?"

"In what I consider my adult life. Okay, no. Actually, that's really not true. There's David Rodriquez."

"The detective?"

"Yes, and I don't like that you knew that."

"I told you. I have to know you to protect you, but I didn't find any evidence you were dating him."

I grimace. "I didn't say I was dating him, or fucking him, for that matter."

"Then I'm confused. How is he your most committed relationship?"

"We've stared at each other across our desks for all of my four years as a detective and for the past six months of that time, we actually said real sentences to each other. He even brings me chocolate on occasion, in an effort to keep me from being bitchy. Now that I think about it, we might be in love."

He gives me a three-second deadpan look. "You win. You're more committed with him than I've ever been with anyone. Ever."

"Do all Green Berets have commitment issues?"

"I own my commitment issues," he says, and obviously eager to get off topic, which we both know is headed toward my cold-case Green Beret, he pulls his MacBook from his bag. "I need a few to pull up the feed," he says.

"Speaking of the feed," I say. "Is Asher shy? He sure ran off quickly."

"The minute we hung up with Savage, he called Asher and asked him for security footage to review as well," he says. "He's taking it over to him. And before you ask, yes, we watch the feed in real time, but Savage wants to do what we're doing. Look for what he might have missed."

It's exactly what I would have done, if I were Savage. "I approve," I say. "Is that what you want to hear?"

"Yes, actually," he says. "And not because I'm arrogant, detective. Because I want you to feel confident that your father is as protected as you are."

Detective.

I am kind of sick of him calling me that, when I should approve. It's formal. It's a wall.

I stand up and head toward the kitchen. "No reply?" he calls after me.

"No reply," I say, and not because I'm being an asshole now myself. Because at that very moment I'm at the island, reaching for the wine bottle when my attention lands on the butterfly. On the broken wing, the warning and threat in that break cutting through me. And while I make a habit of forcing myself to look at crime scene photos, I can't look at that butterfly one more second. Snatching up the bag, I stuff it in a drawer under the island before returning to the living room with my briefcase, my glass, and the bottle of wine.

"Detective," he says softly, only to amend to, "Jewel" and I can feel the way he's looking at me, willing me to look at him, seeing too much, and yet I find myself giving in. I don't fight him.

I glance over at him. "A sincere moment here," I say. "I'm impressed with what your team is doing. I'm relieved that your team is protecting my father, but after that butterfly showed up, catching this creep is all that is going to make me feel better."

His eyes soften and then darken. "Nothing is going to happen to you or your father," he says. "I promise."

"Don't make promises you can't keep."

"I don't."

"You just did," I say, "and I'm not some random woman you're protecting. I've been in my only version of your warzones. Words don't comfort me."

"Then what does?" he asks.

I'm taken aback by the fact that this question is thoughtful. It's not a demand that I just feel relief. "Catching the bad guy."

"But there's always another bad guy."

"Yeah," I say. "There is. What about you?"

He arches a brow. "Me?"

"Yes. You. I know you saw bad things. Did leaving the service give you comfort or peace?"

There is a flicker of some emotion in his eyes I can't quite read, there and gone before I can really even try. "I'm still trying to decide."

There is so much more to that statement than just the words spoken, and I want to ask more, to know more about him, when I should not. He confuses me, challenges me, infuriates me, but perhaps, if I'm honest with myself, that's because I'm drawn to him. And I don't want to be drawn to anyone. I don't want anyone, ever again. But right now, here in this moment, there's just me and him, a man and a woman, both I believe, damaged in our own ways, so I dare to push forward. I dare to ask for more. "What does that mean?"

His phone buzzes with a text. He hesitates, as if he's not ready to leave this moment with me just yet, but then he gives a slight shake of his head, as if scolding himself. And just like that our moment is the next, and our little soul-revealing conversation, is over.

He glances at his screen and then me. "My team in the surveillance truck confirmed they're reviewing the feed again as well." He picks up his wine and takes a sip. "I'd say our target window for review is the window after we left the restaurant until to your arrival here. That's the only way our slayer could have been certain you'd find it."

"Agreed," I say, sliding down to the floor to gain a better view of the screen, which is focused on the front door.

"I started our review at one hour ago," Jacob says, tabbing through the footage, but almost instantly he adds, "Houston, we have a problem." He joins me on the floor, as if trying to gain a closer view himself. "We can't see feet level." He grabs his phone and dials it on speaker. The line rings once before a male voice answers.

"What's up, army dude?"

"We have a problem, Ash," Jacob bites out, almost sounding frustrated, almost, but that would require emotion, of course, that he doesn't show. "This security footage cuts off at knee level. We need to see the ground."

"I'm good at what I do," Asher says. "But I can't create feed that wasn't fucking shot."

"What about cameras on aligned structures?" Jacob counters.

"There aren't any cameras to hack," he says. "It's a residential area, and not a fancy high-rise, high security residential area, either. And even if we captured a random camera, it's not going to show her porch. I'll get with our team and get corrections made."

"Can we make sure those same corrections are made with my father's team?" I ask.

"Done," Asher says before he adds, his keyboard clicking. "I just messaged Savage. And nice to fucking meet you, detective."

Obviously, he talked about me with Savage, and I accept the prompt accordingly. "Nice to fucking meet you too, Asher. Nicer if you can get me footage of our butterfly slayer."

"Nicer indeed," Asher agrees. "I'll hack around and see what I can do, but no promises."

"Call us back to confirm your failure," Jacob snaps, clearly challenging him.

Asher laughs. "Okay, man. I know you're punching my buttons and I'm taking the bait. I'll call back and when I do you'll say thanks for all your fucking badass-ness, Asher—"

Jacob hangs up. "We need to look through the footage and make sure your slayer isn't in the building."

"Agreed," I say. "But then I want to see the notes."

"Understood," he says, but he's focused on the computer screen, already tabbing through the footage, slowing it as two people head inside the building: a pretty blonde and her guest, a man with a beanie and a scarf that blocks his face "That's Sally Moore," I say. "Her bed is a rotation of men that she doesn't know. She'd actually be a perfect target for a male slayer to enter the building."

Sally and her man enter the building and Jacob leaves the now uneventful feed rolling, while pulling up a messenger window and types: *Put cameras on every residential door in the building, starting with Sally Moore on the top floor. In the meantime, if the man she brought home tonight leaves, follow him. Find out who he is.*

The reply from Chow Hound is instant: *On it and on it.*

"Who is Chow Hound?" I ask, as Jacob begins tabbing through footage again.

"Finn," he says. "Ex-Chicago detective, who is now manning the surveillance van. And as you might guess, he is always stuffing his face."

"Do you give everyone nicknames?" I ask.

"Yeah," he says, glancing over at me. "I guess I do. Ash is 'Tat Dude.' He has double sleeves. Royce is "King Kong" because he goes at everything with brute force. Blake is "Fuck Face" because fuck is a verb, noun, and adjective for him. You get the idea."

"But you don't make jokes."

"The nicknames protect their identity," he says, quite seriously.

"Right. Got it. And what's my nickname?"

"You don't have one," he says. "Not yet."

"Any ideas floating around in your head? Because I have a few ideas for a nickname for you. Asshole. Bigfoot. Preacher boy. No. Make that Saint."

"Saint?" he asks, glancing over at me.

I don't answer. I point at the security footage and we're both instantly focused on the feed, where a petite brunette female has appeared on film. "That's Mary Anne," I say, as Jacob slows the action again. "She's a school teacher and complete sweetheart. She lives on three. And her guest list runs the same as mine, which is no one at all." She enters the building and almost instantly, a man appears on the feed.

"Tim Mayfield," I say, of the tall, good looking man in a suit. "He's an attorney who is as arrogant as you are. He's also a man-whore, who I'm pretty sure has done Sally, or she's done him and made him think he did her."

Tim turns and faces the security panel and a realization hits me. "Freeze that."

Jacob hits the space bar and looks at me and says, "We can't see the front of him or his feet."

"Exactly," I say. "And if you look closely, there is a bit of a recessed area at the security panel. That's where I found the butterfly. You can't see that shadowed area on the camera, and even if you could see the ground, I don't think you'd be able to make it out."

"Or see if anyone at the panel dropped something."

"Maybe in the daylight," I suggest. "But not at night."

"That butterfly could have been placed hours before I arrived," I say, as Jacob hits the spacebar again, and Tim enters the building.

"True," Jacob says, "but the only way the slayer could have been certain that you'd be the one who found it would have been to place it right before you arrived."

"And on that note, there I am on the feed and nothing obvious happened before I got there."

"That we can see," Jacob points out.

"I know I'm not crazy," I say, lifting myself up to the couch. "Someone put that butterfly on the porch. Can you give me the security feed to look over before I go to sleep?"

He joins me on the couch again. "We'll have to go through it together. Ash codes our data with a secure link that won't work on any computer he hasn't approved in advance."

That hits me ten shades of wrong. "You're serious?" I don't wait for a reply. "I've agreed to this arrangement despite the many concerns that I've expressed, namely you becoming a trigger for the slayer, but I can't even look at the security footage of my own apartment by myself?"

"I can call Ash, but that means he'll come here and setup your computer, which could bring more of the attention from the slayer, you don't want."

"And we both know that can't happen," I say, feeling as if I'm losing control of a situation that directly affects my father's safety, and I can't let that happen either. "Tell Royce Walker I want to have an official meeting with him tomorrow about how we coordinate this investigation." I reach for my briefcase where it sits on the floor and manage to hit my wine glass that tilts toward Jacob's keyboard.

I lunge for it, and so does he, and in the same moment that he rights the glass, our foreheads collide. He curses softly while I suck in air, and somehow my hand settles on his cheek and his on mine. Our foreheads part but we don't pull back. We linger there together, as if frozen, that push and pull between us all pull now. The anger now lust. The heated words now an invitation for a heated kiss. In this moment, I decide that I most definitely don't hate him. He probably doesn't hate me either, but we'd both be better off if he did, if I did. But it doesn't matter either way. Not now. Not when he smells like winter spice, delicious and addictive. And his breath is a warmth on my lips that I feel in every intimate part of my body.

"You okay?" he asks finally, his voice low, rough, affected for the first time since I've met him.

"I'm a detective," I reply. "Of course, I'm okay."

"You're also human," he says.

"Like *you're* human, Mr. Never-Tells-a-Joke-or-Flirts?"

His hand slides to my neck, where it closes around my braid. "I'm protecting you," he says, his grip tightening around my hair, but not pulling, not tugging my mouth to his. "It's okay," he adds, "to need me. It's okay to be more than the badge. You know that, right?"

He's hit a nerve. A big, deep burning nerve that reaches deep into the past where the word "need" translates to loss, death, and murder. I pull back, breaking our connection, standing as I do. He's on his feet by the time my bag is on my shoulder, and that just feels like he's suffocating me. "The badge is who I am," I say. "There isn't more than my badge and as for needing you. I do. To protect my father. You can sleep in the library upstairs. The couch folds out into a bed but there are no walls or doors. In other words, don't sleep naked." I rotate and start walking, the weight of his stare following me, while the way I can still feel his hand on my face taunts me.

"Detective."

I stop at the open door to my bedroom, but I don't turn. I wait, and he waits, until I say, "Yes?"

"I never sleep naked when I'm alone."

I whirl around to face him. "Is that a joke?"

"I don't joke, remember?" he replies. "I simply state facts." And with that statement, he walks toward me, closing the space that I need between us, but that I don't want. I consider backing up, retreating, but then he has the control that I can't, and won't let go.

And so, I stand my ground and he keeps coming, until we're toe-to-toe. "And the fact is," he adds, "that when I'm on the job, I can't ever let myself be naked, or exposed. Because that means you're exposed."

"I don't need to hear this," I say, curling my fingers in my palm a moment because, for some godforsaken reason, it wants to land on his chest.

"Yes, you do," he says. "Because whatever this is between us—"

"Is nothing," I supply. "There is nothing but this investigation between us."

"And yet there is more," he says.

"I don't do more."

"I don't do denial," he counters. "It backfires, which is why I'm standing here. Which is why I'm saying right now that when this is over—"

"We'll say goodbye," I supply, entering the bedroom and shutting the door. Once it's sealed, I collapse against it, and damn it, I didn't let him finish. I don't know what he was going to say, and why do I regret that so damn much right now? Goodbye is easier when it's said from the very beginning. I've learned that the hard way. And nothing, and no one, not even Jacob's arrogant, good-looking, Green Beret ass is going to make me forget that.

FALLING UNDER

Chapter Twelve

Jewel

Fifteen minutes after I've left Jacob on the other side of my bedroom door, I'm in thermal pajamas, sitting on my bed cross-legged, ready to start my own investigation. My service weapon is also on the nightstand next to my phone where I always keep both ready to use, my version of two bodyguards. Only tonight I have a towering brooding man as my bodyguard as well and I'm trying not to think about how close he came to kissing me, or how much I actually *wanted* him to kiss me. Which would be a distraction that neither of us can afford. Not with the Butterfly Slayer potentially becoming the slayer of someone I love: like my father.

On that note, I refocus and open my MacBook to pull up a blank word document where I type one word: Butterfly.

Where does that lead me?

The past.

Tabitha's murder.

My dead, *murdered*, best friend, who my father didn't even know. That means I'm being led to my past, not his. This is personal. It's about me, not my father. Unless...I thrum the metal beside the spacebar, considering what to type and where this is leading. Many of my friends from the past were headed into a medical field, and my father's merger is in the pharmaceutical industry. It doesn't have to be about me. I could just be the weapon someone is using against my father.

I start keying in names of people from my past who might know about the butterflies, with the intent to search for connections to my father and/or his company. I've typed twenty names when the text message window connected to my phone pops up with a message from Jacob: *Hello?*

Hello, I type.

Nothing on the security feed, he replies.

The security feed I wasn't cleared to review. My lips thin and I type*: You don't know what you're looking for.*

You can come and help me, he offers.

"We both know that's not a good idea," I murmur, as if he can hear me.

And as if he *did* indeed hear me, my cellphone rings with his name on the caller ID. I grimace and hit the answer button. "Are you really texting me from the other room while calling me from the other room?"

"Asher's wife works in forensic psychology. I'll email you her resume but it's impressive. She's looked at the letters and she now knows about the butterfly. She thinks—"

"That butterfly is personal to me, and that makes this about me, not my father."

"Exactly."

"To which I say: possibly. But as we both know, I was headed to medical school back then. I had people in my life who were headed into medical fields, and could now have connections to my father in some way."

"Did Tabitha?"

"Not directly. She wasn't one of the medical students, but she hung out with me and my group."

98

"Darren Michaels?"

"Yes. She knew my then-fiancé well."

"Your then-fiancé who is now a surgeon."

"And married to someone else with two small children. He's an unlikely suspect and I know where you're going with this. I've already started making a list of everyone I knew in college who is in the medical field."

"Save yourself the time. Asher pulled a list of everyone who went to school at the same time as you and Tabitha. He's cross-referencing any connections to you, your father, his company, and anyone connected to the company. And that means digging into extended family member links from every direction. The data search will be extensive and of course, he'll do the deeper dissection of those closest to you. He'll have a report for you in the morning."

"He needs names to know who was close to me."

"There's an internet imprint that shows those connections."

"Right," I say, feeling as if I have absolutely no control over this investigation. "Of course, you can, but yet, I can't see the security footage of my own apartment." I disconnect and look at the time on my screen. It's somehow one a.m. and I have court in the morning. I shut my computer and that's when Jacob knocks on the bedroom door.

Grimacing, I push off the bed and walk to the door, yanking it open to find him crowding the doorway. "The part where I said goodnight and goodbye, didn't sink in, did it?" I challenge.

"You didn't, in fact, say either."

"Okay. Goodnight and goodbye." I try to shut the door.

He catches it. "Not yet," he says, too close now, but I won't back up and risk him joining me in the bedroom. "You hung up on me," he says, "before I could tell you that Savage looked through two days of security footage for your father's work and home locations. There's nothing out of the ordinary."

"I should look at it," I say instead. "I might recognize someone."

"Do you have the time to do that?"

"This is my father's safety. I'll make the time."

"I'll get you all of the security footage you want, and clearance on your computer as of tomorrow. I'm not trying to exclude you. I'm a resource. It's okay to—"

"Use you?" I challenge before he can throw out the "need" card again.

"Yes," he says, his eye glinting, reactive instead of flat and hard. "You can use me, detective."

"Some of the women you protect might find you confusing."

"You mean you."

"I'm simply making an observation."

"If we're going to take the liberty to make observations about each other, here's mine of you. You're a control freak and if using me makes you feel more in control, have at it." He releases the door, and adds, "Goodnight, detective," and nothing more. He simply walks away but there is nothing simple about that reply. I don't know why, but I know that he's angry. In other words, he's finally human. I'm probably too satisfied with that fact.

I shut the door and walk back to the bed and lie down. I stare at the ceiling a moment and then turn off the light. An image of the butterfly flashes in my mind, and with it a memory of Tabitha's funeral. Of a casket. Of tears. Of a sunny afternoon that was so damn hot that my tears evaporated on my cheeks, and that became a challenge to make more.

I shove the memory aside, when I should embrace it, and the clues it might lead me to discover. I dream about my cases. I answer questions in my sleep. It's how this has always worked, but in this case, doing so means embracing the pain and the guilt from the night of Tabitha's death. So much guilt. I could have saved her. I *should* have saved her. "Damn it, Jewel," I murmur. "Stop. This won't solve a case."

I shut my eyes and go ahead and use Jacob. After all, he said I could. I picture him standing in my doorway, broad and all leanly muscled, that perpetual firm set to his mouth. A mouth that was incredibly close to mine just this night. I relive that moment when his hand was on my face and mine was on his. I think of the kiss that didn't happen and won't happen. And tonight, Jacob is my hero. Tonight, he protects me from a brutal memory, a past with guilt, pain and murder. A memory I never let visit me in the darkness of any night, ever.

Sleep begins to overtake me, and it's all Jacob in my mind, until he's not. Suddenly, I am sinking into a nightmare, into the past. Into the exact place I didn't want to go. I try to wake up, but I can't. I'm stuck in the past. I'm back in college, in my dorm room with Tabitha, her sitting at a vanity against the wall. Me on the bed with books in front of me.

"You have to come to the party," she says, spraying a layer of hairspray on her brown, bouncy curls. She rotates in her chair to face me. "Pull all that gorgeous blonde hair of yours from your headband, and fluff it up into a bedhead look."

"A bedhead look? Are you serious?"

"Bedhead is sexy. So do it and then throw on some jeans and red lipstick. Come on. Do it. Come with me."

"I'm preparing for the MCAT. You know that."

She gives me puppy dog eyes. "You know that I get nervous at these parties alone."

"I know but—"

I never finish that sentence. Not this time. Everything goes black again, fading into sleep, ending, only it doesn't end. Suddenly, I'm back in the dorm room and I'm watching her walk out of the room. It's the last moment I'll see her ever again. And so, I live it, over and over and over. I see her open the door and disappear, the memory is on repeat.

There is more blackness and then: I'm standing over her casket, staring down at her, and she won't move. I want to shake her, and I swear I lean in to touch her, to actually shake her, when I'm transported to my uncle's funeral. Back to the graveyard. I can feel the cold wind, the sorrow, the pain. My father's hand on my arm. My gaze lifting and finding the man in the distance, watching us. And then it's darkness again.

Now, I'm back, living that night when I'd seen the stranger again. I'm back at my apartment gate, when I spot him, but I know he will get away. I don't walk as I did the first time to follow him. I run and I shout, "Stop! Stop now! Stop!" I run harder. "Stop now!" I can't see him. I'm in the darkness but I still have a sensation of running. "Stop!"

The bedroom door bursts open, shocking me awake and in a fast move I grab my gun from the nightstand. Twisting around, I aim at the door as Jacob stands there a gun in his hand. "What the hell happened?" he demands, scanning the room.

"Why are you in here with a gun?" I demand, trying to get a grip on the fact that the sunlight beaming through the thick gray curtains to my right means I've been asleep for hours.

"You screamed," he says. "You were shouting at someone. Who?"

"I didn't scream."

"You *did*," he insists, and he doesn't wait for an answer. He's already at the bathroom, entering, and I quickly scramble to my feet when the realization hits me. I'd been screaming at the man in my nightmares.

Since my gun does nothing to battle my nightmares, at least not in the present, I set it down on the nightstand, and freeze with an "oh shit" realization. The butterfly isn't the first thing I've found by that security panel in front of the building. That's what my mind was telling me in that nightmare. Jacob exits the bathroom. "What the hell happened?"

"Nothing," I murmur, but I'm already moving toward the door, rushing away.

I exit the bedroom, crossing the living area, and entering the kitchen to stand in front of the fridge, where that note is still pinned to the center.

"You're not ready yet," I read out loud, and where I'd thought it was a statement that I'd simply chosen to take out of context—perhaps someone late to a date—now I'm not so sure. Maybe the man I'd been chasing left it for me. If that's true, then that leads me to ask two very big questions:

How long has that man been watching me?

And what does he want?

FALLING UNDER

Chapter Thirteen

Jewel

I shake my head. *This is nuts*, I think. That note pinned to my fridge is two years old, and what does it have to do with the butterfly? My mind flashes to the Valentine's card that had read: *Finally, it's our time.* Why am I even going there though? That card was internal; a member of law enforcement gave it to me. It wasn't connected to this note, and yet—it feels connected. I need to go by the office before court. I need to see that card.

I leave the note behind, keeping it here and safe, and then turn, only to run smack into Jacob. My hands landing on the hard wall of his chest, while his big hands catch my arms. "What the hell is going on?" he demands.

"I had a nightmare and now I need to get ready for court. Let go of me."

"Do you have nightmares like that often?"

My defenses flare. "Why is that your business?"

"You were screaming," he bites out, his jaw shadowed, in need of a shave. "I pulled my weapon and I don't pull my weapon unless I intend to kill someone."

He's got a point. He pulled his gun and he did so to protect me. He deserves an answer. "I process my cases in my sleep," I say, my fingers closing around his T-shirt. "I wake up with answers. I didn't—I don't know if I screamed out. I don't remember doing that."

He studies me a moment and then flicks a look at the note on the fridge, before his attention returns to me. "What does that mean to you?"

"Unlike you," I say, "who feels being cocky is a necessity to winning, my uncle told me that the minute I think I'm ready, I'm too cocky, and I'm not."

"I'm confident, not cocky. And no disrespect to what your uncle meant, but if you think you're not ready, you aren't. In other words, I'm releasing but not letting you go. Because you're afraid, even if you won't admit it. I know fear is making you spin out of control and that's why you're pushing against my control. Stop pushing back and tell me what I need to know."

"So you can bulldoze the problem and spook the slayer into killing someone?"

"Don't make me the enemy," he bites out. "I would take a bullet for you, woman."

"I'm not making you the enemy."

"You are, and it can't continue, because whatever this is, whoever is behind it, I'm standing between you and it. And that should earn me trust and communication," He releases me, and turns away, walking toward the living room.

Angry.

Oh yes.

So very angry.

I don't immediately follow, because, damn it, when no one knows how to hit my nerves, he has done so yet again. He's uncovered my fear of being too confident, that at times creates insecurity in me. He's found my doubt in my uncle's words that I don't want to feel. I inhale and glance to my right to discover Jacob headed towards my bedroom, with his bag in his hand. "Hey!" I round the island and head that direction. "What are you doing?"

He turns to stand in my doorway. "There's one shower," he says. "I'm using it first because I'm not giving you a chance to take off while I'm in it later."

He turns and heads into the bedroom. I stop in my doorway, where he was a moment before, and I don't like this push and pull anymore. I think about the butterfly, the note, the nightmare that is telling me this is bigger than a protestor trying to freak out my father. And Jacob who has just opened up the shell I'm living in, and seen so much, so fast. But he also, stayed here with me. He pulled a gun to protect me. No one protects me. I protect them.

But he did.

Damn it.

I enter the bedroom door as the shower turns on, but I don't care. I cross and enter the open door. Jacob is standing in the center of the room, his shirt off, his jeans unbuttoned. Gorgeous. Really, gorgeous with 12-pack abs that only come from hard work and dedication, but I don't let that distract me. It can't. This is bigger than the two of us. It's about my father. It's about other innocent people that could get caught in the crossfire of whatever this is, and *this* feels dangerous.

"You're right," I say.

"What does that mean?" he asks, caution in his tone, which is progress beyond the monotone, unreadable questions, he usually directs my way.

"You deserve communication," I say, "but we have to come up with working rules that you respect."

"I can live with that but those working rules, have to apply in reverse."

"I can live with that as well," I agree. "But that means you don't charge at this investigation alone or with your people, without my input. We act as a team."

"Team," he repeats. "All right. We're a team. Tell me what I need to know."

"All I have right now," I reply, "is a weird hunch and even if I had time to talk about it now, I wouldn't do it when you're half-naked. I shouldn't have come in here now." I turn and walk toward the door and I don't know why but I pause at the archway, and look back at him to find that he's given me his back.

"You staying or going, detective?" he asks, obviously aware I'm still here.

It's a taunt or maybe it's an invitation that he follows up by reaching for his pants. Whatever his intent, staying would be a mistake we'd both have to live with and I don't like mistakes. Staying would make me need him in a far too personal way. And he'll see soon that I don't do need.

And so, I leave, but not without my vivid imagination trying to figure out what the ass that goes with those abs looks like, and the certainty that we need a new rule. I'm just not sure any that I come up with at this very moment would protect either of us. But I don't give it much consideration because my feet have taken me back to the kitchen and I'm standing in front of the fridge reading those damning words on the note: *You're not ready yet.*

Chapter Fourteen

Jewel

As Jacob so eagerly pointed out, I'm a control freak, and on his scale of one to ten I'd rank my control right now at a five. That's what's on my mind as I settle at the island of the kitchen with a steaming cup of chocolate-flavored coffee and power up my MacBook. I need to fix this problem. I need control. When I don't have control, things go wrong. People die. I gulp coffee on that note like it's tequila, because I don't need to be numbed. I need to get my brain fired up. I need to get my shit together and I won't even blame anyone for this but me.

This isn't Jacob's fault. It's not even my father's fault, despite his role in placing a hot, naked man in my shower. It's all mine. I own any moment where I let the bad guys get ahead, and the note on the refrigerator, the butterfly, the focus of all of this on me screams with my own guilt. I didn't suspect that note was a problem. Maybe it's not, but that note didn't even cross my mind. Not one time. I could blame my grief at the time, but I stared at the damn thing for two years, and still saw nothing but motivation.

My screen flashes with new emails as it juices up and I open the window to find the first entry is from Jacob. I open the message to read:

Detective:

As promised. An in-depth report on potential suspects. I've highlighted points of interest.

—Jacob, AKA Not an asshole, but in fact, a man of his word.

"But that doesn't mean you're not an asshole," I murmur, though I'm pretty convinced at this point that he's not, though it's too soon to make any definitive judgments. But he did what he said he would. He got me this list. That matters. The list and his word are noteworthy character markers. They also tell me he isn't intentionally trying to exclude me from this investigation. Or if he was before, he's recognized that as an illogical idea, considering I'm a detective.

I double-click on the attachment Jacob has included and watch it download. I glance at the time while it's working and it's late. I need to get in the shower to get ready for court. The tiny throb in my temples says I also need Excedrin to head off one of the migraines, which I don't admit to battling to anyone. In my world, I can't afford to show weakness, and that's not about being a woman. It's about being one of the humans on this planet who knows what evil walks amongst us.

The file opens on my computer and I immediately go to the summary page with Jacob's notes and five names of interest, all of which he's noted to have relevant connections to me or my father. I scan those names, the first three I don't recognize. They are, however, former classmates, all of whom went on to work in the medical profession, in operations that link in some way to my father's company.

The last two names, Darren Michaels and Tara Michaels, are highlighted, and with good reason. One is my ex-fiancé, and the other is his wife, who at one point, had been my jealous friend. Jacob's note reads: *The wife works for the pharmaceutical company that is being merged with your father's.*

My brow furrows with rejection of Darren as the man behind all of this. It doesn't fit him, and while I'm not a fan of Tara, the build of my watcher at the funeral was male. I'm sure of it. Not that either of them couldn't have hired someone to follow me, or hell, even kill me, but I'm not connecting with this premise. My gut isn't screaming in this direction.

That throb in my head is though, and I walk to the cabinet, pull out a bottle and down two Excedrin with a gulp of coffee that amounts to half a cup. I reach behind me and tug free the braids I slept in last night, certain they're the culprit, and not sure I can dare wear my hair back today without risking a full-blown head explosion. I've just finished fingering my way through the waves the braid created in my otherwise straight blonde hair when Jacob exits the bedroom, now dressed in black jeans, boots and a black collared shirt. His bag is not in his hand, which tells me it's still in my bathroom, because he's basically living here right now.

He heads toward the living area, where he's left his MacBook, and I cross to meet him on the opposite side of the coffee table. "I have cereal, milk, and coffee in the house," I say as I pass him. "There might be peanut butter."

"There was," he says.

I settle my hands on my hips. "You ate all of my peanut butter?"

"And a box of stale pastries."

"Those were really old." I laugh. "Were they good?"

"No," he says, shutting his Mac and straightening, "but I was desperate. It takes a lot of calories to be this big."

"That was a joke," I accuse.

"I don't joke," he says, all stone faced and robot like.

"It *was* a joke," I say, liking the way he's starting to let me see the real him. "But more importantly," I add, eager for more of him, "let's talk about your use of the word 'desperate'. It's so very human of you."

"I am," he says, "in fact, human."

"Hmm, well. The jury is out on that one, but I don't want to starve you. Then you might not be able to boss me around and generally be obnoxious."

"So, you *do* like me."

"I'm obnoxiously in like with you, so have some cereal on me. I have Rice Krispies in the cabinet."

"There's no milk."

"Orange juice is underrated on cereal. Try it." I tilt my head and give his clean-shaven, handsome face a once over. He arches a brow and I head toward the bedroom before calling out, "I liked the whiskers. They helped make you more human." I enter the bedroom and shut the door, leaning against it with a pulse of pain in the front of my forehead that does nothing to diminish my growing interest in the man beneath the robot. No one is as cold and hard as he is without a reason. And the truth is, I know the reason: death. Death has made him that way. I get it a little too well.

Pushing off the door, I head into the bathroom and since I shut the bedroom door, I don't shut this one. I'm about to strip for a shower, when I spy Jacob's razor and a few toiletries on the counter. I'm not even sure how to react. I've actually never had a man leave items at my place but right now, there is this funny feeling in my belly, I reject and reject quickly. My gaze lifts to the mirror, and I grimace with the realization that I still have on yesterday's make up, and it's all in the wrong places on my face now. My freshly freed hair is no different as it now points in about five random directions. I could write a book on destroying relationships before they ever start.

"I like your hair loose like this."

At the sound of Jacob's voice, and the low, gravely quality of his normally monotone voice, I slowly rotate to face him, my right hand settling on the counter. "Shut doors don't mean anything to you, do they?" I say, rejecting that funny feeling in my belly all over again.

"I forgot my watch," he says walking toward me, the bathroom suddenly small, when compared to most New York City apartments, it's quite large. He stops two small steps from our collision, and opens a drawer to remove his watch; an elegant silver number with a black band, and an inscription on the back. "Someone special gave it to you," I suggest, wondering if it was the special woman he claims he's never had.

He freezes with the clasp at his fingers, glancing up at me for two unreadable beats before finishing his task and then says, "Yes. Someone special gave it to me."

"Who?"

"You're nosy, aren't you?"

"Says the man who stalked me."

"To protect you."

"Then you'll appreciate that I can't protect myself without knowing the stranger in my house." I counter.

"My sister."

My brow furrows. "What?"

"My sister gave me the watch."

"You have a sister?"

"Had," he says, his hands settling at his hips, as he firmly jumps past the sister topic. "What was the Excedrin for?"

"Fighting with you gives me a headache," I say, deflecting as he just deflected.

"Don't fight with me," he suggests. "Headaches solved."

"Don't give me a reason to fight with you. Work with me, not above me."

"I *am* working with you, detective. In fact, I'm going to take over your computer while you're in the shower, and get it coded to match our data systems."

"How? Is Asher coming here?"

"He can do it remotely."

"I won't ask how. But fine. Do it. And don't nose around my documents."

"I'd tell you not to nose around, but since you're a saint, I'm sure you don't do that, either."

His eyes glint surprisingly hard. "Don't start thinking I'm anything close to a saint," he says. "We'll both end up disappointed." And with that, he turns and disappears through the archway, his footsteps heavy before the bedroom door opens and shuts.

I could blow off that comment about him not being anything close to a saint or I could let it lead me to naughty places that it's hard not to go to with a man like Jacob King. Just as it's hard for someone like me, who knows death, not to see the pain in his deflection over his sister. But most unpleasantly, with his anti-saint comment, my mind goes elsewhere: to the alleyway behind the restaurant, and to him burning Jesse Marks's file—a man who killed his family. A man Jacob doesn't want me to hunt down, and yet he has to know, I can't turn away. Not from the Jesse Marks mystery and not, it seems, anything to do with Jacob King. A man who is a puzzle I want to solve, and perhaps, that's why he interests me more than any other man in a very long time.

Chapter Fifteen

JACOB

I'm no damn saint, I think, exiting the detective's bedroom, proven by the fact that I'd like to shut up her smart mouth with my mouth. Not to mention all the creative ways I could think of to get rid of her headache. Like spanking her pretty little ass for being such a pain in mine. All thoughts that a man protecting her should not be having. And yet, I am. Every fucking moment I'm with her.

I shut the door, and damn it, setting aside the fact that I want to fuck her, I have no idea why I told her about my sister at all. Hell, why I told her about my life. Duty means being professional, unemotional—it means she's unfuckable no matter how damn fuckable I want her to be.

I round the island in the kitchen and press my hands to the counter. "Fuck. Fuck. Fuck." I grimace. Holy hell, now I sound like Blake Walker, who can't fucking say anything but fuck, which is just more proof that there is something about this woman that affects me. I should remove myself from this assignment, and if I was a saint, maybe I would, but I don't want to remove myself and even if I did, that's not even an option. Not with Jesse Marks on her radar, and her potentially on the wrong radar because of Jesse Marks.

Walking to the Keurig on the counter behind me, I grab a cup from the cabinet above the machine and then inspect

115

the pods. I have a choice between chocolate and chocolate, because the detective has a sweet tooth. Not that I'm complaining. Chocolate works for me. I stick the pod into the machine, wait for my cup to fill, then step to the refrigerator where I open the door and pour in creamer. I shut the door again, and stare at that note on the door: *You're not ready yet.* I assume it's in her uncle's writing and I get that the man was a great detective, but as far as I'm concerned, those are words that create hesitation in the face of danger and hesitation gets people killed.

My cellphone buzzes with a text and I set my cup on the island and dig my phone out to find a message from Asher that reads: *It's done. She logged onto her computer and I took over.*

I won't be telling the detective that Ash took it upon himself to hack her computer without her permission. I down a slug of coffee and set my cup aside again, about to reply to Ash when my phone rings with an unknown number. My jaw clenches with the certainty that this is the call I've been expecting. I answer the line. "Yes?"

"We have a problem, Major King," a male voice says. "And you're in her house right now. That seems quite a coincidence."

"It's an indication that I've ensured that she's not a problem."

"That better be the case, major. *Handle her* or we will."

The line disconnects.

I inhale and let the air trickle from my lips, aware that any call I make immediately after that one, will indicate a potential communication about Jesse Marks. It will connect whoever I communicate with to the problem and that's not an option. I set my phone on the island and open my MacBook, typing to Asher on iMessage. I'm connected to

"Tat Dude" almost instantly and he lets me know. *What's up, big boy?*

Past life experience coming back to haunt me, I reply. I need to see Royce in person. No phones. No online communication.

Fuck is Asher's response, because he's a man of brilliant words, and he's also an ex-SEAL, who served on the elite Team Six. He knows what "past life" means. And that's exactly why his only other reply is: *When and where?*

The courthouse, I type.

Confirmation pending, Asher replies.

My lips thin and I sit there, thinking through the tasks ahead of me. I need to silence a woman who won't be silenced, who I don't want to hurt. That's the complicated part, the not wanting to hurt her. Otherwise, I know how to make someone shut up and quit. I'm good at those things. Really damn good at those things. With my enemies, I look at it as pain for them equals results for me. However, Detective Jewel Carpenter is not my enemy, nor am I hers.

Over the next half hour, I work to formulate part one of a plan of action, while downing my coffee, and making another cup. I've just gotten a message from Asher with my confirmation when the bedroom door opens. I shut my computer as Jewel, *Detective Carpenter,* damn it, walks out of her bedroom in a black pantsuit, with her long, blonde hair loose at her shoulders. I stand up and she walks toward me, her steps weighted when they're normally light, her expression strained, but not angry. I know the tension etched in her face all too well, both from personal experience and observation: she's in pain.

She closes in on me and steps to the endcap of the island to my left. "Are we set?" she asks, indicating her MacBook.

"Yes," I confirm. "I can now officially share data with you."

"Did you snoop?" she asks, attempting her normal snark but her voice is weak, and the whites of her eyes are bloodshot.

"There wasn't time," I say dryly, and testing her pain level, I push for more of that snark of hers I apparently like, because I keep asking for it. "But," I add, "Asher downloaded all of your files for my review later tonight."

"Of course he did," she says dryly. "Because you're an asshole."

"I guess one of us already has a nickname."

"I have a few for you, actually," she says. "But as directed, I marked saint off the list." She walks to the counter, presenting me with her back, but I don't miss her scooping up that Excedrin and slipping it in her bag. "We should head out," she says, and when she would return to the endcap of the island, I don't allow it.

I snag her wrist. I would never randomly touch another woman I was protecting, but then, I'm no saint, and she's not another woman. She's the one fucking my head ten ways to Sunday.

"What are you doing?" she demands, her crystal blue eyes wide, but of notable interest, is the ease at which she allows me to walk her to me. Which speaks of pain or interest, or perhaps a combination of both.

"You have a migraine," I say, my hands settling on her shoulders. "That's why your hair is down when you wear it back to downplay being a woman. But you can't risk the pressure on your head today making the pain worse."

"You have no idea what you're talking about."

"I get headaches," I say. "Which is why I know a beast of one when I see it."

"Mr. Green Beret gets headaches?"

"I've had my head used as a punching bag a few times."

"Right," she breathes out. "I shouldn't have joked about that. You're really a hero. You fought in real wars."

"You're fighting in real wars, too, detective," I say, damn near calling her "sweetheart" when that never happens to me.

"I'm not," she says.

"You are. Just a different kind."

"I investigate. I ask questions. You put your life on the line every day, and I need to take a moment right now to say, that despite all my Green Beret comments, I respect your service."

"Does that mean you'll stop fighting with me?"

"Are you going to stop fighting with me?" she challenges.

"Good," I approve.

"Good? How does that fit the context of the conversation?"

"You're still sharp enough to deliver verbal punches so this should do the trick." I reach in my pocket and present her with a BC powder, which is just powdered aspirin. "Have you ever tried these?"

"No, but you actually carry those with you? How bad are your headaches?"

"Bad enough," I say, not really interested in where a more detailed answer would lead her. "The powder works if you catch the headache early enough, but it tastes like shit." I open the thin rectangular package for her. "Toss it back and then down the coffee. The caffeine boost will help the powder work faster, and you're going to want something that tastes good anyway."

"I'll try anything at this point." She downs the powder and makes a horrible face that is adorably sexy.

"Help," she chokes out, accepting the cup in my hand. "Wait. It's yours."

I laugh and order, "Drink it," and she doesn't need to be told twice.

She tips it back and gulps several swallows. "That really was nasty."

"Yes," I say, taking the cup from her and setting it on the island, "but by the time we get you to the courthouse, your headache will be bearable."

"Eck." She makes another face. "I can still taste it." I laugh again, I can't help it. She grabs the mug again and gulps more coffee, looking over the rim to glare at me. "Really? You chose to finally laugh and it's at my misery?" She sets the cup down and punches my shoulder. "Your nickname fits. *Asshole*."

"Finally laugh?"

"Yes. Stop being the robot you think you have to be to protect me. It doesn't work for me and it has to suck for you."

I stopped being a robot to the job the minute I met this woman, but I don't think sharing that is the right decision. Instead, I move on, glancing at my watch instead, and noting the time. "We should go."

"Fine. I get the blow off I was just delivered. Continue the robot routine and I will continue to pretend you are not doing it, until you stop doing it." She grabs her Mac, sticking it into the bag resting at her hip. "Are you taking your Mac?"

"I need to be mobile," I say. "I'll leave mine here."

"Mobile," she repeats, facing me again. "To protect me."

"Yes," I confirm. "To protect you. Be it by way of providing BC powder or be it to end a bigger asshole than me that means to hurt you."

"Thank you," she surprises me by saying, her mood instantly serious, and when I look at her there is a punch of awareness between us, and far more in her eyes now than pain. A soft, warm something that says she let me pull her close, because she wants to be close, the way I want her close. But then I already knew that. We've been fire and ice from the moment we met. "For the BC powder," she adds, "and for pulling your gun this morning to protect me, even if I didn't need protection."

"That's a good thing. The not needing the protection."

"Yes," she says. "Agreed. Jacob, no one knows about my headaches, so can you—"

"Your secret is safe with me."

"I appreciate that," she says. "I—Is that why you left the Army? The headaches?"

"No. I had them for years before I left. Adrenaline will kill even the worst of a headache, which I'm sure you know."

"Yes. I know. Do you tell people that you get headaches?"

"I don't tell people anything about me."

"But you have me," she says, and I shouldn't be surprised at the observation. She sees things. She gets things. She gets me like I do her, even if she doesn't realize that yet. Or ever. Fuck. Where the hell am I going with this woman?

"You have me," she repeats.

"You just nag it right out of me."

"Asshole," she says, but it's more of a tease than an insult at this point.

"Yes," I say, "but I'm *your* personal asshole for now. Let's talk about what comes next."

"Yes. Let's. To be clear," she says. "I'm not stupid. The butterfly freaks me out, as it should. If it turns out to be a real problem, I'll be glad you're my shadow."

"But you're still concerned that my nearness will make your slayer attack elsewhere," I say, seeing where she's leading me.

"You *have* to admit that's a concern."

"What I know is that whoever this is, is fixated on you. Whoever this is, is also smart enough to drop that butterfly by the door without Walker knowing. And we're damn good at what we do. That means this person is damn good, too."

"If this person really left the butterfly," she supplies.

"We all have to assume they did."

"I don't disagree," she says "Like I said. I'm not stupid."

"And we have to assume that the slayer will eventually come for you," I continue. "But I am not easy to go through which is why I don't give two fucks about being a trigger when there could be ten others, and my distance leaves you exposed. I'm staying close. Don't argue. You won't win."

"Thanks to this headache, I really don't have it in me to argue with you *and* potentially the judge at the hearing this morning. So, what's the plan right now, this morning?"

"I say we go with your plan. If I was your protector, I'd hide. I'm not hiding. I'm just the guy you're fucking."

She blanches. "Not literally."

"Fine. I'm the guy you're dating."

"I don't date," she says. "No one would believe that."

"All right then," I say. "I'm just the guy you're fucking." I arch a brow, and there's a question there I shouldn't be asking, and yet, I wait for her answer.

"Fine then," she says, her eyes warm, her voice hinting at a rasp that tells me what I want to know. "We're fucking," she adds, and with those words, her gaze meets mine for a jolt of a moment, before she rounds the island and heads for the door.

Running from the connection, she wasn't running from a moment ago, and I make a decision right then. I can't let her run. She might run to the wrong place, and end up dead. And so, I pursue her, grabbing my jacket as I go, and I'm at the door by the time she's there, opening it for her. She exits, and I lock up, catching up with her on the stairs, stepping to her side where I intend to stay. We head down the stairs in silence, and me pulling on my jacket does nothing to dilute our little conversation about fucking that is in the air, right along with an expectation of danger. Every step we take, I'm more in tune with her and with my gut feeling. She's in danger, and after that phone call, not just from the slayer. We reach the end of the steps, and I pause at the door, and make another decision.

"Me first," I say, my intent to shield her, and I don't give her time to object. I step outside and I rotate to face her, forcing her to step directly in front of me. The instant she does, I reach for her, one hand at her hip, the other under her hair at her neck, dragging her close.

"What are you doing?" she demands, sounding breathless, her hand flattening on my chest. Holy hell, I really like her hand on my chest.

"Showing anyone watching that this just got personal for me," I say, leaning in, our lips a breath a part.

"Don't kiss me," she whispers, a moment before I would.

"Sorry, detective," I say. "But this is for your own good." I close my mouth down on hers, and I intend one quick slide of tongue to tongue but my intention goes full-on to hell and quickly. The minute I taste her, I need more. My hand slides to her back, between her shoulder blades, and I deepen the kiss. Drinking her in, savoring the sweetness of a woman who is all fire and ice. And she tries to be ice now, stiff for just a lick, before her arms soften. Until she is responding, sinking into the kiss, a soft little moan escaping her lips that is the submission I didn't know I craved from her. I feel it in my cock. I feel it in the adrenaline coursing through my veins that is too hot, too demanding for right here and now. I drag my mouth from hers before I go too far, and I want to go too far.

Our lips part and we linger there a moment, breathing together, the heat between us damn near combustible. "I don't—" she begins.

"I did," I supply, "and I don't have any regrets." I take her hand and we head down the stairs, and yes, I feel the eyes of the Walker team, but there is more. I feel the eyes of the enemy, heavy, attentive, and calculating.

Chapter Sixteen

JACOB

Still holding the detective's hand, I lead her in the direction of the subway three blocks from her apartment, and for a full sixty seconds, things are uneventful. The instant we're crossing the first roadway that changes when she tugs unsuccessfully against me, trying to separate our hands. I hold onto her, bending our elbows and dragging her next to me. "Don't go blowing the cover story I just set up for us," I warn as we step onto the sidewalk again. "We're fucking, remember?"

"What happened to being professional, Mr. Robot?"

"It was my professional assessment that we should kiss."

"Really?" She glances over and up at me. "That was a professional decision? To kiss me and not ask in advance?"

"It was absolutely a professional judgment that I kiss you at that very moment," I confirm. "I just happen to be enjoying my job a little more than usual today. And judging from the way you kissed me back, you are, too."

She cuts her gaze, but not before I spy the heat in her cheeks. "I don't know why I kissed you back."

"Because you wanted to?"

She cuts me a sharp look. "I considered kneeing you instead."

"Because you didn't actually *want* to kiss me," I press.

"You shouldn't have turned us into a peep show."

I stop and pull her around in front of me. "Us?" I demand softy, liking the sound of that far more than I should.

"My mistake," she amends. "Me. You made me a peep show."

"I made you mine to everyone watching."

"I'm not yours or anyone else's."

"Now you are," I say, my tone damn near guttural and I don't even know the fuck why.

"I don't want anyone to think I'm weak enough to be your bimbo."

"And here I thought you were empowered enough to make me your fuck buddy, not the other way around. I didn't warn you because I needed you to be authentic."

"What if I really would have kneed you? Then what?"

"I gambled on you wanting to kiss me."

"Because everyone you protect wants to kiss you?" she challenges.

"Do you think that's who I am, detective?" I bite out.

"You barely know me, and you kissed me," she says, jabbing at my chest, as if she wants to be certain that everyone watching knows that we're fighting.

"I barely know you, woman, and I've talked to you about things I never talk to anyone about."

"Am I supposed to believe that? Why would you do that?"

"I've been trying to figure that out myself," I say.

"You—"

"Wanted to kiss you? Yes. If you don't want to admit that you wanted to kiss me, don't. If you don't want me to do it again, I won't. It was done until you started this confrontation and that means it has to happen again. After that, dig for your phone and you'll have an excuse to ignore my hand when we start walking again."

"After what?"

I pull her to me and kiss her firmly on the lips. "That. After that and since you seem to hate my fucking kisses, I made it quick. Now, if you want it done, it's done. I'm going to let you go. Do as I say. Dig for your phone."

But that's not what she does. I let her go and her hand that rests on my chest curls around my shirt, and she steps closer, her legs pressed to mine. "Kissing me, and me kissing you back, does not give you the right to overstep boundaries that we have yet to set."

"Understood," I say.

"I don't think you do."

"Understood, detective," I repeat more firmly. "We'll set the boundaries together. We'll do this, all of this, together."

"If you mean that, then I'm in. If you don't, your Green Beret skills won't save you. I will hurt you."

"As much I might enjoy that," I say, because she's standing so fucking close to me right now, it already hurts, "I'm a man of my word."

"Good," she says. "Because I have questions for you that I expect real answers to."

"I'm aware of that," I reply, also aware that she's talking about Jesse Marks.

"This doesn't, and won't, stop me from looking into that case file," she adds.

"Don't you need to get to court?" I ask, because now would not be the right time to tell her that her investigation is permanently closed.

"I'm only letting you get away with dodging a direct answer because yes, I need to get to a bail hearing."

She tries to pull her hand back and I catch it, covering it with my own. "Did you want to kiss me, *detective*?"

"Yes, *asshole*, I wanted to *fucking* kiss you."

I arch a brow. "Asshole?"

"It's your nickname, remember? Spoken fondly, of course."

"Fondly," I say, fighting a smile. "Got it." I wrap my arm around her neck, keeping her in front of me, my cheek sliding to hers, lips by her ear. "You feel it, right?" I ask, and I'm not talking about how much I want to kiss her again.

"Yes," she says, and when I pull back to look at her, she confirms her understanding. "We're being watched," she adds softly, "and not just by your people."

"And now they know they have to come through me to get to you," I say. "You might not see the value in that, but your slayer does, I promise you." I don't give her time for her normal bravado, that one way or the other she'll figure out she doesn't need with me. "Come on," I say, turning her, my arm settling around her shoulders, and setting us back in motion.

"What if you're wrong?" she asks as we cross the next intersection. "What if you just pulled that trigger with the slayer that I've been trying to avoid?"

"I'm more worried that I've driven him into a hole. Someone this smart, and this devious, is better lured out than left to plot and plan on their own."

"And if he acts rashly?"

"If he was meticulous enough to find out about a butterfly fetish that is years old, that's unlikely. But if he does, is rash really better than calculated?"

"Calculated would most likely be focused on me."

"How do you know that calculated doesn't equal exactly what you fear?"

"Meaning what?"

"A well-planned attack on your precinct. Or on your father's business or home. My point here, is there is that we're both guessing. And I say drive the slayer out while you have an army of the Walker Security team as a shield."

"I get it," she says, looking at me. "There's no right or wrong answer. I just hope yours is the right one, because you've set us on that path."

I hold my reply as we round the subway wall, joining a crush of people on the downward stairwell and perhaps this would be a good time to let go of her. I don't. I hold onto her until we're swiping our cards through the payment gates. On the other side, I don't reach for her again, but we have a matched pace, side by side as we hurry down the stairs toward the proper gate, arriving as the doors to our packed train open.

Now, I snag Jewel's hand again, done calling her detective at this point, at least in my mind, and I lead her onto the busy car into a tight corner, grabbing the strap above us with one hand. Jewel turns to face the general population, her back to me, but she doesn't have the luxury of my six feet four inches which allows me a substantially better view. I watch several people shove into the crowd. I can't see who might enter from the other side of the car, but I don't sense a problem. The car begins to move, throwing Jewel backward into me. I catch her, my hand settling on her belly, and for just a moment, she doesn't move. In fact, she tilts her head back onto my shoulder, her hand covering mine, and fuck. I *want* this woman, and when she turns to face me, her hands settling on my chest, her legs still tightly aligned with mine, it's clear she wants me, too.

I cup her face and lean down, my lips finding her ear. "How's your head?"

"Better since you kissed me," she says. "Adrenaline and all, you know?"

I smile against her cheek. Hell. I don't remember the last time I spontaneously smiled because of a woman. "Are you flirting with me, detective?" I tease.

"Of course not," she says, leaning back to look up at me. "I'm a professional."

I laugh and she laughs, and for a blink, I have a glimpse of Jewel without her many walls, a vulnerable side of her that I'm not even sure she knows she's shown me. "I need you to trust me," I say, seizing the moment, and thinking of our conversation before we entered the subway. "I'm not going to let anything bad happen."

"That's a big promise but then you're all about big. Big words. Big attitude. Big—"

"Big?"

She laughs at the corner she's painted herself in as the car jolts to a stop, and just like last night, our foreheads collide. And just like then as well, our hands settle on each other's faces again, lips close, the sexual tension between us in that moment utterly combustible. The instant the door announcement comes though, I pull back, ready for anything new to come our way. Keeping her close and safe, I lace my fingers with hers, but once we're outside the car, in proximity of the courthouse, in her professional territory, I release her.

Side by side, we walk up through the terminal and a block street-side, before she grabs my arm and pulls me to the side of a building. "Detectives don't have fuck buddies following them around. I can't have you do that without creating questions that I don't want to answer. As it is, I feel obligated to tell my boss that I'm investigating these threats."

"I'm escorting you to the courthouse," I say, "and the bail hearing."

"You're carrying a weapon," she says. "I felt your gun under your jacket. You can't get into the courthouse."

"I'm disarming."

"How can you disarm on a New York City street?"

"Like this," I say, as a man in a gray suit with dark wavy hair steps to our side. "Detective Carpenter," I say, "meet Adam." I remove my weapon and hand it to him. "Adam, meet Detective Carpenter."

"Nice to meet you, detective," he says, holstering my firearm in a holster under his jacket. "If you need me, I'll be there. No song lyrics included with that statement."

"Was that a joke?" Jewel asks, glancing at me and then Adam again.

Adam gives her a stone-faced look. "I don't do jokes," he says. "I'm always professional." He laughs and looks at me, not her.

Jewel laughs and looks at me, too. "You have a reputation that extends beyond me, I see."

"Apparently," I say dryly. "But then, Adam and I are a different species. He's an ex-SEAL."

"We are," Adam says. "Divided by those who can swim and those who cannot."

"A bunch of wet SEAL boys," I say. "You know what we call those, don't you?"

"You're the pussy, Beret," he says, and he glances at Jewel. "I assume you don't have virgin ears, detective, so I won't apologize."

"We're done here," I say, taking her arm, and guiding her away from him and onto the walkway.

"You're not as dry as I thought you were," she teases.

"Aren't you funny?" I ask, releasing her as we hit our stride.

"Not usually, actually," she says. "My skill lies in my ability to be snarky and demanding." She rushes forward, only to step in front of me in a backward walk, before planting her feet. "You can't go to the courthouse with me. Do your invisible man routine. I'll call you before I leave and all that stuff I know you'll demand." She doesn't wait for my argument. She rotates and takes off walking. I let her pull ahead, following her but giving her space, but I don't intend to give it to her for long.

Once she starts up the heavy high concrete steps leading to the courthouse, I close the distance between us, weaving through the crowded path. Watching anyone and everyone as I do. Watching *her*. Aware of Adam as he steps to my right rear, who obviously has already handed off my weapon, and his, to Finn. And man of disguise that he is, his suit helps him blend into the legal crowd, his appearance the opposite of mine, by intention. We never fit together, and yet despite his newness to our team, the ground pounder and the sea monkey have found we work together perfectly. Jewel enters the courthouse, and I enter just behind her and three other people. She clears security, and I manage to do so right behind her, without my shoulder strap even being noticed, which is exactly why no one is ever safe in this place except today, with my team here.

A few steps behind her, I'm on the stairs leading to the next level, and in the center of a cluster of people. She turns a corner, and I cut right and double step to catch up with her. I'm literally right behind her and she reaches around her to jab my leg, letting me know that she knows where I am this time. She senses me now. She wasn't aware enough before and she needed to be because she won't have the chemistry she has with me to connect to with someone else.

She enters the courtroom and I step to the side of the door, and Adam follows her inside, with not a hint of a look in my direction, but he drops a toothpick: a message that tells me I have a meet up in the stairwell next to the bathroom. I cut a look right, find the sign, and walk in that direction, following it right. The expected exit sign is next to it, and I enter the stairwell to find Royce waiting on me, his long dark hair tied at his nape, his suit blue, and tie also blue.

He doesn't speak. That's not his thing. He's a man of few words, but when he chooses words, they're thoughtful and usually hard, but I find I want to hear what he speaks. "Thanks to her interest in me," I say. "Detective Carpenter decided to dive into a top-secret case concerning a scandal the government doesn't want uncovered. The kind I can't explain to you and the kind that means trouble for her. The kind you don't come back from."

"What do you need from me?"

"She's working cold cases. I need to be contracted in to work cold cases, and now."

"Done. The NYPD is always happy to claim free help, especially from us. By the time she gets out of court, you're her new partner. How's she going to respond to that news is the question."

"I'll handle her."

"I hear you have quite the technique for handling her," he says, obviously indicating the kiss.

"I sent a message. Come for her, you go through me."

He gives me a three-second, hard-ass stare. "You're a professional. I'm not going to tell you not to fuck on the job, because you don't fuck up on the job. But don't make this a

133

first." He turns and starts walking down the stairs and it's not him I'm worried about fucking up with. It's Jewel. I told her she could trust me, and now I'm about to sideswipe her, but I have no choice. I can't risk her fighting me on this. Because I have to know what she is doing at all times. It could be a matter of life and death.

Chapter Seventeen

Jewel

Jacob King is more than one kiss and a lot of pissing me off. That becomes utterly, completely obvious when, in the midst of a courtroom that is press-laden, he's chaos in an unexpected way. I sit in the front row, just behind Evelyn, where she sits at her DA assigned table and despite the buzzing crowd all enthralled by the billionaire CEO and his dead wife and child, I know the moment he enters the courtroom. I have this sudden, intense, overwhelming awareness of him that I've never had with any other person in my life. I fight the urge to turn and look behind me, certain he's close, perhaps in the row directly behind me, but I resist my need for confirmation. I'm simply not willing to let anyone know that I'm looking for him, especially since he's not the only one I feel. The slayer is here. I know because I sense him, too. I can't explain how I know that either, but somehow I really do have a stalker, but his name is not Jacob, and he's here now, too.

I pull my phone from my jacket and text Jacob the exact words he spoke to me earlier: *You feel it, right?*

His reply is instant. Yes, but I don't have a visual.

I am more relieved than I should be at his reply and confirmation that he is here. I'm not supposed to need comfort. I'm supposed to give it, and usually that works out well. I've learned, like most detectives, how to remain sympathetic to those I help, but also know how to tune out the parts of my job that would destroy me: those human parts that I can't allow to exist, and survive this job. But that talent is failing me now. The idea of being watched for years, and not knowing it, has shaken me in ways that I don't ever want to be shaken, and having Jacob at my back isn't all that bad after all. Kissing him isn't all that bad either.

I type a reply: *Where are you?* but before I hit send, a loud rumble of murmurs draws my attention to the door to the left of the judge's podium where the defendant is being escorted into the room. That defendant being Bruce Norton, the tall, dark, and obviously deadly, thirty-eight-year-old tech CEO billionaire who I damn sure know killed his wife and unborn child. The pretty boy who's now traded in the orange jumpsuit I put him in for one of his ten-thousand-dollar suits. I want him back in that jumpsuit.

Sticking my phone back in my pocket, I watch Norton's attorney, pretty boy Davis York, re-enter the courtroom after a previous departure, from the same door Norton had entered. In a blue suit that competes in price tag with his client's, he and his client take side by side seats at their table. I wonder how York looks at himself in the mirror every morning, but then, men like him tend to look in their wallets, at their cash, not at themselves. Though I have a feeling both of these slime bags tell themselves how gorgeous they are, how inferior the rest of the world is to them, every single day of their lives. I decide right then that I don't like pretty men. On the other hand, I apparently do, in fact, like ruggedly handsome men, which is what I'd called Jacob, a conclusion I base on the fact that, I sure as hell did kiss him back and enjoyed every damn moment of it. Well, until afterward, when I had to hear him point out how much I enjoyed it.

York looks over at the DA's table, and gives Evelyn a wink sure to be reported in the news. I watch Evelyn's perfectly manicured fingers tightening around her pencil, indicating her well-communicated dislike for the bastard, as well. She leans over and speaks to her co-counsel, her long blonde silky hair draped down her navy suit dress and I imagine her saying just that: *bastard.*

The judge is announced and the packed courtroom is instantly on its feet. The insanity of shoulder-to-shoulder bodies here for a bail-related event, proof that a good-looking billionaire always steals the show. In this case, the lives of his wife and unborn child, as well.

York stands. "Judge, my client is the CEO of a company that not only provides jobs for this state, but contributes substantially in taxes. By leaving him out of the driver's seat, and behind bars, the performance of that high-performing employer is in jeopardy, thus so are jobs and tax dollars." He lifts a folder. "I have fifty character references for your review."

Prepared for just this action, Evelyn stands up to present the counter that she and I prepared. "Aside from the fact that the defendant is filthy rich, and has the means to flee the country, he stands to inherit even more money from his wealthy, deceased wife."

"Objection," York says. "We don't have the bodies. She may well have used her money and ran away."

"We'll show evidence that clearly shows the defendant killed his young, beautiful, rich wife, and her unborn child. As for a flight risks," she holds up a folder of her own, "I have the only character reference that will matter. The female detective on the case who the defendant attempted to seduce."

"Objection, judge," York calls out yet again. "Do you know how many women proposition my client daily? When he turns them down, they get vicious. And that's what this entire case is about. A jealous female detective who lashed out when she didn't get a sugar daddy."

I don't react but Evelyn laughs, offering a quick, well prepared rebuttal. "Should I object to the ridiculousness of that statement," she asks, "or the sexist narrative, or how about I just let the court know that the detective in question recorded the conversation?" She flaps the folder in the air. "I have the transcript right here."

The judge, a fifty-something distinguished-looking man with dark salt-and-pepper hair, motions to the court clerk. "Bring it to me."

"Objection," York shouts. "I have not had the opportunity to review the transcript."

"I have a copy for you," Evelyn says sweetly, walking one to him, while the clerk hands one off to the judge.

York studies the statement, but I can't make out his face. He sets the file down and the courtroom watches the judge read his file, before looking up sharply, focused on Evelyn. "Is Detective Carpenter present?"

"She is," Evelyn replies.

"I'd like her to validate this statement."

"Objection, judge," York calls out. "This is highly irregular and—"

"Overruled," the judge bites out.

I stand up and walk toward the gate, while Evelyn directs the appropriate people to allow my passage. Both pretty boys turn to look at me, and in turn, I give them both direct, cold stares. I join Evelyn, who has a hard look on her face, and together we face the judge.

"Detective Carpenter," the judge addresses.

"Yes, your Honor?" I say.

"Please tell me in your own words what took place."

"Evidence directed my focus to the defendant. When my questions became uncomfortable for him, he tried to kiss me, and then asked me to leave the country, and the investigation behind to travel to Europe with him."

"To which you said?" the judge asks.

"I asked him who would find his dead wife and unborn child's bodies while we were gone? And of course, judge, at this point, I wonder who would run his company. Obviously, that wasn't the same concern just one month ago, when this took place, that it is now."

York pops to his feet. "Objection. Snark is not evidential testimony."

"Fortunately," the judge states, "this is an informal proceeding." He looks at me again. "Detective, do you believe he meant to flee the country?"

"I believe he meant to ensure he didn't have to flee the country by winning my favor, which unfortunately for him, belongs to his dead wife and child."

The judge studies me for several beats and then says, "You're dismissed, detective."

I nod and exchange a look with Evelyn, a nervous but confident energy between us, before I return to my seat, but before I even sit back down, I hear, "No bail." There are murmurs in the court and the judge hammers his desktop. Chaos erupts, and Evelyn gives me a celebratory thumbs-up, but as pleased as I am with the ruling, it's not over. For the next fifteen minutes, I am trapped in the center of chatter, objections, and finally, finality in the judge's decision. When it's all said and done, I push my way through the crowd, but not before pretty boy attorney catches my gaze, and surprisingly, there's amusement in his eyes. Almost like he's playing some cat and mouse game and we just took the bait he wanted us to take. But we won. His client is stuck behind bars. Unease rolls through me. What does he know that we don't?

He turns away and I make my way through the crowd, but I don't see or feel Jacob anymore. I don't see or feel the slayer either, which leads me to the conclusion, that maybe, just maybe, Jacob found him, and he's now following him. I'd find comfort in that, but I have this sense of disorder that started with pretty boy attorney and his smile. I head toward the stairwell, and I'm one flight down when my cellphone rings. I glance at the caller ID, unfazed by the unknown number, considering I hand out my card freely.

"Detective Carpenter," I say, exiting the courthouse.

"Detective," a mildly familiar male voice states. "Interesting. Are you fucking with me? Is this a game?"

"Who is this and what do you want?"

"Davis York," he confirms, "but you know that, right?"

I stop walking and freeze. Pretty boy attorney? "How did you get my number?"

"I had a message that it was urgent that I call this number, no name given."

"Who gave you the message?" I ask. "Your billionaire baby-killing client?"

"He's innocent, detective. And a security guard gave me your number. You weren't behind it?"

"If I wanted to talk to you, I'd walk right up to you."

"Uh," he says. "Someone must think they're entertaining."

I fight the urge to glance around me and look for that someone, if there is a someone other than his client. "Perhaps they saw the smirk you gave me in the courtroom," I say, heading down the stairs.

"Smirk. Interesting. I never have considered myself a smirking kind of guy. But why don't we have coffee and talk about it?"

I hang up before he can try to get information from me, only to find Detective Rodriquez, waiting for me at the bottom of the stairs, and he does not have a donut to offer me this time. "What a coincidence, Rodriquez," I say, joining him. "I think you're the only grown man I know that can pull off a black suede jacket and dress pants and not look like he's going to junior high prom."

"Coincidence?" he scowls, ignoring my commentary on his attire. "What the fuck? I got a message you needed back-up."

"What are you talking about? Who gave you that message and when?"

"You wanted me to meet you here." He pulls his phone from the blazer he's wearing and shows me the message from the front desk at the precinct: *Carpenter needs backup. Meet her on the courthouse steps when the bail hearing adjourns.*

A foreboding feeling slides through me but I downplay it to Rodriquez. "The switchboard owes you a donut. That message wasn't for you." I turn and start walking toward the subway, hoping to get rid of him and call Jacob, but it doesn't work. Rodriquez falls into step beside me.

"Who the fuck was it for then?"

"Someone taller, bigger, and a better kisser than you," I say, trying to distract him from a problem I don't want him in the middle of now or ever.

141

"You've never kissed me," he points out. "You don't know that."

"I've heard."

"Says the virgin detective."

"Why are you still with me right now?" I ask, not about to be lured into a conversation about my sex life, or lack thereof, with Rodriquez.

"Any lead on finding the rich dude's dead wife?"

"No," I say, glancing over at him. "Why?"

"I know a guy." He reaches in his pocket and hands me a name and number. "You need to know him, too."

I glace at the white piece of paper with a name and number written on it. "Why do I need to know this guy?"

"He makes problems disappear," he says, as we approach the entrance to the subway. "If your billionaire CEO made his dead wife go away, he'd be the one to make it happen."

"And you know this how?" I ask, stopping at one of a dozen gates that require a card to be swiped before they open.

"I'm supposed to know shit," he says.

"But why do you know this guy?" I ask.

"It's my damn job, Little C."

I swipe my card through the gate and walk through, expecting him to do the same, but on the other side, he's not there. I turn and find him walking backward, away from the terminal, but still facing me. "I forgot a meeting I need to be at," he says, giving me a two-finger wave. "Call my guy. He can help." He turns and leaves.

Meeting, my ass, I think. He just doesn't want to tell me how he knows this guy, and now I have no service, which means I've missed the chance to call Jacob about whatever the hell these weird games are that someone is playing with me. And where is Jacob, who stalked me until I actually wanted to find him? I head into the terminal and once I'm on my crowded train, I set my Spidey senses into action, and I just don't think he's here. Someone from Walker Security must be, but I don't know who or where.

The ride is short and I'm street-side quickly, a short walk from the station, with service returned to my phone. As soon as I hit the sidewalk, I expect my cellphone to ring or Jacob to step to my side. He doesn't. A bad feeling rushes over me. What if Jacob *was* a trigger and the slayer went after *him*? I take my phone from my pocket and dial his number. It goes to voicemail and I have a sudden realization. He is Mr. Professional, but he kissed me. Shortly after Adam showed up and made himself known to me. Either Jacob asked to be removed from my protective order or he was pulled by Royce Walker. Or he was killed by the slayer.

Arriving at the precinct door, I stop walking and lean on the wall, quickly locating the Walker Security phone number. I punch it into my cell, only to be greeted by an answering service. "I need to have Royce Walker and Jacob King call me. It's Detective Jewel Carpenter and it's urgent."

Concerned for Jacob, I consider calling my father, but I don't want to worry him, and surely the answering service will get the message to Royce for me and quickly. I decide I'll give them fifteen minutes and no more. If necessary, I'll go find a Walker Brother to help me. And Jacob is a Green Beret. He's not a boy scout, as proven by his handling of his weapon, not to mention the kiss.

I head inside the building, and remember that stack of cards on my old desk. I head to that level and today everyone is gone or has their head down, with only one stray "Little C" shout before I arrive at my desk. Rodriquez is nowhere in sight, but then neither is the card I'd left on my desk. Which is odd. Really damn odd. The others are here. Maybe I took it to my new office and just don't remember, but I don't think that is the case. "Detective Carpenter!"

At the sound of Lieutenant Ross, or rather, my boss, shouting my name, I rotate to find him standing in his doorway. "Get in here."

I assume he wants to talk about the bodies I have yet to produce for the trial, rather than the good news that the billionaire killer is still behind bars. That's his job. Push me. And push some more. Unfortunately, I think, crossing toward him where he waits for me in the doorway, I have an obligation to tell him about the slayer. Upon my arrival, he steps back and allows my entry. I clear the doorway and cut left to the seats, only to find Jacob standing in front of the desk, facing me. Adrenaline races through me, driven by anger and betrayal, and with my boss at my back, I walk up to him, and say, "Asshole" in a semi-low voice before Lieutenant Ross's door shuts.

Jacob gives me a cool gray stare, but he doesn't react, because of course Mr. Robot is back, though not to stay. I'm going to take care of Jacob King like he's never been taken care of before. And soon.

He's going to find out that I'm also more than the kiss he used to manipulate me. I'm the kiss he's never going to forget.

Chapter Eighteen

Jewel

Jesse Marks.

That is the name that comes to my mind as I stare at Jacob, trapped in silence by our location in my boss's office, my gut telling me now that every move Jacob has made since I showed him that file is about *that* file. My boss, Lieutenant Ross, joins us, claiming his rightful spot behind his desk where he sits down. Jacob gives me a small nod and then turns away, claiming his seat. It's all I can do to force myself to face forward and sit my butt in a chair. I do it though, but I'm aware of Jacob beside me, his leg so very close to mine. I am so damn aware of the man who almost made it to my bed before he sideswiped me that I want to hurt him, especially when I think of his promise that we were "doing this together."

My boss looks between us, a curious look on his face, and no doubt he feels my combustible energy with Jacob, but he leaves it alone. "I understand your father contracted Jacob and his team to beef up security, thus you have met," he says.

"That is correct," I state.

"What else?" he asks.

I look at Jacob. "Why don't you answer that question," I say, since I have no idea what kind of ditch he's driven me into. Just that I'm in one.

"Royce notified him about the notes you've been receiving," Jacob states, clearly trying to tell me that he didn't do this, but he didn't warn me either. "Both he and Lieutenant Ross felt my involvement in a more intimate way would be useful."

Intimate, my ass, I think, but I say, "The notes that *my father* has been receiving."

"That target you," Jacob counters. "We both know you're the real target."

"We don't know," I say, looking at my boss. "But yes," I add, as if he's asked, because he will, "I do suspect I'm the target, which is why I was going to tell you on my own this morning. I would have preferred to tell you myself. It's not like this is my first threat. I know the procedures."

"Royce Walker would not call me and get involved if there wasn't a real threat," he says.

"I didn't suggest it wasn't real," I quip back at the inferred suggestion. "I assume all threats are real."

"I understand this one seems to have intimate details about your life," Lieutenant Ross challenges.

"That's not verified," I say, thinking I might just cuff Jacob and stick a sock in his mouth.

"It's personal or it's not," my boss presses, trying to back me into a confessional corner.

He fails. "I can't validate that it is or is not," I reply. "A random incident might be nothing more than my paranoid creation. I have no facts to back that up."

"You don't get paranoid," he points out.

"My father's close to this," I tell him. "And considering my history, this is an exception."

"What does your gut tell you?" he presses. "How serious is this?"

I want to lie, but I hate lies, and I respect Lieutenant Ross, which means trust is my only option. "My gut says that this is the real deal. This is a problem."

"Your gut feelings have solved forty cases," he reminds me. "I choose to bet on you, and that means keeping you alive." I open my mouth to argue, when he adds, "And everyone around you," which shuts me up. I can't, and won't, risk other people's lives and he knows it.

"Jacob here will be your shadow," he adds. "The story to the department is that Walker is helping with cold cases. Jacob will provide those man hours by helping you with those cases and any open investigations while his team offers our team support. In a perfect world, you two are golden together, and you find the bodies of a woman and her child and convict a billionaire CEO." He glances at his watch. "And on that note. I have an IA asshole to deal with on an unrelated matter. That means you two need to get out of here."

I ignore the order to get out. "I work best alone," I state, feeling as if Jacob is taking over my life and my good senses, based on my early trust. "I'll work off-site. I'll—"

"Don't finish that sentence," he says, leaning forward to rest his arms on his desk. "You're close to this. You feel paranoid. You are not yourself. In other words, you don't work alone this time and if I let you, your uncle would crawl out of his grave and beat my face in. But yes. You work off-site, at the Walker offices, where they can protect you, which protects the rest of the team."

"With all due respect, Lieutenant Ross," I begin. "This is not—"

"—up for discussion," he supplies. "We aren't turning down free services that offer you protection, and us man hours to solve cases." He points to the door. "Go."

Letting out a heavy breath, I accept my obvious defeat, and really truly, just hours ago, I felt I needed Walker Security, but now—now I question Jacob's motivation, and that becomes a problem on top of a problem. But that is between me and him, and outside of this room, thus why I stand up. Jacob does the same beside me, and when I head for the door, my boss calls out, "Great job in court today, detective. Now use this asshole to find those bodies."

In other words, he heard me call Jacob an asshole, but I don't care. Jacob *is* an asshole. The one I trusted. The one I kissed. The one I would have fucked, but he fucked me instead. He won't fuck me again, or ever, if we're being literal. I open the door and exit, walking through the workspaces and past my old desk, without stopping. I keep going, turning right into the hallway and by the time I'm on the steps, headed down to the basement, Jacob is by my side, big as usual, which I decide works for me. Further for him to tumble and harder for him to fall, which is exactly what will happen when were alone. I don't plot how that will happen, though. I'm confident the right moves will just come to me.

We clear the steps and once we're at the file room entrance, I'm thankful to find that Becca is not at her desk. I reach for the door, and Jacob is there first, our hands colliding, a charge between us that jolts me to the core and tells me one thing. He closes his hand on the knob, but doesn't open it. He does, however, crowd me from behind. "I didn't plan that."

"Not a conversation I want to have for the cameras," I bite out.

I can almost hear him curse in his mind before he turns the knob. I push the door open and I'm inside the reception area a step later. I pass Becca's desk and head down a row, created by shelves of files, on either side of me. Jacob is by my side in an instant, and damn it, our paces seem to naturally align. A lot about me and this man naturally align except for the big one: he's trying to protect Jesse Marks while I'm trying to put him behind bars.

At the end of the path I cut to my right.

I enter the room, and of course, my robot is still with me. We pass through two rows of files, a path that feels like it goes on and on forever, while the charge between myself and Jacob is downright combustible for about ten different reasons. I open my office door and enter. And while I fully intend to put the desk between us, I'm not even slightly surprised I never get the chance. Jacob shuts the door and catches my arm. And so, the war is on and Jacob, The Robot Betrayer, is about to find out Green Berets have weaknesses.

I rotate and shove him against the door, my hand on the hard wall of his chest, heat seeping through his shirt to my palm. "I'm a pretty good judge of people," I say, "which I've proven again with you because I was right. You're an asshole. *We'll do it together* wasn't an offer. It was the only warning I got about that meeting."

"I never denied my willingness to be an asshole to protect you."

"Protect me? Or keep my cold case on Jesse Marks cold? Because we both know his name on my lips is when you decided to put your lips on mine. To control me. And it won't work."

"If you weren't controlling me, I'd never have kissed you. I wouldn't want to kiss you so damn badly now."

"You kissed me to control me."

149

"I kissed you because I wanted to kiss you."

"Right. Just like you told me we'll do this together and I was going to do this together when I don't do together."

"We are doing this together."

"This is how you do together?"

He shackles my hips and pulls me to him, and I could fight him, but he *is* a Green Beret. And I really won't win a brute force battle. "I couldn't risk you shutting me out," he says, as my hands go to his wrists to avoid his chest again, but it doesn't help. Now heat is rushing up my arms and over my chest. "We both know," he adds, "that you're safer with me by your side."

"Because you're my personal Green Beret bodyguard, right?"

"Yes, detective. I am."

"And you'll fuck me and then if I cross you on Jesse Marks, you'll make me beg you to kill me?"

"If I make you beg, it won't be for death."

"I don't beg. Ever. For anything. As for right now, I'm going to work from my apartment, not Walker Security. We both know you're coming with me, so you need to know this. I can fuck you, I can enjoy it, and I can arrest you the minute it's over. I might even get off on it. And you can let go of me now."

"Not until you hear what I have to say. I'm here to stay. I'm releasing you, but I'm not letting you go. You won't get rid of me and you can take that to the bank." His hands fall away.

I don't immediately move away. I stand there, a lean from touching him, and I stare into those cool gray eyes of his. "I'm going to get what I want," I say, thinking of that burned file.

"As will I," he says. "You can bank on that, too. And then we both win."

The heat that sizzles between us in the moment after that exchange says that we want each other, but we both want more. We both intend to get more. "We'll see, won't we?" I say, and on that note, I turn away from him and walk to my uncle's desk, and key my computer to life. I go to the file search and right when I'm about to pull up the Jesse Marks file, Jacob grabs the keyboard and moves it away from me. I look up as he presses two hands on the desk across from me.

"If you think," he says, "that I'm going to let you pull that file, you are wrong."

"That's fine," I say, standing up and forcing him to straighten to keep a dominant position. "We both know the information I need is in your head and the battle we need to fight can't happen here." I grab a box, fill it with as many files as I can stuff inside, and then I round the desk and shove it at him. "My uncle had a lot of files and you're big boy. Let's go to my apartment, where we can be alone."

"Whatever you want, detective," Jacob replies.

"Yes. Whatever *I want.*" I head to the door, with every intention of taking this man to my apartment, where I might just go ahead and cuff him. From there, I'll get my answers, one way or the other.

FALLING UNDER

Chapter Nineteen

Jewel

By the time I'm in the file room, walking between two rows of files again, Jacob is back by my side. We don't speak, and he follows my lead to the rear exit of the precinct. It's not long before we're a few blocks away, and inside a semi-vacant subway train. I claim a pole and Jacob is immediately at it with me, despite having two others he could use. He sets the box on the ground and grabs the pole, our hands now stacked but not touching, that push and pull between us thick in the air, the reasons I shouldn't touch him, many. The reasons I should, in my mind right now, just as many.

The train begins to move, and both of us instinctively stick a foot to the box to hold it in place. We do a lot of things alike, to be so different. I want to understand that and him. "Where exactly are you from?" I ask, deciding it's time to be a detective with this man.

"You didn't read that in my file?"

"I want to hear it from you," I counter.

"Long Island," he says.

"Tell me about your sister."

"I don't want to talk about my sister, but before you read into that, there's nothing scandalous there. I just don't talk about it."

Like I don't talk about a lot of things myself. I don't like it, but I get it, so I move on. "Why did you get out of the army?"

"I told you," he says. "It was time."

"Your entire life was based around the army and it was just time?"

"Everything ends," he says, his tone a bit haunted. "If anyone understands that the way I do, you do."

He's right. I do. Too well. And for that reason, among others, I don't doubt the attraction between us. I don't doubt that chemistry bouncing between us like a ping pong ball is real. It is. But just because something is real doesn't mean it can't be used against you. It doesn't mean that it can't be used to hurt you. Anything this powerful and immediate can be dangerous. Anyone as skilled as Jacob King is dangerous. And he's who I chose to affect me. He's who I've let work himself beneath my surface and make me want and need. He's the person I wanted to trust until he reminded me that I cannot.

The train stops and my body lunges toward the pole, while Jacob's stays steady, aligned with it, and now with me. He catches my hip, steadying me too, while that familiar jolt that is every touch with this man hits me hard this time. I don't look at him, or reach for him, but I can feel him all over, everywhere he's touching and even where he's not. My nipples are hard. My breasts heavy. My sex tight. I *do* want him, and he knows it. But ultimately, he's trying to control me and I'm trying to control him. That kind of game between us is actually liberating. I can get naked with him and there is no fear that I'll fall under a spell and fall for him. Because I don't want to fall. I don't want to care for anyone ever again.

The doors open and his fingers flex at my hip as if he doesn't want to release me. My gaze lifts and find his, and with that connection, I see the same in his eyes. He doesn't want to let me go, and the truth is, despite how angry I am with him, I have never wanted a man the way I want this one: so instantly, so intensely. But he does let me go. His hand slides away and he grabs the box. Not long after, we've done the trudge through the station, and we're on the sidewalk above, walking in silence toward my apartment, the anticipation of a confrontation between us, that may or may not be resolved while naked, pulsing between us. For my part, I'll confront him about Jesse Marks. For his part, he'll expect it. He'll try to shut me down.

We reach my gate and enter, walking up the sidewalk and then the steps. I turn to key in the code, when my gaze falls to the dark corner of the wall that no camera could capture, with the certainty that something is lying in the corner. "What is it?" Jacob asks, stepping closer.

"I don't know," I say, opening my leather case at my hip and pulling out a plastic bag. Sticking my hand inside it, I bend down and scoop whatever it is up. Turning the bag inside out to cover it, I stare at the item, freezing with the sight of a pink paper umbrella, which one might find in a cocktail, but it's not in a drink. It's here and it's here for a reason. For me. It's here for me.

I stand up, shaken enough that I don't turn and look at Jacob. I stick the bag in my case and key in the code. Jacob opens the door and the instant we're on the stairs, he asks the inevitable. "What does it mean to you? And don't tell me nothing. I've been with you around the clock now. This isn't nothing."

"I'm trying to figure that out," I say. "I need to think."

"What do you *think* it means?" he presses.

"I'm trying to figure it out," I repeat, a ball of emotion in my chest that I hate I've let this bastard playing with my head create. I have to get it under control. I have to get myself under control.

We reach the door and I open it, and without waiting on Jacob, I enter the apartment and head to the island. Jacob is the one who flips on the lights, but by that time, I'm already headed up the stairs to the library. Once I'm there, I flip a switch and a lamp splays light over a cozy room just big enough for an overstuffed brown couch framed by two bookshelves right and left, while black and white abstracts fill the wall above it. I like black and white. I see enough of the wrong colors in my job.

I pull off my bag and set it on the floor, then walk left to the bookshelf. Locating what I am looking for, I grab the memory album I made several years back but haven't opened since. The front reads: *Martha Carpenter's Life*. My mother's life. I'd made it as part of the healing process and inside I have memories that range from her childhood to the end. I flip to a photo of my mother standing in front of her bakery, holding one of the pink umbrellas she sold there. A photo that was in a well-published advertisement, so it would not be hard to find. It was public knowledge, but it's still a countdown to me, a list in order of those who have died in my life. It's meant to get my attention or my father's, but it feels like me. The message seems to be leading to my uncle, and then me.

Jacob's footsteps sound on the stairs behind me and I stick the book back on the shelf and turn to watch him join me on the landing. And just that fast, the already tiny room is smaller, and he is bigger, and not in size. This man consumes me when he is near, and I both resent that reaction he stirs, and crave more of it—of him. But what I want and crave isn't the issue. Not now. Not with all I have going on in my life, not with my duty in the forefront. "What does that umbrella mean to you?" he asks, his voice managing to be low, but still a rough demand.

"What does Jesse Marks mean to you?" I counter.

"Tell me about the umbrella," he says, closing the few steps this room allows between us, and stepping toe-to-toe with me, that spicy wonderful scent of him filling the room. *He* fills the room.

"So you can make it a public service announcement?" I demand.

"You knew that the Walker crew knew about the butterfly. They were all looking through the security feed. Tell me about the umbrella. I need to know and you need me."

"You know, I'd decided that I needed you. As my Lieutenant said, this is personal. I'm objective enough to know that affects my judgment. I'm too close to this. But then you sideswiped me. You made me look bad to my boss." I poke his ridiculously hard chest. "You made me feel like it's me against the slayer and you."

He stares down at me with one of his hard robot looks on his stupid handsome face.

"Cat got your tongue?" I demand, when he is slow to answer.

"Every move I've made," he replies tightly. "I've made to protect you."

"Is that right?" I challenge, not liking where this is leading me. "Then that means you kissed me to protect me?"

"I told you—"

"That you wanted to send a message to those watching me and us. Got it. You made the move to protect me. How many women have you kissed to protect? How many did you kiss to shut them up, like you did me? How many—"

He steps into me, one hand on my hip, while the other tangles into my hair. "I have never kissed a woman I protected, ever. You were the first."

"And how do I know that?" I demand, my hand on his chest, his heart thundering beneath my palm. "Your heart is racing. That could mean a lie."

"I don't lie. I have never kissed a woman I was protecting," he repeats.

"Then you just kissed me to shut me up."

"I kissed you because—"

"You wanted to."

"Yes. Because I wanted to. And I have never wanted to kiss any woman as much as I do you right this minute and that is the God's honest truth. But tell me. What do you want? That is what you said this visit to your apartment is about, right? You getting what you want?"

"Yes," I say. "That's exactly why I brought you here."

"Then I repeat," he says. "What do you want, detective?"

Chapter Twenty

Jewel

"What I want is for you to stop calling me detective. It makes me feel like you have some creepy schoolteacher fetish, only for detectives."

"For your information, *Jewel*," he says. "My only apparent fetish involves you being a bitch to me and giving me hell all the damn time."

I have no idea why him saying my name turns me on so damn much, but it does. My fingers curl around his shirt. "Are you going to kiss me, asshole, or what?" I demand.

He smiles a moment before his mouth closes down on mine, when he never smiles. And I have just a moment to think about how damn sexy it is that he did so now because I told him to kiss me, before he licks into my mouth. Before the first wicked taste of him explodes into my mouth, drugging me with raw masculinity and the hunger I taste on his lips. His hunger. Mine. I moan softly, and he pulls back, his lips lingering just above mine.

"Just to be clear," he says, his voice low and rough. "I'm breaking every rule I own with you. I don't fuck women I'm protecting."

"You could hand me over to someone else," I suggest, "and it won't matter."

"Not a chance in hell," he says, his hand sliding under my hair to cup my neck. "We'll break the rules together."

"I'm not sure I like how you do 'together'."

"I'll make sure you do," he promises, his lips slanting over mine, and this time he kisses me like he owns me, like he wants to control me, and like I really *am* his, like I belong to him, and in this very moment, I can honestly say I am. I want him, and I can't get enough of him.

And how can it ever be enough when he's this damn impossibly hot, and he's such a damn good kisser. The way he makes me want his mouth on every part of me and the way he makes me want my mouth on every part of him. And so, there it is. I'm his, but I'm going to make damn sure he's mine, too. I kiss him back as passionately as he's kissing me. I meet him stroke for stroke, arching into him, telling him I am here and present, and I'm not even close to afraid of him or of this. He doesn't get to control me. He isn't making me do this. I control me, and I choose him and this.

Arching into him, his shoulder holster and mine are in the way, and I want them gone. I want him naked. Just to be certain that he knows that's where I want this to go, my hand presses between us and I stroke the hard line of his shaft. He groans low in his throat, a sexy rough sound that tells me he gets the point. This isn't his show. It's ours. It's us together, or there is no show, with or without our clothes on.

His reaction is to tear his mouth from mine, his lips lingering there though, as if he wants to kiss me again, and just when I would kiss *him* again, he leans away just enough to shrug out of his jacket. I take one step backward, and do the same with my blazer. I reach down and pull off my boots and he does the same. Next, we disconnect our shoulder holsters, and the truth is, it's the first time I've ever been with a man who is probably more armed than me. That feels significant when it perhaps is not. He's not a cop. He's not that kind of career complication. He's a Green-fucking-Beret, and one hell of a hot one, for that matter.

He sets his weapon on the couch and snags my hand, walking me toward him and taking my holster and weapon as he does. "Just making sure you don't end up shooting me before this is over," he says, setting it with his before shackling my hip.

"I told you I'll wait until after the orgasms."

"Careful," he says, a hint of a smile on his lips again. "I might hold that orgasm and you captive."

"You can try," I say, but my head isn't in the game in this moment, and somehow my hand is on his face, right by the almost smile, that seems to have complicated what should be sex, an escape, a way to pull back the emotions that umbrella stirred in me. That smile reminds me that Mr. Robot is his wall, his way to cope with death, with whatever makes him protect Jesse Marks.

He captures my hand. "What are you thinking?"

"That you have on too many clothes," I say, before I let this go someplace emotional, somewhere that two people like us never want to go.

My hands press under his shirt, but he doesn't immediately give me what I want. He studies me for several beats and then kisses me hard and fast. Too fast, but I get over it when he pulls his shirt off, tossing it aside, and given me a delicious view his perfect torso, and that shoulder tattoo that is gorgeously crafted: an eagle, a flag, the words Semper Fidelis, which is not just significant to the marines, but to law enforcement as well. It means "always loyal" and only a man dedicated to his job and his country has that tattooed on his body.

I step to him, and caress a path down the tattoo. "You were a proud soldier when you got this."

"I still am. Getting out doesn't change that."

"But you—"

He cups my face and kisses me, his hand sliding up my shirt, his touch fire that has me helping him pull my shirt over my head. Letting him drag me to him where he now sits on the couch. I straddle him, my bra somehow gone by the time I'm there. But my hands press to his shoulders, and I hold him at bay. "I will still arrest you if I need to," I promise. "This doesn't change that."

"You aren't going to arrest me any more than you hate me." He glances down at my chest, his gaze a hot caress as it rakes over my breasts, my nipples, before his eyes meet mine. "Because you know I'm protecting you."

I ignore the ache between my thighs. Or I try. "From what? The slayer or the Jesse Marks damage patrol?"

His hand slides between my shoulder blades and he molds my chest to his. "Do you really want to talk about Jesse Marks right now? Because if you ask me questions, I'm going to ask you questions when I'd much rather be inside you, giving you as many reasons as I can not to arrest me. But you pick. Conversation or fucking."

"Both," I say, because it's the truth. I want answers and I want the conversation my emotions are having in my head to shut up. "Fucking first." I push away from him and stand up, unbuttoning my pants, sliding them down my hips, and he watches me with that unreadable, robot expression that is admittedly sexy as hell. I press my lips to his and that's all it takes.

We are crazy, hot, kissing, his hands on my breasts, my nipples, my neck. I can't touch him enough. I can't feel him enough, can't get close enough, and that's new to me. I don't need anyone the way I feel I need this man. I don't want to need anyone this much, but it's too late. At least, right here, right now, I do. He rolls us to our sides, facing one another, the wide cushion of the couch more than holding us and the next kiss isn't fast and frenzied. It's long, drugging, and somewhere in the midst of his tongue stroking my tongue, I end up on my back with the heavy weight of him on top of me, his hands on either side of my head. Those gray eyes of his bore into me. "I have one condom. We have to make it count."

"I get the birth control shot, but I have a question before I give up that condom. When you weren't fucking women you were protecting, how many women were you fucking?"

"I don't fuck around. I don't have time, but if that occasion presented itself, I used a condom. And a woman gets a shot for one man or a lot of men. You won't let a lot of men get close to you."

"I had a fuck buddy. He's gone."

"Who?" he demands.

"Just—a fireman. He's *gone*."

"How long and when did it end?"

"He was a fuck buddy, Jacob. There was nothing to end."

"When did it end?" he asks.

"Six months ago."

"*Why* did it end?"

My brows furrow. "Why does it matter?"

"Holy fuck, I don't know, but it does."

"What does that mean?"

"Why did it—"

"He was too nice, and he wanted more and I just didn't."

"What was wrong with him?"

"I told you. He was nice."

"Nice is bad?"

"Okay, he was *too* nice. I don't do nice. Nothing in my world is nice. And you're not nice. In fact, you're so far from nice that I might have to arrest you and I hate that I want you, but I do."

"You aren't going to have to arrest me. I'm a lot of things, many you might not like, but I'm not that guy. I'm the guy who will die to protect you if I have to."

My hand goes to the tattoo on his shoulder. "You'd die to protect anyone," I say, which only backs up his words. He's not the guy I have to arrest. I don't want him to be the guy I have to arrest.

"You're not just anyone or I wouldn't be here, like this, with you right now."

"I don't know what that means."

"Neither do I," he says, and he doesn't give me time to process that statement or reply. He kisses me again, and I decide, "good kisser" is once again the proper description for this man. No, I decide, as his mouth travels down my neck to my nipple, where he licks and suckles—good with his mouth. Good, so very good, and everywhere. My sworn testimony to that fact is his mouth on my belly, and his tongue dipping low beneath my waistband.

He catches the string of my silk panties at my hips, and caresses them down my hips, but he stops mid-thigh, lingering there just long enough to give my clit a lick. I gasp, and arch my back, and he suckles my nub, sending darts of pleasure straight to my nipples. His tongue follows again, swirling and teasing, until his mouth is gone, and moments later, so are my pants. The instant my ankles are free, he's standing, reaching for his pants. I sit up, not because I feel out of control—oddly—I've forgotten that battle that felt so very real when this started. I've forgotten what I was angry about, what I was afraid of. I sit up because I want to watch him, and by the time my feet settle on the ground with my knees pressed together with the ache in my sex, his pants and underwear are gone. And it's not the jut of his cock—which like the rest of him is impressively big—that has my attention, but rather the much larger, deep scar that runs the length of his thigh and calf.

The horror of how he must have gotten that shakes me, and reminds me that he is a *Green Beret,* he is a *hero.* He walks toward me and the minute he's in reach, one of my hands comes down on that scar, and the other around his cock. I trace the scar with my fingers, and it is deep, so very deep. I look up at him and he is watching me, his expression hooded, jaw hard. Cock even harder, and I lean in and give him a lick.

"Fuck," he breathes out, and I like it. I like him sounding rough and out of control. I *want* him rough and out of control. But when I go to take him in my mouth, he moves, and in a blink, we're back on the couch, on our sides facing each other.

"My cock in your mouth right now, means I come, and you'll think I'm more of an asshole than you already do. And I'm not that damn selfish." He kisses me and then presses his cheek to mine, his lips near my ear. "I'm going to fuck you now, hard and fast, because we both need hard and fast right now, but later," he nips my lobe, "later, I'm going to taste you again. Lick you again." His breath is a warm trickle on my neck. "Everywhere. But right now—" He strokes his cock along the wet seam of my body. "There is this." He presses inside me, and I grab his shoulder with the sensation of him entering me, stretching me, until he's in the deepest depths of me.

Our foreheads come together, and his hands settle between my shoulder blades, molding me closer. We don't move though, we just linger there, and I swear I feel something happening between us. Or maybe it's me that it's happening to. Maybe I'm more affected by the slayer than I realize, more vulnerable to Jacob's appeal than I intended to become. Maybe alone isn't as good right now as together.

"What are you doing to me, woman?" he asks, as if he's thinking what I'm thinking. Like he feels this too, but I don't even try to reply. I don't know what this is, and I can't think now. Not when the thick ridge of his erection is caressing a path backward until I think he is going to pull out to move away. I arch forward, desperate to bring him back, and he slides my leg up, over his hip, and answers me with a hard thrust. I pant, trying to catch my breath, moaning as his hand slides to my backside, pulling me closer, driving deeper. I want him to drive in again, but he leans in and kisses me, a slow, drink-me-in kind of kiss, his hips doing this kind of slide and grind against mine.

Our lips part and for a moment we breathe together before he thrusts again, and the explosion of sensation I feel has me panting out his name, and digging fingers into his arms. He thrusts again, and with that, a frenzied need erupts between us. He starts to pump into me over and over and I feel him shaking, or maybe it's me who is shaking. His gaze rakes over my breasts, and he kisses me in between another pump and grind. And another. And another. I don't want this to end, and yet I need him to keep hitting that crazy sweet spot that promises bliss. I need it to the point that I move into him, pull him closer, lean into every move he makes.

And then it happens. I am there and without warning. I am never there without warning. I'm honestly rarely there at all. I usually just hope to get there. But I am now. Suddenly, intensely there, my sex clamping down on Jacob

166

inside me, spasming with the most intense orgasm of my life. He growls low in his throat and drives into me before I feel the wet, hot heat of his release. We tremble into release, clinging to each other. Our naked bodies meld together intimately, our foreheads connected.

And for the first time in my adult life, I don't know what I want to come next. I don't know what to do with that. I don't know what he's making me feel. I need to think, which isn't going to happen with this man naked and all over me. I try to roll away, but he captures me. "What just happened?"

"I don't know what you're talking about. The couch. I need tissue."

He reaches behind us and grabs tissue, pulls out of me and stuffs it between my legs. "Problem solved. Now. What just happened?"

"We had sex," I say, trying to get my head back on straight. "Just sex. That's what happened."

He cups my face and kisses me, this drugging, seductive kiss that is somehow all about sex, and yet, not about sex at all. "That didn't feel like just sex to me," he says. "But maybe it is. Maybe you needed to forget the slayer and maybe I just wanted you to forget Jesse Marks, which I do, I don't deny that. But I can tell you that I plan to fuck you again. I plan to lick you every place I can possibly lick you. And I plan to make sure you can't even remember that firefighter's name." He rolls me to my back and hovers over me. "So is it just sex?" he asks. "Maybe. Or maybe it's something else and since I've done something else, I think I'll try it on for size and take you with me." And with that, he stands up and walks to get his pants, giving me a perfect view of his perfect ass.

He's such a damn asshole.

An asshole that is definitely making me feel something else.

Chapter Twenty-One

JACOB

I've gone too far with Jewel. I know this, but I can't turn back. I want her. I'm fucking obsessed with this woman when that's not my way. I don't obsess. I don't crave. I don't have to have anything, and yet I do feel every bit of that with her. I want her that fucking badly, and I can't explain it. I could keep her naked in bed for a solid week, and I know that wouldn't be enough *to be enough*.

But right now, she has a real stalker, and I need to end that person. And so, I let her dress, no doubt hammering away at her wall as she rebuilds it, while second guessing me and herself for wanting to trust me. We reach for our shoulder holsters and once we settle them back into place, we're both back on the job.

"Tell me about the umbrella," I order softly.

"Tell me about your scar," she says, and I almost smile at her brilliant dodge and deflect.

I could do quid pro quo and promise her an answer for an answer, but I've torn down her trust by sideswiping her today with her boss. I need, and want, it back. "It was a Cuban mission," I say. "I pissed off the wrong guy. Does it bother you?"

She softens instantly. "No. God, no. Of course, it doesn't bother me. It's a part of you."

"You seemed quite obsessed with it," I comment.

"You were naked. I was obsessed with all of you."

Obsessed. There is that word that was in my head, now on her lips.

"Were you a prisoner?" she asks, before I can comment.

"Yes," I say. "I was."

"How long?"

"Seventy-two hours, until my team showed up."

"Did you kill the person who did that to you?"

"Yes," I say again. "I did."

"Was Jesse Marks on the rescue team?"

And there it is. Proof of how good she is at her job. She hit me from the side. "That mission was top secret, and I can't tell you that."

"That's a yes," she assumes.

"Sorry, detective. I've been questioned and cornered while being tortured. Your questions and assumptions don't faze me, nor does my lack of an answer constitute an answer at all."

I reach behind me and pull the book out that she was holding when I followed her up here. "Tell me about the umbrella and this book."

She closes the space between me and her and grabs the book. I shackle her free hand and pull her to me. "I can't protect you if you don't tell me what is going on. We have to do this together."

"Your version of together and mine don't work. And spilling details of an investigation to an army of people leads to mistakes, miscalculation, and problems."

"This is about Royce going to your boss."

"You went to Royce," she says, "or he would not have gone to my boss."

"I don't deny that. But would you feel better about me leaving you exposed?"

"Don't be an asshole and go around me."

"I will do what I have to, to protect you." I say.

"You mean you will do what you have to do to ensure you know what I'm doing with Jesse Marks."

"Damn straight, detective. Because Jesse Marks will end you. Not your career—*you*. Back off while you still can."

"Is that a threat?"

"That's a fact," I bite out. "A cold, hard, brutal fact that will get you killed."

"I'm a—"

"Detective," I supply. "Yes. I know."

"Then you know that I can't just walk away from this. I need more than that. I need details."

"Details are top secret, just like his file."

"But you know the details?"

"Yes."

"So you served with him."

"Yes. I served with him."

"You're protecting him."

"Not a chance in hell. I'm protecting you."

"You're protecting him," she hisses, angry now.

"The government does not let its secrets get uncovered."

"You're saying they'd kill me?"

"Yes. I am. And I will continue to say this over and over, and hope like hell one day I don't have to prove it. I *am* the guy who will die for you, Jewel. Set Jesse aside right now. Set it aside and let's catch the slayer *together*."

"I told you, I don't like your version of together."

"Come on, sweetheart," I say, releasing her hand and settling mine on her shoulder. "Forgive me like you fucked me. All the way. Let me in. You said yourself you need me."

She studies me for several long beats. "I need to be able to trust you. I need together to mean something."

"One slip and you'll be dead, and I couldn't wait for you to decide to trust me."

"Don't do that to me again," she says. "Together means together. Talk to *me,* not my boss, not my father. Not your team."

"My team is protecting you, too."

"I get that. I do. But humans make mistakes and the more humans who are involved, the more those mistakes multiply and whoever this is we're facing is scary smart."

"All right. I'll concede there is truth to that statement, but my people are not average people. They're the elite of the elite, and I don't think your problem is what they know. I think if you're honest with yourself and me, your problem is still what happened today with your boss. And Jewel, I've been frank and honest about why I did that. Put Jesse Marks aside for now. I need you to talk to me about that umbrella." I lift the book. "Why did it take you to this book?"

She studies me for several more intense beats, before she takes the book, the tension around her brow telling me her headache is back. "I'll show you, but downstairs. There's a piece of the puzzle there as well." She twists out of my arms and heads down the stairs.

I don't hesitate to follow, hoping whatever piece of the puzzle she has leads us to the slayer. I find her behind the island, the book in front of her. I join her on the opposite side, and she reaches into her briefcase at her hip and tosses down the pink paper umbrella that she bagged.

I glance at it and then her. "What does it mean to you?"

She opens the book and flips to a page before turning it toward me. "My mother did an advertisement for the bakery holding a pink umbrella. People wanted those pink umbrellas and she started selling them in her bakery."

I study the advertisement, and then glance at Jewel. "Another very personal message."

"It is, but the ads were everywhere so this wouldn't be hard to discover. Now, Tabitha's love of butterflies is another story. This person still has to have intimate knowledge of my life."

I glance at the date of the newspaper clipping. "This campaign took place while you were in college. That's where this is leading us."

"Or that's where this person wants to lead us," she says, shoving a wayward strand of blonde hair from her eyes and pressing her fingers to her temples. "That seems too obvious." Her voice is heavy again.

I reach in my pocket and grab the last BC powder I have with me, before setting it on the counter in front of her. "You need this."

"That obvious?"

"To me, yes. To others, you'd just seem like a stone-cold bitch, which I imagine in your job, works for you."

"Says the man who is the king of the stone-cold bitch look."

"Bitch does not sit well with a man," I say. "I prefer stone-cold asshole, spoken affectionately, of course."

She smiles but then frowns, pressing fingers to her temple. "I do not have time for this," she murmurs.

"And on that note," I say, we need to order lunch, groceries and more BC powder, because I'm out."

"Groceries?" she asks, attempting to sound off with her usual teasing snark and failing. "You don't like cereal?"

"Funny thing about me. I like milk with my cereal."

"I knew there was something suspicious about you," she jokes but her lashes lower on the delivery and she reaches for the BC powder.

I round the island and open the fridge, snagging her a bottle of water. "Take that powder," I order, joining her and twisting the top off the water.

She nods, tears open the pouch and downs the medication, grabbing the bottle from me and gulping water afterward. "Still nasty," she murmurs, making a disgusted face. "Ah God. It's horrible, but it works." She rotates to face me and rests a hand on the counter. "Thank you, Jacob."

"You're welcome, Jewel," I say, reaching up and wiping a droplet of water from her lip, when I really want to kiss it away.

She catches my hand, and despite her headache, and a fuck session behind us, that touch sets off ten degrees of heat between us. "I like you better naked and with stubble," she says. "In case I didn't fully express that up to this point."

"I like you better naked and with your hair down," I reply, aware that she is always looking for a reaction in me. Even more aware of the fact that she always gets it, even if she doesn't know it. "In case I didn't fully express that up to this point," I add.

"I like it when you laugh," she says. "It's a good laugh, all sexy and deep. Almost awkward, like it's unfamiliar to you."

"Always trying to kill my tough guy routine, aren't you?"

"I don't want to kill the tough guy routine," she says. "I just want to see beneath it."

"You have. You are." I shackle her waist and walk her backward, easing her onto the barstool behind her. "Now," I say, my hands on the wood arms, framing her body, "let me see beneath yours. What don't I know about you and your slayer, Jewel?"

She looks upward, eyes to the ceiling, seeming to battle with whatever this has become for her, before she looks at me again. "It's ridiculous. It's a crazy theory that I would normally keep to myself until I had more time to investigate."

"Crazy ideas, have saved my life more than a few times, sweetheart. Tell me."

"Okay then." She breathes out. "Crazy it is. When I was at my uncle's funeral, I looked up to find a man standing a good distance away. He was wearing a hat and trench coat. I couldn't make him out. The funeral was a big deal with uniforms, the playing of taps, and a big tribute in general, to my uncle. I thought maybe he was just watching that."

"How does that tie to this, now?"

"When I got home after the funeral, I was about to go into the gated area when I saw him again. He was standing far enough away to make it impossible for me to make him out. I thought maybe he was one of my uncle's informants, looking to me in his absence. I went after him, but he disappeared around a corner. I couldn't find him. When I was returning to my building a few days later, I got to the security panel and found a sticky note on it. I didn't connect it to the man, but now, I think I might."

"What did the note say?"

She walks around me, and I turn to find her standing at the refrigerator and indicating the note I'd noticed before. "This is it," she says. "*You're not ready yet,*" she reads and then looks at me. "I thought it was about someone being late to a date or something like that. But now, I'm not sure anymore. You know this, but my uncle always told me that if I thought I was ready, I was being overly confident."

"Therefore, you weren't ready," I say, not even trying to hide the disapproval in my voice. "Yes. You told me."

"And you told me, you disagree with that way of thinking. I get that but that isn't the point. My uncle's words are why that note hit home: You're not ready yet, is what I always tell myself to make myself work harder. Maybe it hit a little too close to home."

"How are you connecting this note with the butterfly and the umbrella?" I ask. "Aside from the fact that all three items were found by the security panel."

"I know they appeared years apart. I know there is no obvious connection, except me, but I'm a big connection, an obvious connection, I have a gut feeling about this. That note, that man, is a part of this. And there's one more piece of this puzzle anyway."

"I'm listening," I say, dragging the stool behind me closer to her and perching on the edge.

"Every Valentine's Day, the guys at the precinct write me love letters. Or love letters to Little C. My uncle was Big C. This year I got this strange card. It read: *Finally, it's our time*, with my name on the front. No one there calls me Jewel."

"Was it internal or sent through the postal system?"

"Internal. No postmark which is why I tried, and failed, to blow it off."

"Where is the card?"

"That's the thing. I left it on my old desk in the general population. I went back to get it, and it was gone." She points at the note. "*You're not ready yet* and then, *finally, it's our time.*"

"I see the potential connection," I say, "but tying in the items found at your door, feels like a stretch."

"Not to me. To me it feels connected. It does. They do." She balls her fists at her chest. "I feel it."

"Then we go with your gut. We operate on the premise that the person who left that note, left the butterfly and the umbrella."

"That means this person has been watching me for two years and I'm not going to lie. It's screwing with my head. I'm not supposed to let things screw with my head. This job is how I keep things from screwing with my head. I'm doing something. I'm fixing something."

My hands come down on the arms of her stool again. "I get it, sweetheart. I do. More than most people and I think you know that. But both of us are human, even if we don't want to admit it."

"If I let him, whoever he is, get to me, then he wins."

"That's not true, but don't fight what you feel. Feed it. Get angry. Hurt him before he can hurt you. I've been in some fucked up situations, and when I hid from what I feared, I almost lost. Embrace it and stop fucking telling yourself you're not ready."

"My uncle—"

"Was a damn good detective and man, but you are your own person. Be you because it's you in this war, right here and right now, not him. Could you make out any of this man's features?"

"Not much but—" She considers a moment. "He was lean, and he was agile."

"You know that we need to tell the Walker team about this. They need to know what to look for, not just for your safety but for your father's."

"Yes. Okay. Tell them. And I need to run prints on the umbrella though I know there won't be any."

"Walker can take care of that," I say. "Where is it?"

"In my bag, in the library. The butterfly is in the drawer here beside me."

My cellphone rings and I pull it from my pocket. "Asher," I say. "I called him about the security footage before I went upstairs with you." I answer on speaker phone. "I'm here with Detective Carpenter," I say, setting my phone on the counter between us. "What do you have for us?"

"Hey ho, this all blows," he says. "I do not have good news. We have extra cameras all over that place, and not a damn thing to show for it but the bag of chocolate Finn ate while we were scanning through the feed. He's the garbage disposal of Walker Security, detective. In fact, if he wasn't a sharpshooter and booby-trap expert, he'd probably work at a candy store."

"Forget Finn," I say tightly. "Define cameras all over this place. Do we have a full ground view next to the security panel?"

"We did and we do," Asher says, "but that area by the security panel is recessed and dark. In shot after shot, the position of the legs and feet, blocked camera views. Detective Carpenter—"

"Jewel," she says. "Just call me Jewel."

"Jewel," he says. "I'm going to email you, and the stone-faced dude there with you, the names of everyone who entered the building for the timeline we have footage for now. The list will hit your inboxes in the next few minutes. But I can tell you this now. There's no one on the footage that doesn't live in the building, except the mailman, who we've been monitoring for days now."

The obvious hits me, my gaze shoots to Jewel's. "Are you thinking what I'm thinking?"

"Whoever is leaving those gifts by the door has to be close," she says. "As in right here in this building."

Chapter Twenty-Two

JACOB

The "slayer" as Jewel calls him, actually lives in this building, or has intimate access to someone who lives in this building. And if she's right, and this person has been watching her for two years, that's a whole new level of fucked up and dangerous. "If the stalker is in the building," Asher says, "we need to get you the fuck out of there, Jewel."

"We'll call you back, Asher," I say, disconnecting the line and focusing on Jewel. "He's right. Pack a bag. You're coming to my place. You'll be safe there."

"We need to think about this. And I know that your first reaction is to protect me. That's your job and—"

I stand up and press my hands on the arms of her stool again. "Don't do that," I say. "Don't turn us fucking into me using my job to get you naked."

"No. Jacob, I didn't mean it like that. My point is that your first instinct is to protect me, to take cover and guard me. My first reaction is to go door-to-door and question everyone because I'm not a civilian. I don't react to things like a civilian."

"You're human. You die, just like everyone else."

"I know that. Believe me, *I know that*. I've seen enough in this job, to know stupidity doesn't pay. That's why I said that I know I need help. But I've also learned, that every action has a reaction. Showing brute force, and driving the slayer into a hole for another two years isn't protecting me. And the idea that he might live in the building has holes. It doesn't explain the card at my office. No one here could get inside there."

"You don't know that the card is connected."

"We don't know a lot of things. We're going with my gut and my gut says that the card is connected. And if I'm right, then somehow this person has access to be wherever I go."

"All right. Assuming you are right, this is exactly why you need to be with me, at my apartment. The Walker building is a fortress."

"If I'm right and that card was from him, then he says I'm ready now. Ready for what? This feels like a game and he knows the rules and we're just charging down the field, perhaps running in the wrong direction."

"Staying here could be the wrong direction."

"He's *playing a game*. The messages indicate his desire to have me play, too. If I'm there, the game is over. At least for now. He's patient. He's proven that. He'll be back when you're gone."

"When I'm gone," I repeat, and those words illogically bug the fuck out of me. I just met Jewel, but I damn sure don't want to give her up right now. I push away from the stool but she grabs my T-shirt. "You're not gone now," she says, as if she's reading my mind. "I do need you. And your gun."

I cup her face. "Yes. You do need me." I kiss her, a quick slide of tongue, before I add, "And my gun, as well as my team. Walker Security includes some of the best in every field of law enforcement. We're going to talk to them. We're going to come up with a plan we all agree on. Non-negotiable."

"Non-negotiable," she says. "You know, you're more of a control freak than me. I think that might be a problem for us."

"As long as I win all arguments," I say, my hands settling on her shoulders. "It won't be a problem at all."

"You need a name tag that says: *Controlling Asshole* to warn people."

"Why would I want to warn anyone? And your eyes are bloodshot again. You need to go lay down and kick that headache."

"I don't need to lay down. I need—"

"To lay down. You're human, *detective*. I get that you pretend that you aren't to the rest of the world and I even get why you hide the headaches, but use me, remember? Nap and I'll kill anyone who tries to join you that isn't me. In the meantime, I'll send off the prints, arrange some conversations with the team, and get us some damn groceries ordered."

"I don't—"

"You do. You're in pain." I tilt her head back. "It's *okay* to be human," I repeat. "I won't tell if you don't. I got you. I got this. Okay?"

She inhales and lets a breath out. "I—I don't know how to do whatever this is we're doing."

"Neither do I but I have confidence that we're both smart. We'll figure it out, but after you get rid of this headache." I pick her up and start walking.

"Are you really carrying me?"

"Yeah. I've never carried a woman who wasn't bleeding or in the middle of a warzone. I thought I'd give it a go." I enter the bedroom and cross to the bed, setting her down on top, and sitting down next to her. "Take a nap."

"You aren't as hard as I thought you were."

She hits a nerve, and I lean over, pressing my hand to the bed on the opposite side of her head. "I am hard, Jewel. I'm heartless. I'm demanding. I'm not as gentle as I was with you today when we were naked and I'm not as gentle as I seem right now. If you make me something other than that, I'll disappoint you. I'll hurt you. And I don't want to do that."

I stand up and start walking toward the door.

"Jacob," she murmurs, pain in her voice that stops me in my path.

"Yes?" I ask without turning, because I really just want to strip her naked and show her how not fucking gentle I am.

"If you were as hard as you say you are, you wouldn't care if you hurt me."

I grab the doorframe and shut my eyes. She's right. I don't know what the hell she's doing to me, but there's a heart in my chest I forgot existed. I turn to find her eyes shut and her weapon now by her side. Because she doesn't know she doesn't need it. She doesn't know she's safe with me. And I have to decide if I want her to feel that safe with me. I have to decide if I really want to open the door between us that damn wide.

I cross the living room and to the island and open my computer, keying it to life, while I dial Ash again. "Are we convoying her to Walker?" he asks when I answer.

"We're not doing anything until we talk this through. Where's Sierra?"

"She's right here with me," he says, he hits the speaker button. "You're on live with wifey."

"Hey Jacob," Sierra says. "What's happening? How can I help?"

"First," I say. "Let me bring you both up to speed." I run through the entire story with them. The man. The gifts. The notes. The umbrella connection. The limited description.

"Holy fuck," Ash says. "Does Savage know any of this?"

"No. I need you to update him and tighten her father's security. This person, this man if Jewel is right, is fixated on her, but that doesn't mean he won't go after her father to hurt her."

"I don't like the idea that he has access to her at home and at work," Sierra says. "This is very concerning, but I reluctantly agree with Jewel. We need to think through reactions to our actions and be ready."

"Right," I say. "But doing nothing isn't an option either. I don't do the sitting duck routine unless I'm luring in my prey. Which is where you come into play."

"I'm listening," she says.

"I need you to talk to Jewel later this evening, and between the two of you, decide how our actions become reactions for this freak."

"I can do that. When?"

I glance at the closed door. "Jewel can't do it now. I'll call you when she is free."

"That works for me. That gives me some time to take notes and write out some questions for her."

"Until then," I say, "for the next however many hours, all her slayer can possibly know, is that I'm working with Jewel, and that has led to us getting up close and personal. The team needs to stay off the radar until we analyze the facts, and we all, Jewel included, decide what comes next."

"Let me remind everyone that someone who lives in that building is helping him. There is no other way or other option. They key in their code, and drop the gifts in the shadowed area. That also means they understand the camera placement and limitations."

"Which means educated and intelligent," I say. "Someone involved in technology or crime scene processing."

"The latter feels more on target," Sierra suggests.

"Agreed," I say. "And circling back to you, Asher, and those gifts. I have the newest one that needs to be checked for prints."

"I doubt we will get a hit," Asher says. "But we have to try. Order food. We'll deliver."

"I'm going to order groceries because a man cannot live on cereal with no milk," I say.

"Milk does the body good," Asher says. "But so does other things." He clicks off speaker. "I heard your tongue somehow got in the pretty detective's mouth. How personal has this gotten for you?"

My lips thin. "I don't do personal."

"That fucking personal, huh?"

"Yeah," I say, because he gets me. He knows me. "That fucking personal."

"First, I got your back and hers. But I cannot help but state the obvious. The Tin Man actually has a heart and a weakness. I am, in fact, going to hang up and savor that for just a moment." And he does. He hangs up.

I grimace and set my phone down, pressing my hands onto the counter. Why the fuck did he have to call her a weakness? That hit a nerve. I swore I'd never have a weakness again when I left the clusterfuck of my last few months in the army. She can't be a weakness. That means I have feelings for her. I just met the woman, but Jesse Marks, or no Jesse Marks, I damn sure can't walk away from her, either. I need to get Jesse Marks out of the picture and I need to catch this bastard stalking her before I get any deeper with Jewel.

I glance at the umbrella, aware that the team is waiting for an excuse to pick it up. Focusing on my Mac, I pull up a local grocery delivery site, keying in my account. I order enough food to last for several days, but if I have my way, we'll be at my place by tomorrow.

Or better yet, I think, refocusing on the umbrella, the slayer will be gone, one way or the other. Jewel is right. He's following a path. Her friend. Her mother. Her uncle, by way of that card at her office, where she aspires to be just like him. I walk to the refrigerator and stare at that note and focus on the words. *You're not ready yet.*

It's as if her uncle spoke to her from the grave. Her uncle is the center of this. I text Ash: *Look at the uncle. His friends. Co-workers. Anyone in his life.*

Already thought of it, Ash replies. On it.

I grab the box filled with his files and I start typing a list of every name associated with each case. We need to search those cases for connections to Jewel, her mother, her friend, and her father. Hell, we need any case he ever worked, but the ones that were on his desk seem the most relevant and a good start. I email Asher the list, and then text him: *See email. I sent you a list of the uncle's cases, to cross reference to every fucking thing you can.*

Got it, Asher replies. *EVERY FUCKING THING I CAN.*

"Smart ass," I murmur, and stick my phone back in my pocket.

I've just started a cup of coffee brewing when a soft three-punch knock sounds on the door, a Walker code that tells me the groceries have arrived, delivered by one of our men. I cross to the door and open it to find Adam, master of disguise that he is, no longer in his suit and tie. He's now in ripped jeans, a baseball hat turned backwards, sneakers, and his favorite New York Jets Jersey. "I better be getting a good damn tip," he murmurs, shoving the store bags at me.

"Here's your tip," I say, handing him the umbrella. "But as an added bonus. The Jets Suck. Join the Pats club and actually win." I shut the door on him and lock up before putting away the groceries. I glance at my watch. *Fuck.* Jewel's been asleep for two hours. My gaze lifts to the shut bedroom door. She's not a weakness. She's a job. That's what this should have stayed. That's how I protect her. I grab a bottle of water and think of the homeless man that was following her that most likely wasn't a homeless man at all.

Suddenly, I don't like her closed bedroom door, or how long it's been shut, one fucking bit. I start walking toward her room.

Chapter Twenty-Three

JACOB

I reach Jewel's bedroom, and I'm about to open the door when it flies open and she rushes out and smacks right into me. "Oh," she gasps, as I catch her arms, heat charging between us that appears in-fucking-escapable. "I didn't know you were there," she adds, catching herself with a firmly placed hand on my chest, and just that easily, I'm hard and hot, and if not for Asher's "weakness" comment, she'd be halfway naked already.

Fuck.

I release her, one hand planted on the doorway to keep it off her damn, perfect body. "How's your head?"

"Better," she says. "Thank you for the BC powder and convincing me to nap. I feel guilty for sleeping too long, though. I was just coming to find out what was happening."

"Nothing eventful," I say. "Mostly data collection, but let's eat something and I'll update you."

"God, yes," she says. "I could chew my own arm off right now."

It's a joke but neither of us laugh. We just stand there, staring at each other, those naked moments we'd shared earlier between us again now, tempting us, telling us we want more. "You're not gentle?" she asks, proving her mind is right where mine is, and it's not on work.

"No," I say, not about to sugarcoat who, and what, I am to her, or anyone, for that matter. "I'm not even close to gentle."

"Right," she says. "You're hard."

"Yes."

"You're fucked up."

"Ten shades of fucked up," I assure her.

"I'm fucked up, too, you know," she says.

"About twenty shades of fucked up," I comment dryly.

"Well then," she says, "if that's true, together we're thirty shades of fucked up. That seems like a problem. That and you are a control freak and—"

"—so are you."

"Yes. I don't like giving it up. I'd always be fighting you for it."

"And you'd never win."

"Of course, I would," she says, a smile hinting at her lips, which are lipstick free because I kissed it all away.

But I don't smile. I'm not amused at all with where my thoughts go. "I'm not your fireman, sweetheart. I won't break. I won't give. I won't make you feel normal or good, even for a little while. I'll make you feel all thirty shades of fucked up, sometimes double. Because I don't pretend to be what I'm not."

"Mr. Robot just shuts everyone out."

"I didn't shut you out."

"Yes, you did. That 'I'm not gentle' remark was all about scaring me."

"Are you scared?" I ask, waiting a little too anxiously for her reply when I do nothing anxiously, ever.

"I don't scare easily. Not anymore. Not for a long, long time. I guess that's where my twenty shades of fucked up comes from. But let's just face it. Two fucked up people make really fucked up people."

I feel those words like a punch I don't expect. It's obvious where she's going. It's obvious she's the one putting up the roadblock between us. I should celebrate. This is what I need. This is what keeps her from mattering to me, and yet all I want to do is carry her right back to that bed, and join her this time. Which is exactly why I turn and walk away, heading back to the kitchen.

By the time I'm on the other side, sitting on the stool that I've been using while working, she's standing across from me. "What did that reply even mean?" she demands, her blonde hair in sexy disarray around her shoulders, when I'd like it to be on my naked body, preferably my stomach, with her mouth back on my cock.

I cut off the fantasy of her licking me again. It gets me nowhere but more fucked up after fucking her. "I didn't reply at all," I say.

"No reply *is* a reply, and you know it," she counters.

"There's a reason you gravitate to your normal, good guy, fireman."

"What? Where did that come from? I told you. It's over with him mostly because he *is* a normal, good guy, fireman."

"But you need someone like him to make you feel normal. To give you a dose of straight up good. I told you. That's not me."

"I don't want a damn good guy fireman," she repeats. "And I don't need anyone."

"Two fucked up people make really fucked up people," I say, repeating her words. "You're right. We're just going to fuck with each other. We're a distraction that can't exist or one or both of us will end up dead. Which is why, right now, we need to decide if we stay here or go to my place. Here's your update. The team is researching connections to your uncle and I've sent a list of the case files you brought home with you. I have them looking for connections to you. Asher's wife, Sierra, can Skype with you when you're ready to profile the slayer and talk through actions and reactions."

She leans over the counter, close to me, that damn floral scent of hers teasing my nostrils. "What I was going to say," she says, "is that fucked up is the only way I live in my world. Fucked up is the only thing that fits me, which is why the fireman does not. And more. I was going to dare to say more, but I'll just stop right there." She pushes off the island. "Set up the call." She grabs her briefcase and sticks it in the box. "I'll be in my bedroom working." She turns and walks away.

I watch every step she takes to depart, every single one of them tempting me to follow her, repeating her taunt: *I was going to dare to say more.* I want to know what more is. I just want fucking more of fucking her. I sit there a moment and consider staying where I'm at for all of thirty seconds. That isn't going to happen. I pull Asher up on my messages: *Set the meeting for seven-thirty.*

Done, he replies. Skype me. I'll put Sierra on.

I stand up and walk to the fridge, grab the bag of sandwiches I ordered from the grocery deli, two bottles of water and my MacBook, before I head toward the bedroom. The door is shut, and I don't knock. I open it and find her on the bed, legs crossed, her boots on the floor, and her Mac open in her lap. I cross to stand beside her, setting her water on the nightstand. "Drink. It will help your head."

"You didn't knock," she says. "What if I was changing?"

"I'm not that nice of a guy, remember? And I assure you that had you been changing, I would have enjoyed the view." I reach into the bag and hand her the sandwich. "The best chicken salad on a croissant in the city." I walk to the chair in the corner by the windowless wall—which works out just fine when it comes to protecting, not so fine if she needed to escape—and sit down. "If you don't want that sandwich, I'll eat it."

"You aren't getting my sandwich," she says, opening the container.

"Okay then. Skype is at seven-thirty. Groceries are in the fridge."

"And you're in my bedroom," she says.

"We're doing this together. That means a door doesn't separate us."

"Just a world," she says, looking at her computer screen.

Only we aren't a world apart. Not even close. We're so damn close that I can practically taste her, and it's killing me. But she's right. Fucked up, makes fucked up, or I wouldn't be fucking her on the job. Correction: wouldn't have fucked her on the job. I can't do that again. Ironically, it's because she's her, while I wouldn't have done it at all if she was anyone else. We eat in silence and neither of us work. There's just me and her and the damn bed that she's in without me.

"You're right," she says as we finish up. "It was a great sandwich. You have pretty good taste for an arrogant—"

"Asshole?"

"I was going to say: heartless, never gentle, hard-ass. Do you prefer asshole?"

"Considering you're the only woman who's ever gone at me like you do, and the only woman I couldn't say no to, apparently, I do."

"What?" she demands. "You say that like I seduced you into fucking me, Jacob," she says, and the use of my name, over "asshole" actually tells me just how pissed she really is.

As if proving that point, she starts to scoot off the bed, and damn it, I can't leave her alone.

I'm on my feet and standing over her by the time she's on her feet. "We got to me. *We*. Us. This. Whatever the fuck it is."

"Well then, we'll fix that. Remove yourself from this assignment."

"You know I won't and don't say that's about Jesse Marks. It's about you. I'm the one who's going to do the up close and personal side of protecting you."

"You don't *need* to be in my bedroom to protect me. We don't need that distraction, remember?"

"I need to keep you close," I say and it's a confession to her and myself.

"No one can get past your team and my front door, and live. You don't *need* to be in my bedroom."

"You're right," I say, "but I'm not leaving and you don't want to and you don't really want me to either."

"According to *you*, I want the fireman here, not you."

"I don't want you with that fucking fireman." I pause for effect. "Ever."

"What happened to me being the distraction that will get us killed?"

"Do you know what Asher said to me?" I don't wait for a reply. "He said the Tin Man finally grew a heart and a weakness."

She pales. "Me?"

"Yes. You."

"Why would he say that? Because you kissed me?"

"Because when he asked me how personal this had gotten I told him 'real fucking personal.'"

"But I'm a weakness."

I close the small space between us and slide my hand under her hair to her neck, my other hand at her lower back. "I let his words fuck with me, but I was wrong. He was wrong. Because yes, this is personal, but what that means is that if anyone comes at you that's personal, too. And only a few people have hit that nerve with me, and they didn't live to talk about it. Tell me the more you didn't tell me before."

"I don't want gentle. I don't like being treated like I'll break because I don't want to start thinking I'll break."

"And yet you believe you're never ready?"

"Maybe that's why I don't want to be treated like I'll break. I don't *want* the good guy, nice fireman. I want you, but how about you protect me, but don't fuck me like you're protecting me?"

"You really want to go down this path with me?"

"Who's scared now?" she challenges.

I don't need to be convinced. I want her. Incredibly, some part of me needs her, when I don't let myself need anyone. And I need to taste her need really fucking badly. My mouth closes down on hers, and that's exactly what I do. I kiss her. I kiss her like I'll never kiss her again; like I can't get enough of her, because I can't. She moans, and melts into me, soft curves, making me harder and hotter, adrenaline burning through me, but none of this steals my control. None of this drives me over the edge, for one reason and one reason only. I still feel the wall between us. I still feel her restraint and I want what I don't have. I want her to give up control. I want her trust and that means submission.

With that need burning through me with the adrenaline, I tear my mouth from hers. "Undress for me," I order, setting her away from me.

"Are you going to undress?" she asks, more challenge in her voice.

"When the time is right," I say. "Right now, I want to watch *you* undress."

"Watch me," she repeats.

"Yes," I confirm. "Watch you."

She studies me for a moment, maybe two, and then pulls her blouse over her head, tossing it onto the bed. Her pants are next, and her panties go with them. I barely have time to appreciate that sweet V of her body, or her long legs that I want on my shoulders, and around my waist, before she unhooks her bra.

"Now what?" she says, tossing it aside, and giving me a view of her beautiful high breasts, and puckered nipples. Her eyes meeting mine, but there is no sign of submission, just more bravado, that I now see as a wall between us. And I not only want it torn down, I'm *going* to tear it down.

I pull my shirt over my head, tossing it, and grabbing her wrists, pulling her to me, her breasts nuzzling my chest. "Where are the cuffs?" I ask. "I know you have some here."

"I don't know you well enough to give you that kind of trust."

"Sounds like a good way to fast forward the trust that I might need one day."

She pulls back. "Because of Jesse Marks?"

"Quit going to him for everything. We said—"

"We'd put him aside for now. I know. I'm trying."

"Try harder. And the answer to your question: Why do I need your trust? Because that's the only way, I become your escape. Your safe place. That's the only way that you can stop being Detective Carpenter. I want you to know that you can be vulnerable and not pay a price. That is, unless you're just too afraid of me."

"I know what you just did," she says. "I know that was a challenge, meant to hit a nerve, and it still worked. I'm *not* scared. Top drawer. And it's not a kinky thing. I keep my gun and cuffs nearby."

That confession tells me how on edge she lives, how much she lives with the monsters of her work, and her past, every moment of every day. And this realization, not only makes me want her trust more, it makes me want to be safe for her. It makes me want to show her it's okay to let go with me. I reach around her and open the drawer, finding both a set of steel cuffs and another pair of the plastic breakable cuffs. I choose the plastic, because I know they will feel less intimidating to her. Shutting the drawer, I pull Jewel's hands together, and she laces her fingers. Her gaze lifts, and she looks at me, and despite more of that bravado in her stare, I find nerves and that vulnerability I want her to willingly embrace. It hits me then that binding a woman because she wants to be fucked and binding a woman who is daring to give me trust she gives no one else is a whole different ballgame. It's a responsibility. It's a promise, to be worthy of that trust. And I want that trust, no matter how unreasonable that demand, no matter how soon I'm asking for it. But I don't seem to care that it's soon, or that it pushes her limits. I just want her. All of her. And right now, I'm nowhere near having her.

I bind her wrists.

"I can get out of these cuffs, just like you," she says.

"I know you can but I'm going to make sure you have plenty of reasons to keep them on."

Chapter Twenty-Four

Jewel

Jacob pulls me flush against the long, hard lines of his body again and adrenaline surges through me at the idea that I've actually given up this much control. But then he kisses me, and I can't think. This is not just any kiss. Not a kiss we've shared before. He kisses me like he owns me: possessive, intense, and yet somehow he's savoring me, drinking me in. And once again I think, *oh God, the man can kiss. Oh God, I'm so wet.* My nipples ache. My body thrums and yet nervous energy radiates through me, and won't let me just relax into him.

"Relax, Jewel," he says softly, clearly reading my mind, his hands stroking my hair in what might actually be a gentle touch, if he was a gentle man. But he's not gentle, he's something else I cannot explain. Something that works for me in a way I didn't want anyone to work for me.

"I'm relaxed," I say. "Well, as relaxed as a control freak gets, cuffed, by the only man she's ever let cuff her. Who she's just met."

He tilts my face to his. "You can break the cuffs. You just said that, but you don't have to. You want free, you tell me. Okay?"

I like this question. I like the vehement way he's asked it. Like he needs to know this is my choice. Instead of needing to know he's in control. "Yes," I say. "Okay."

"The idea here is that next time you don't let me cuff you. You want me to do it. Because this is about pleasure and escape. Blocking out Detective Carpenter and Major—"

"Robot?"

"Yes." His lips quirk at the corners. "You don't have to be tough. You don't have to push back. The idea is to just let go."

"I can't just let go. It's not—it's just not who I am."

"You can," he says, reaching in his pocket and pulling out his phone.

My heart races. "What are you doing?"

"Easy, sweetheart. I'm just putting on some music." He brushes his lips over mine. "I don't want you to have room to think of anything but the music and me."

"Right. Yes. I guess I am a little on edge."

"Nervous?" he supplies.

"Or something."

He responds by punching a few buttons on his phone, before setting it down on the night stand, while Imagine Dragons "Believer" starts to play, the words filling the air:

First things first

I'ma say all the words inside my head

He grips my wrists with one hand and pulls me to him, but he doesn't kiss me. He watches me, his free hand stroking over my breast and then down my ribcage, over my backside, before he leans in, his cheek next to mine, lips at my ear. "The many ways I want to fuck you," he says, "can't even begin to start tonight."

I breathe out with the intimacy of those words that are somehow naughtier because they came from him and I actually *want* him to do what he promises. His lips find my lips, a breath from touching, as he asks, "You sure you don't want gentle?"

"If I wanted gentle, the fireman would be here right now."

"You had to taunt me, didn't you?"

"I like taunting you."

"Probably not a smart choice when I decide when you come, not the nice guy fireman. Who I suspect would be happy with a fake orgasm because he can't tell the real thing."

He's right. I have faked. A few times, but I don't reply. I can't. Jacob's fingers find my nipple and he starts tugging and teasing it. My sex clenches and just when I would squeeze my thighs together, his leg wedges between them.

"Don't do that," he says, his hand sliding down my belly to my sex, where he caresses my nub. "Because then I can't do this." His fingers press along the wet, now aching, seam of my body, and I swear, I could come so very easily right now. As if he knows where my head is, and my body, yet again, his hand suddenly moves and settles on my hip and he kisses me again, turning my back to the bed at the same time.

We go down on the mattress and he's on top of me, and he's pressed my wrists over my head. "Keep them there," he orders, his hands on my arms, slowly traveling downward, until one of them is on my breast, and he's kissing me, tongue stroking against mine, lips then caressing a path over my cheek. Down my jaw, to my neck, and then lower. He cups both of my breasts and licks each nipple, sucking and repeating, left to right. I arch into his touch, his mouth, and he travels up my body and kisses me before returning to my puckered nipple. His fingers settle between my legs, stroking, teasing, driving me crazy, and just when his mouth has teased a path to join his fingers, he stops. His hand goes to my hips and he shifts us, and then me, turning me to my stomach, and I tuck my hands beneath me, ready to lift myself. He's over me before I can, hands on either side of me. "Don't move, or my mouth won't go where we both want it to."

"Next time you wear the cuffs," I whisper.

He laughs, a low sexy sound that makes me smile at the same moment that he smacks my ass. I gasp and then laugh, and oh my God, I'm so aroused it hurts. He leans into me again, near my ear. "If you move, I might even spank you. And you'd like it."

"Like I'm going to beg for you to kill me?"

"How about I make you beg for that spanking?"

"That's never going to happen," I promise, my words denying the ache in my sex.

"No?" he challenges.

"No," I say, and damn it, why am I this aroused by this conversation? I don't do kink. I don't do spankings. But then, I don't do cuffs either and I'm in them now.

"Maybe not tonight," he says. "But soon."

With that promise, he moves away, and the ache in my sex is the only thing that keeps me laying there. Spanking? No. That will never happen. My ass tingles with the very thought, and I find myself pressing my arms against the sides of my aching breasts. Behind me, the sounds of Jacob undressing begin. The rustle of clothing. His boot thumping to the ground. His belt clinking. The music shifts and I laugh again because it's gnash's *i hate u, i love u,* that pretty much sums up how I feel about Jacob. Well, the hate part doesn't feel much like hate at all.

The bed shifts and he is back over me, the hard length of his erection settling against my backside, while his hands settle by my shoulders. His lips are by my ear. "I'm back," he says softly, as if I am not fully aware of his naked body pressed to my naked body. He nips my earlobe before his hands are dragging down my back until he shackles my hip and lifts me to my knees, forcing me to hold my weight on my hands. He kisses my backside and scrapes his teeth across one delicate cheek. And right when he literally lays on his back, and pulls my sex to his mouth, my cellphone chooses to ring.

"Oh no," I breathe out. "I'm on rotation. I have to get that. I can't believe this, but I have to get that."

"I'm getting it," Jacob says, as if this is just fine, not a problem at all, when I'm eighty percent to orgasm and have no control of my hands.

Before I can even consider which way to move, Jacob turns off the music and hands me the phone. I settle on my elbows, my ass still in the air, and when I would roll over, Jacob is back between my legs, holding me in place, his breath hot on my clit. And I still have to answer. I hit answer, and without looking at the caller ID, say, "Detective Carpenter."

"Detective," my boss says, at the same moment, that Jacob licks me.

I hold back a pant. "Yes, Lieutenant?" I bite out, squeezing Jacob's head only to have him laugh and lick me again.

"Why do you sound breathless?" he demands.

"I'm running," I say. "You know I run when I'm," Jacob licks me again, and I bite my lip, "when I'm thinking through cases."

"You can't find bodies on a run."

I clench my fist at the way Jacob is now stroking my clit, looking down at him with a glare he can't see because he's facing in the other direction. "I'll find the bodies," I promise. "I'm working on leads."

"There is pressure from all kinds of directions on this. We need a conviction and so does the DA's office."

"I know," I say, my voice cracking. "I know. I—"

"Finish your damn run, and get back to work." He hangs up. I drop the phone.

"Jacob, damn it," I hiss. "I cannot believe I was doggystyle, in cuffs, talking to my boss about dead bodies when you were—"

He suckles me and I have no words left. I just give in to the pleasure. It's here. It's there. It's everywhere. My entire body is charged and the minute his fingers slide inside me, I'm done. I tumble over into orgasm with such force that my body jerks. Jacob does this slow, perfect lick and eases me down, as if he reads exactly what I need when I need it, but the minute I come back to the present, I whisper, "I hate you right now." He laughs again, and I scowl even though he can't see it since I'm facedown on the blanket. "And you laugh at my torture."

He turns me over and slides up my body, the sweet weight of him settling on top of me. "This would not be a good time to tell you that I'm pretty sure you didn't disconnect the line, right?"

"What? No. Tell me no." I grab my phone and it's disconnected now. "I hope he hung right up."

"Just tell him it was a really good run," he says, his lips lowering to mine.

"I really do hate you right now."

He kisses me, a long, salty, slide of his tongue, before he whispers. "Does it taste like I hate you?" He presses inside me, sliding deep, stroking all those sensitive nerves on the way, before he settles in and repeats, "Does it feel like I hate you?"

I grip his shoulders, my lashes lowering with the feel of him inside me. "You are—"

"I'm what?" he asks pulling back, doing a slow slide until he all but pulls out. "I'm what, Jewel?"

"Gentle," I say, because I can't help myself. "Too damn gentle."

He thrusts into me, his lips lingering above mine. "Is that right?"

"Yes. Fuck me already, will you?"

He doesn't immediately move, and I don't know why, or what he's thinking, but when his mouth crashes onto mine, it's rough with demand, his tongue stroking deep, the taste of him raw, hot. Addictive. Arousing. Overwhelmingly right in every way. I arch into him and he thrusts into me and it's a wild, crazy, intense rush of bodies grinding together, lips touching, tongues licking. Teeth scraping. There is nothing but him. Nothing but this and us and I can't get enough of him, until finally, I can't hold back. I can't stop the rush of need that tumbles into another orgasm. I gasp and my sex clenches around him. He lets out a low, guttural groan that fills the room while he fills me with the heat of his release.

We melt into each other in utter sated completion, his weight resting on me and his arms. "Are you still afraid?" he teases near my ear.

"I was never afraid," I scoff, when my phone rings again. "Not again," I say, reaching for it and this time I look at the ID. "My boss again." I answer. "Lieutenant."

"One more thing," he says, as Jacob pulls out of me and stuffs tissue between my legs. "You're off rotation."

"What?" I ask, sitting up, shocked at this new turn of events. "We're short-staffed. Why would you do that?"

"Find me the bodies and deal with your stalker. Don't argue. The decision is final." He hangs up. "Damn it." I look at Jacob. "I need these cuffs off." I scoot to the edge of the bed and he grabs them and yanks them apart.

"What happened?" he asks, reaching for his pants.

I stand up and toss the tissues. "He's pissed. That's what happened." I can't find my underwear and I just grab my pants and pull them on. "He took me out of the rotation," I add as Jacob pulls on his shirt, and hands me my bra.

"And that's a bad thing?"

"Yes," I say, taking my bra and putting it on. "I'm off rotation and I'm not allowed at the station and that's your fault. That's not where I'm going with this."

"You're a damn good detective," he says, as we both pull on our shoes and holsters.

"Good or bad, I'm basically on leave. He said to find the mother and her unborn child, and get him a conviction before I come back. Oh and end this slayer threat." I press my fingers to my forehead. "This is not good. This is what I do and it feels like this is the prelude to undoing what I do. I don't know how to operate outside this box." I pull on my jacket.

He steps in front of me, his hands settling on my waist beneath it. "Because this is how you cope with knowing how many monsters live in this world."

"You see too much."

"Because I understand. I know what you need and how you feel."

"Because that's what the army did for you."

"Yes," he confirms.

"But you got out."

204

"And that story about me getting out, which you obviously want to hear, will require that trust I don't have yet."

"Because Jesse Marks is involved?"

"Jesse Marks isn't why I got out."

My cellphone rings again and I grab it from the bed where I'd left it. "Rodriquez," I say, frowning.

"The guy that shared a workspace with you?" he asks.

"Yes. And he never calls me, so he must have gotten my rotation and wants to bitch me out." I hit answer. "Rodriquez."

"That guy I told you about. The one who does shit for people. He called me. Says he's in danger. I'm headed that way. How about backing me up and then you can hit him up about your case, too?"

"Yes. Of course. Now?"

"Now. I'm almost there. You have the address?"

"Text it to me to be safe."

"Will do." He hangs up and I look at Jacob, my brow furrowing again.

"What is it?" he asks.

"We need to go out but—you see, Rodriquez told me about a guy that was 'the guy' to get rid of bodies. He wouldn't tell me how he knew him, which was odd. Now he tells me that same guy called him in distress, in some kind of danger."

"And he's on his way there and wants you to back him up," he assumes.

"Yes. And that feels—"

"Off," he supplies. "Agreed."

"Then Rodriquez could be walking into a trap," I say. "We have to go." I step around him and head for the living room. Jacob is right behind me and as soon as we're on the stairs outside the apartment, he's by my side, dialing his phone. "Yeah, Ash," he says. "That call with Sierra is off for now. We're headed to back up a detective Jewel works with." I hand him the card Rodriquez gave me and he takes it. "Check out this guy," he tells Asher, "and tell the team this is where we're going." He reads off the address and name and he's off the phone by the time we reach the street.

"It's clear across town," I say. "The fastest way is going to be the subway."

"Agreed," he says again, and we hurry into a station.

Once we're in the subway, on a car, sharing another pole, he says, "You do know that we could be headed into a trap, too, right?"

"Yes. But that's okay. I have a big bad Green Beret with me."

Chapter Twenty-Five

Jewel

The instant Jacob and I step out of the subway terminal and onto the sidewalk, his phone buzzes. He pulls it from his pocket and glances at me before answering. "Royce. I'll put him on speaker." I nod and he hits the answer button. "Jewel's on the line," he announces.

"Good," Royce says. "You both need to hear this. This guy you're going to see, Gerome Smith, is a licensed PI in California, not New York. He's been here six months, but he hasn't applied for a license. On a gut feeling, I made a quick call to one of my ex-co-workers at the FBI. Turns out, prior to moving here he was in LA, and the feds suspected him of aiding more than one felony cover-up. There is reason to believe he had a connection to the former DA. As in the DA wanted a case to go his way, and Gerome helped him make it happen. That DA left office, and Gerome quickly got out of dodge. Word is he's operated on a cash-only basis, and off the books. Watch your backs. He's a tricky little bastard. I'll be on standby if you need me."

"Copy that, boss," Jacob says, disconnecting the line.

"Okay," I say, processing what we know. "So, Rodriquez must have had an informant that he didn't want to share with me that hooked him up with Gerome."

"Or he has something on Gerome and decided to use it to get him to do work for him."

He's right. That makes sense. Maybe Rodriquez even covered up crimes for Gerome. Maybe he helped Rodriquez cover up a crime. It's not a place I want to go, but there are dirty cops. That's just a fact. Jacob and I fall into silence, passing a closed topless bar that is the only eyesore in a neighborhood that is residential, with high-end shops a few short blocks away, and a half-dozen Starbucks somewhere within walking distance.

A half-block past the bar, we stop at the front door of our destination building, a fifteen-story heap of old brick, with a buzzer door system, like so many of the locations in the city. Someone exits the door, and Jacob grabs it before it shuts. "Good catch," I murmur, entering the foyer that is basically a walkway surrounded by walls. Jacob joins me and we make our way to the elevator that is one of those steel slow moving boxes.

The elevator slowly opens and we enter the car. Jacob snags Gerome's card from his pocket, glances at it and punches the tenth floor before we stand side-by-side waiting on the dinosaur doors to shut. We don't speak, both of us focused, ready for trouble. I'm comfortable with this silence. I'm comfortable with him right here with me, too. He doesn't feel like an intrusion as I'd expected him to and that has nothing to do with my need for protection. I haven't even thought of the slayer for hours until this moment. But slayer or not, I have only known Jacob a short while and yet I'm one hundred percent confident that he would take a bullet for me. On the other hand, I can't say that about many of the badges I've worked with daily, which is proof that a job, duty as one might call it, doesn't give you courage or honor. That I can count on Jacob matters to me. I think he has the potential to really matter to me.

"I'd take a bullet for you, too," I say, without looking at him.

"What?" he asks, and I feel his attention on me now, not the doors.

I glance over at him. "I just want you to know that I know you'd take a bullet for me and it's a mutual thing. I've got your back, too."

"I don't want you to take a bullet for me, Jewel. I protect you. You don't protect me."

"Sorry, Jacob. That's just not how this works. And I don't want you to take a bullet for me, either. But there is something about knowing that the person by your side would."

The elevator dings and I can feel him fighting an urge to pull me close. "We're going to talk about this conversation later," he says, his tone hard, something unreadable in his eyes.

"Talk all you want," I say. "Conversation won't change who I am or what I believe."

The doors finally open and I step forward, only to have Jacob catch my arm. "Ladies don't go first into danger."

"I'm a—"

"Don't say detective," he says. "Because that conversation, as you say, changes nothing." He pulls me behind him.

I grimace but he's already stepping into the hallway, blocking my path several beats, giving me space to join him, and motioning me forward.

Once I'm at his side, he points to the hallway several feet ahead, and right. We walk in that direction and, of course, he rounds the corner first before we continue on toward

Smith's office. We locate the proper room number to find the office door cracked open. Instinct has my hand going to my weapon, and Jacob does the same. We glance at each other and give a ready nod.

Both of us flatten on the wall. "Hello?" I call out, while Jacob kicks open the door and reclaims his spot out of the line of sight. "Hello?!" I call out again, easing around the doorframe just enough to get a visual that sets my heart to racing. Not only is a man that I assume to be Gerome lying on the floor in a pool of blood, Rodriquez is next to him and he's not moving. "Rodriquez!" I shout. "Rodriquez, damn it, answer me!"

He doesn't move and I share a look with Jacob, who motions to the door, a moment before he enters, his weapon ahead of him, scanning left and right. "Don't touch anything," I order, trusting him to cover me as I make a beeline for Rodriquez, and the bullet hole I spot between Gerome's eyes does not make me hopeful. But as I squat down in a blood-free zone next to Rodriquez, hope forms with the absence of an obvious injury anywhere on his body. I press my fingers to his neck, but there is no pulse to be found. "Damn it," I murmur, moving my fingers and trying again. "He's dead!" I call out and then murmur again, "Damn it, he's dead."

"We're clear," Jacob calls out, while I frown at the sight of a piece of paper lying on top of Rodriquez's legs. I scoot down in that direction to find handwriting that reads: *I'm sorry, Jewel. He knew things you just weren't ready to know. If you were, you'd have seen what I already showed you.*

My spine stiffens with the words "weren't ready."

"Jacob!" I call out, reaching in my bag for gloves.

LISA RENEE JONES

"I'm here," Jacob says, kneeling beside me, and the instant his gaze hits the note, he curses. "Is that the Rodriquez's writing?"

"Yes."

"'Not ready'? Either Rodriquez is your slayer, or this isn't a murder/suicide as that note suggests. It's murder, and that's a message to you."

"He's not the slayer," I say, my gut screaming with that reply. "And the slayer is too smart to believe I'd believe that." I rotate to face him, pulling on my gloves. "I need to hear that my father is okay. Please call Savage while I'm calling this in." I hand him a pair of gloves. "You need to wear these."

He takes them and grabs my hand a moment. "Your father is safe, but I'll go call and check in with Savage. Are you okay?"

"Yeah. I'm always okay at a crime scene. I have to be."

He studies me a moment in which I'm certain he wants to point out that this isn't a normal crime scene, but he doesn't. All he says is, "I'll be back," before he pushes to his feet and walks toward the door.

I stand up and grab my phone, connecting to the station, scanning the few pieces of furniture in the room. A desk. A credenza. Two chairs. "This is Detective Carpenter," I say when the line is answered. "I have a double homicide with a detective involved and dead." I answer a series of questions, and give them the address, before standing up and dialing the Lieutenant, scanning around the bodies.

"Detective," he says. "If this is about rotation—"

"Rodriquez is dead. I'm at the scene."

"Holy fuck. Give me the address. I'm walking toward the exit now to come to you."

211

I give him the address. "It's Gerome Smith's office." And because I know his next questions before he asks them, I supply details. "I'm not sure if Gerome was an informant or what exactly. He was going to meet him and asked me to back him up."

"And Gerome killed him," he assumes.

"No," I say. "He and Gerome are both dead. It looks like a murder/suicide with Rodriquez as the trigger. Without forensic input to confirm, it appears he may have shot Gerome and took some sort of toxin, which of course, will take weeks to confirm."

He's silent a beat. "Did he do it?" he asks gravely.

"My professional opinion is no. It's a set-up."

"Facts," he orders. "Back that up. Tell me what you do know."

I give him the rundown on Gerome and the theories I'd discussed with Jacob. "You're telling me that Rodriquez might have been dirty?"

"I'm telling you that I want this case and that I have to use that as a working hypothesis."

"That hypothesis," he argues rightfully, "supports a murder/suicide."

"I know that," I say. "But it wasn't."

"Don't make me work for this Carpenter," he snaps. "*Back it up.*"

"He left a note addressed to me and while it's his handwriting, it reads like something my stalker would write."

"Okay. I am going to put that bombshell aside because your head is fucked by this stalker. Rodriquez called you for back up and the note was addressed to you. That sounds like he, himself, planned it."

"With all due respect," I bite out, "My head is not fucked up, Lieutenant."

"Why did he call you, of all people, to back him up?" he demands.

"He told me that Gerome was 'the guy' to go to hide a body. He wouldn't tell me more but as I think this through, I assume Rodriguez had something on the guy and was using him to solve cases. It's the only thing that makes sense."

Sirens sound in the near distance. "Deal with the forensic team," he says. "Check any cameras. I'll be there in fifteen." He hangs up and I shove my phone inside my bag, and study the body, looking for signs of trauma that just don't exist.

"Your father's fine," Jacob says, rejoining me. "And Savage is going to stay the night in his apartment with him." He glances down at the body, tilting his head to the side, and then looking at me again. "No bullet wound?"

"No," I say. "No obvious trauma at all. Which means—"

"Pills or poison," he supplies. "Which one could reason, was because he was afraid to pull the trigger on himself."

"No," I say, rejecting that idea. "This is no murder/suicide, but it was made to look like one. And if the forensics agree, I'm going to have a hard time proving otherwise. I will, though. I will prove it and I will get him. I know this was the slayer."

"I don't disagree," Jacob say, "but the first question we have to ask is, to what end game?"

FALLING UNDER

Chapter Twenty-Six

Jewel

When one of our own dies, the city takes notice, and an army of law enforcement sweep down on the murder scene at Gerome's office. I take the lead, and with Jacob never far away, I direct the teams, looking for answers my way. The cameras are checked and no help. The scene empty of many clues but I take photos of handwriting samples and random documents I find in Gerome's desk. The lieutenant arrives much later than expected, an hour into the investigation, and with no explanation. But once he does, it's his team. His man. His lead. He gives directions, walks the scene and then motions for me to head to the hallway.

Jacob stays by my side, obviously trying to be as informed as possible, but this time, my boss isn't having it. "We need a moment, son," he says gruffly, scrubbing the graying whiskers on his hard-set square jaw.

"Yes, sir," Jacob says, reluctance in the speed of his steps.

"Were you fucking him?" he demands.

I blanch, the anger that follows barely contained. "What? Did you really just ask me that?"

"Were you?" he demands again.

"No. Never. Even. Close."

"Why did he write a suicide note to you?"

"He didn't," I bite out. "I told you. My stalker used that same wording. The words 'you're not ready.' That's a theme."

He narrows his eyes on me. "You're saying they were murdered by your stalker?"

"You ask that now as if I haven't already said that to you. So yes. I'm saying that both myself and Jacob think it's on the table as an option."

"Why kill Gerome?"

"I don't know."

"I told you on the phone, or I think I did. He was my lead to find the bodies in our billionaire CEO case."

"Why would he want to stop you from finding those bodies?

"I don't have the answers," I bite out. "Maybe he's just fucking with me and my career"

"Or?"

"Or Gerome had something on Rodriquez and was blackmailing him and Rodriquez just lost it."

He looks around me and motions Jacob back. I don't turn, but Jacob is standing next to me moments later and I'm not threatened by his presence or my boss's interest in his opinion. I'm damn glad for the backup. "You and your team believe this could be a result of her stalker?" the lieutenant asks.

"We do," Jacob says, his tone absolute.

My boss's lips thin and he refocuses on me. "Why would your stalker choose Gerome as the murder victim?"

"Rodriquez said that this guy is the guy to make bodies disappear," I say. "Gerome was on my radar as a person of interest. I wanted to talk to him."

"Why would your stalker care about that case?" he asks.

"He doesn't," Jacob says. "He cares about her. He's obsessed with her."

The lieutenant looks between us. "Do we know who he is?"

"No," I say. "We do not."

"Lieutenant!" someone shouts.

"Damn it," he grumbles, looking at Jacob. "Are you with her around the clock?"

"Yes, sir. She's well protected."

"Good," he says, looking at me. "Get out of here for now. We'll talk about how to keep anyone else from getting hurt tomorrow."

"I want this case," I argue. "I need to take this one."

"You're too close to this," he says. "So not no, but hell no. Get out of here."

"I need to at least go to his apartment. I need—"

"I sent a team there before I ever got here. I'll send you the reports. For now, you may be in danger and you may be putting others in danger. I need to deal with Rodriquez and his family tonight."

"What family?"

"He has a brother and pre-teen daughter that lives with her mother in Long Island."

My throat thickens. "Rodriquez has a daughter?"

"Yes. He *had* a daughter. Go home. We'll regroup tomorrow." He turns and walks away.

I inhale and let it out, a ball of emotion in my chest that I don't want to feel. I don't look at Jacob or anyone. I need out of here. I need to breathe. I rotate to start walking and a body bag is suddenly being rolled in front of me, one of the two men, who died because of me, inside. Jacob gently nudges my arm, stopping short of actually holding onto me, and obviously reading me, points at the stairwell, understanding that I need an escape and I need it now.

We start walking and enter the stairwell, and when I would continue downward, Jacob grabs me and pulls me to him. "Are you okay?"

"He had a daughter, Jacob. He had a fucking daughter."

"No one takes a job like ours without knowing the risks."

"No one takes a job like ours and intends to die, either. I need to be on this case."

"We'll talk to your boss tomorrow. We'll make the argument that our team is supporting this investigation."

I press my hand to my forehead. "He died because of me. Both of those men died because of me."

"Are you sure the slayer wasn't Rodriquez?"

"It's not him. He didn't walk like him. He didn't feel like him. The bottom line here that we both know, but don't want to say: the slayer killed Rodriquez to taunt me. Maybe even a way to punish me for having you involved. You have to back off before someone else gets killed."

"If I have to tie you to your bed and keep you there while my team finds him, that's what I'll do. You are not going to be stupid enough to do what he wants you to do."

"I'm not trying to be stupid." I grab his jacket. "I can't live with the idea that someone else dies because of me. A little girl will never see her father again."

His hands come down on my face. "I know. I understand. You're emotional right now, and for justified reasons, but that's why we make decisions tomorrow."

"Pretend you're not with me. Cover me from a distance."

"I'm not leaving room for him to get to you, without coming through me."

My fist balls on his chest. "We just need to catch him and then this conversation won't matter. Now. Right now."

"How do you suggest we do that?"

"He made a mistake. Everyone makes a mistake. We have to figure out what it was."

The doors below open and voices sound, coming in our direction. I twist away from Jacob and we both start walking, giving quick waves to the uniforms headed up while we go down. We exit to the street and the chaos of emergency staff and press, and make our way past the yellow tape, dodging several reporters, before we enter a subway entrance. "Where are we going?" Jacob asks, keeping pace next to me on the stairs leading into the tunnel.

"The precinct."

"You aren't allowed to be there right now," he reminds me. "Your boss—"

"Can fire me if he so desires, but I'm searching Rodriquez's desk before anyone else gets to it."

He doesn't reply. He doesn't fight me on this because he knows this has to be done. In fact, he doesn't speak at all until we're in an otherwise empty train, sharing a pole again, hands stacked. "Are you okay?" he asks, his powerful leg hugging mine, that intimacy between us affecting me now more than ever, and I can't say why. It just does.

"I told you," I say. "I'm always okay at a crime scene."

"Sweetheart, we aren't at a crime scene. We're alone, just you and me." His hand comes down on my hip. "Deep breathe a moment and then talk to me."

"I can't deep breathe. I'm still living the adrenaline rush of it all."

"How well did you know Rodriquez?"

"Not well at all apparently. I didn't know about his daughter." I laugh without humor. "He brought me a donut on Valentine's Day in the hopes I'd be less of a bitch.

Obviously, it didn't work." My voice cracks. "Damn it. I can't believe he's dead. I can't believe he's dead because of me."

"When you say that, the slayer wins. He's fucking with your head. Rodriquez is dead because of the slayer, not you."

"But you know—"

"No buts, Jewel. I know you know I'm right. Logically you know, but in times like this it can be hard to see the truth above the guilt."

"Even for the Tin Man?"

"Hell yeah, sweetheart. I'm human, too. But being human is what makes us different from the slayers of the world."

The train jerks to the side and I grab his jacket, when I would never automatically reach for anyone else in my life, past or present. Because Jacob is different and I want the chance to know how and why. "What if he comes after you?"

"Then he dies and this is over. And maybe that's exactly how we catch him. We make him come to me."

"How?"

"That's a question for you and Sierra. Profile him. Decide how we trip his trigger and drive his attention to me."

"No," I say. "No. I won't let you do this. I don't want you to do this."

"I'm—"

"Don't say you're a Green Beret. Rodriquez was a sharpshooter. He had a black belt in karate, and he was a ten-year veteran of the force. Gerome hid dead bodies for a living. They're both dead."

The car screeches to a halt and Jacob presses his lips to my ear. "Believe in me as much as you believe in him."

I don't look at him. I don't know what he'll see in my face or what I even feel. I don't want to care about someone who is going to die, again. I can't. And he's trying to get himself killed. The doors open and I pull away from the pole and him. He doesn't stop me, but as it seems he always is now, he's immediately by my side. We exit to the street and start walking, cold seeping into my bones, proof that my adrenaline has come down a notch, since I felt hot all over before the train ride. "Do you feel him?"

"No. Do you?"

"No," I say as we approach the precinct. "But if he's been watching me for two years, maybe I'm used to how he feels."

"I don't, though," he says, opening the door for me. "Which is why you can call me an asshole all you want, but you're stuck with me, sweetheart."

I rub the back of my neck and pass him by, guilt-ridden by how much relief I feel in those words. He's making himself a target. I'm making him a target. That isn't okay. It's that thought that drives my footsteps and I waste no time clearing us past security and hurrying up the stairs. We reach my old desk, and I ignore it and sit at Rodriquez's. Jacob joins me and opens a drawer, and the two of us start a search. We're about to give up and I actually fill a box with all of his things, when I lift the pad on top of the desk.

That's when I find the Valentine's Day card that went missing from my desk.

FALLING UNDER

Chapter Twenty-Seven

Jewel

I stare at the card which, despite my rejection of the premise, all but declares Rodriquez to be the slayer. Taking a mental step back, I admit to myself that the truth is that the card had no postmark. In other words, how else but by way of an insider, could it get to my desk and then to his desk? It had to be an internal action. But the bottom line here is that nothing in my gut connects with the idea of Rodriquez as the slayer. Jacob kneels next to me and hands me a pen. "Open it," he orders softly, obviously aware of the sparse, but populated, sea of desks around us.

I accept the pen, using it as intended to flip open the card, and prevent further compromising fingerprints. Jacob grabs a form filled out by Rodriquez from the edge of the desk and lays it next to the card. Together, we study the two sets of writing and I shake my head. "They don't match," I say, "and yet—look at the loops in the bottom of the Y's. God. Maybe it does. Maybe it was him. I mean, it's on his desk. Like he left it as confirmation."

"Maybe," Jacob says, sounding skeptical. "Or maybe that's what we're supposed to think."

I grab my phone and find the photo of the suicide note that I'd taken at the scene of the crime, setting it on the desk to allow us both to compare samples. "The script on the suicide note matches Rodriquez's script for sure," he says.

"But not the card," I add. "That writing is different. This makes no sense. Why would he have a card he didn't give me?"

"Either he had it written by someone else so you wouldn't recognize the writing, he was working with the real slayer, or he was set up. Whatever the case, the intent here is a mind fuck."

He's right. It is, and I don't like it. I swipe to another photo. "This is Gerome's writing." We both study the samples. "And," I say. "It's not even a close match to anything else we're looking at."

"Agreed," Jacob says. "We need an expert opinion and Royce has already stepped up to help. He called in a favor from a pal at the FBI. They're going to have a handwriting expert help us out." He motions to the desk. "Grab some samples of Rodriquez's writing and then let's get out of here. Preferably before your boss rains hell down on Walker Security for me letting you come here."

I glance over at him. "Letting me?"

"Sweetheart, I'm on your team, holding on tight for whatever ride we decide to take together, but so is *my boss*, who will get hell from *your boss*. Let's avoid the ass-chewing from both ends."

"Right. I forgot that you have people to answer to as well." I glance over at him, this pushy arrogant man who is only trying to help. "Thank you for helping me."

His eyes flicker with surprise, and then soften. "It's a rough night when a soldier, or I should say a badge, goes down, be it the right or wrong side of the law."

He cuts his eyes, and while "soldier" is an easy slip of the tongue for a soldier, I have this sense that he hit a nerve he didn't mean to reveal. I'm curious but I would never ask him about it anywhere but alone. For now, I try to jab him out of that memory. "But you're still an asshole," I tease.

He glances over at me, and whatever was in his eyes moments before is now gone. "Say that when we're alone."

My brow furrows. "Why?"

"Because apparently it turns me on."

My cheeks that never heat, heat, and I look away. Not because I care at this point that he knows how he affects me, but because two men died tonight and more could follow if we don't stop that from happening. That means solving the slayer mystery, and on that note, I take a couple of photos of the card and the desk in general, as well as multiple documents signed by Rodriquez. Once I'm done, I flip the card shut again and shove it between two sheets of paper, before slipping it into an envelope. I stuff it into my bag and then open a drawer to glance at a personal bill inside, confirming Rodriquez's address in my mind, though I'm fairly certain that Walker already has it.

Jacob motions toward the rear exit, and I nod, falling into step with him, and the idea that I missed what was in front of me starts to eat away at me hard and fast. We head down the rear stairs toward my office and fortunately, no one steps into our path before we exit to the garage where I turn to face Jacob. "I sat across from him for years," I say, expressing my thoughts to him before I explode. "I never felt the slayer watch me. I never saw or felt Rodriquez looking at me when he thought I wasn't looking and yet, no matter how wrong it feels, it has to be him."

"You're making yourself crazy right now," he says, his hands settling on my shoulders. "Your first reaction was to tell me it wasn't him. Both when we found the bodies and when you found that card on Rodriquez's desk."

"My gut says it's not him, but the facts say that it is."

"There are no facts," he says. "There are just possibilities and I know you know that. Let the FBI handwriting expert tell us if all the written pieces of the puzzle come together, but right now, you need to recognize that someone you know is dead. That's not the same as dealing with a crime scene and a stranger. I know because I've lived both in the form of warzones. You don't have your detective hat on right now."

"I do. I can handle this, and I need to handle it now. Work is sanity for me."

"I'm not suggesting that you can't handle it. I'm suggesting your boss wasn't wrong. Right now, you need to step back and breathe. Think about where we are, process. You said that the slayer wants to play a game with you. Well, the slayer is playing you and this is the biggest mind fuck of all."

"If it's Rodriquez," I say following his lead, "then he's made me doubt that it's him. He's mind fucked me into chasing a dead man. If it's not Rodriquez, he's making me focus on Rodriquez."

"And if it's Rodriquez and he's dead, you don't need protection."

"And then I'm left exposed," I say, seeing where he's going with this.

"Exactly."

"But he's smart. He expected I'd have protection. "

"Maybe we were more than he expected. Or maybe it's all about breaking you down. You're safe. You're not safe. You're safe again."

"We solve the case now or I'll never be able to know I'm safe, or anyone around me is safe, again." I start walking and he pulls me back, right in front of him.

"Where are you going?"

"The note said that Gerome knew things that I wasn't ready to know. I need to go to Gerome's place."

"There's going to be a forensic team and if he killed Gerome to keep you from finding something, he got rid of it. And we're making decisions together, remember?"

"I know, but—"

He drags me against him.

"No buts. We talk this through. We do this together."

"Yes," I say. "But—"

He leans in and kisses me. "Stop saying but."

"Contrary to popular belief, *your belief*, kissing me does not make me compliant."

"No?"

"No, it—"

His mouth closes over mine again, his hands at the back of my head, tongue licking against mine in a couple of quick, delicious strokes that curl my toes, before he says, "You were saying?"

"I have no idea, asshole," I whisper, but the asshole really comes out like a breathless "please kiss me again" which pretty much blows the impact.

"If taking an opportunity to kiss you makes me an asshole, I will gladly be an asshole." He strokes my hair from my face. "Don't push so hard, sweetheart. I'm not the bad guy."

"I know that."

"Do you? Because I really fucking need you to know that."

"Are we talking about the slayer right now?"

"We're talking about trust."

"Again. Are we talking about the slayer right now?"

His cellphone rings.

"Saved by the bell," I say.

"I can't be saved," he says, as if that was something he's just accepted, but I don't get the chance to ask what he means. He reaches in his pocket and pulls his phone out, glancing at the caller ID and then me. "Royce," he says, before hitting the answer button. "Yes, boss." He listens a moment and there is a brief, impossible-to-understand exchange, before he hangs up and sticks his phone back in his pocket. "Royce wants us at the Walker building."

"Why?" My hand goes to my throat. "Is—my father—is he okay?"

"He's currently playing chess with Savage because Savage told him he would kick his ass."

I breathe out and then frown. "He took a break from work to play chess? That can't be right."

He pulls his phone out and shows me a photo taken by Savage of my father, pondering a move on the chess board.

"Well, there's some good news in a sea of bad. Since my mother died, he insulates himself from everything but work."

"Sounds familiar," Jacob says.

"Do you mean me or you?"

"I meant you but we're two sides of the same coin, sweetheart."

"You shut people out."

"And you push them away."

"You don't take being pushed very well," I observe.

"You take silence very well, but I assume that serves you well as a detective."

"And with you."

"Yes," he agrees, warmth in his voice. "And with me." He motions me forward. "Let's go get that handwriting sample from your apartment and get to the Walker offices."

We start walking. "Do you have an idea what Royce wants?" I ask.

"I know he talked to your boss about sharing the investigation material. Other than that, he just said they have critical information and need your input."

"I really need to go to Gerome's apartment."

"Everything worth finding out about Gerome we'll find out by hacking, calling in favors, and working around the obvious, which is happening right now at Walker. They're putting together a monstrous pile of data to go over with us."

We head out of the parking lot into what has become a night worthy of a coat. I shiver and Jacob pulls me close, under his arm.

"I'd offer you my coat, but it would impair your ability to get to your gun, which is why I assume you grin and bear it when you can."

He's right. That's exactly why I avoid a coat unless it's a brutally cold day. I want to be ready. I always assume I won't be ready. But I go back to my previous thought. I'm not ready because the slayer has watched me for at least two years, and I never knew. That thought is the one that stays with me for the short walk to the subway, and as we pile into the packed car, Jacob holding the strap above him and me holding him, it doesn't fade.

Once we're at street level again, we don't speak, both of us in tune with our surroundings. I send out my Spidey senses, looking for a familiar malice, but I find none. We're quickly at my apartment and Jacob opens the gate. I move forward and he's by my side by the time I've taken two steps. We approach the porch and nerves that I rarely feel jostle through me. Together, Jacob and I walk the steps and when I step to the security panel, I stare down at the ground.

"Jacob," I say, but he is already right there, at my shoulder.

"What do you see that I don't see?" he asks, shining the flashlight on his phone at the ground.

"Nothing," I say. "I don't know why, but I expected to see something." I glance up at him. "Even if the slayer is dead, I'd have thought he'd have left a message. It feels like he would."

"He left the card on Rodriquez's desk."

"Right," I say, keying in the security code, but my mind is trying to lead me to ten different places.

The door buzzes open and Jacob and I enter the building, walking up the stairs. Once we're at my door, I let Jacob do the protector routine, and enter first. Once we're inside and locked up, he heads to the bedroom to clear the apartment. I pull my phone from my pocket and walk toward the refrigerator. I stare at that note: *You're not ready yet.* The script doesn't feel familiar. It never has and when I compare it to the photos of the script for Rodriquez, the card, the suicide note, and Gerome, only the card and the suicide note have possible similarities.

Jacob walks in. "Well?"

I hand him my phone and walk to the island, pressing my hands to the countertop. A good minute later, Jacob joins me and sets the phone next to me. "They don't match."

"No," I say, and we face each other, elbows on the island. "That means the writer of the original note might not be connected to this at all."

"Or he had an army of helpers."

"Why would anyone help him stalk me?"

"If we could answer that question, it would lead us to the slayer."

I push off the island and walk to the refrigerator to stare at the words again. *You're not ready yet.* There's the taunt I now see in what has long seemed inspiring. Jacob steps to my side. "Did you feel him?" I ask again, glancing over at him. "When we were on our way here?"

"No, I didn't. Did you?"

"No, but I really don't feel in tune with him at all." I turn to face him. "When you followed me, I didn't know you were there at first, but I do now. I feel you close. I know that has to do with our connection, but it's new and fresh, and I still feel you when you walk into the room."

"Some would argue that's because new and fresh means that every moment we're together is charged because of that connection."

"Okay. Yes. Agreed. But I've always sensed things. It's part of what makes me a damn good detective. Maybe he's military like you."

"Whatever he is, he's dangerous. He's invisible. And he's coming for you."

"If he's alive."

"We're assuming he's alive until we know otherwise."

"Then me going to Walker Security tells him I'm insulated and he can't get to me directly. What if that makes him kill someone else?"

"When you start leaving a trail of bodies, you make yourself a target. I don't think he's that stupid."

"But he could be that crazy."

"Exactly why you're packing a bag and coming home with me."

"And if I say no?"

"I won't let you. Because you see, sweetheart, you might be a damn good detective, but I'm damn good at killing

231

people and staying alive. And I'm going to keep us both alive."

"If he's alive, he needs to feel like I let my guard down. That will lure him out."

"Pack a bag," he repeats. "You're coming with me. End of conversation."

Chapter Twenty-Eight

Jewel

"Did you really just say that to me?" I demand.

"Yes. I really just said that to you."

"Do you expect me to reply with 'yes sir, you hot, arrogant man, you'?"

"You can save that for the bedroom, sweetheart. But to be clear. You want to fight, bring it on. I'm still going to win. Otherwise, just go pack a bag."

"Okay," I say.

He arches a brow. "Okay?"

I hold up a finger. "On one condition and a deal."

He closes the small space between us but doesn't touch me. He just makes me wish he was touching me, the heat between us sparking hard and fast. "Does anything you're going to offer include us being naked?" he asks, his eyes dark, hard, and hot.

"The right answer," I say, "is 'what do you have in mind, Jewel?'"

"I think we'll both enjoy what I have in mind better," he says.

My hand settles on the hard wall of his chest. "You're doing that thing you do again."

"The part where I make you want to fuck me the way I want to fuck you, or the part where I piss you off?"

"The part where you immediately try to stick me in a hole that you're protecting, and I'll admit that maybe that *is* the right decision. I'll even pack a bag and go with you right now. If you would please—note the word *please*, which I rarely use—admit that you might not be objective about me because of us, and we might need to do this differently. Maybe, just maybe, we need to set a trap and convince the slayer this is over in our minds and that I'm alone. I'm unprotected."

"If anyone is going to be bait," he says. "I am."

"I accept that could be an option, even if I reject it as a good one. The point is that we *have* options. Let's talk to your team, and to Sierra, and see what she thinks will be the best plan based on the slayer's psychological profile. But the deal is: I'll agree to live with whatever decision we all make together, but you have to, too."

His hands come down on my hips and he pulls me to him. "You'll live with the team's decision?"

"Yes," I say, narrowing my eyes on him, "and why do I think I just lost this argument?"

"Because you did. The team believes you should take shelter. That came from Royce after he pulled together the best of our team, and they debated your safety. You can hear that from them yourself, but to be clear, if that changes, if they change their mind, I won't change mine. I won't agree to anything that puts you in danger."

"And I won't agree to anything that puts you in danger."

"I'm a—"

"Green Beret. I'm aware of that, but to me you're Jacob." I push to my toes and kiss him. "And believe it or not, you can still die. So to be clear—"

I don't get to finish that sentence. He kisses me and it's no gentle kiss. It's hard, demanding and possessive, but there is more. There is another nerve I've hit, an internal struggle inside him that I don't try to contain. I want to know it. I want to know him. I slide my hands under his shirt, hot, hard muscle beneath my palms. He pulls his mouth from mine. "We don't have time—"

"I know, I just—"

"Ah fuck it," he says, pulling my shirt over my head, and tossing it moments before his mouth closes down on mine. Then his hands are on my breasts, shoving down my bra, teasing my nipples.

My hand finds his zipper, stroking the hard length of him, and that seems to set him off. He drags my pants down and licks my clit on the way to pulling them off my feet. A moment later, I'm on top of the counter by the refrigerator, legs wide, his hands cupping my breasts, before he's suckling my nipples and I'm holding onto his head, wishing the man's military cut left more hair for my fingers.

"Jacob," I whisper, arching my back into him.

He's kissing me a moment later, and touching me, and I don't even know how or when his pants come down. Just that he is pressing inside me and lifting me off the counter, holding all my weight. Holding me in more ways than just my body, and in ways I let no one hold me. He's consuming me in every way. A part of my life, in a split second, and he won't let go. I don't want him to let me go. I bury my face against his neck, but he doesn't let me seek sanctuary there.

"Press your hands on the counter, behind you," he orders.

I lean back, trusting him to hold onto me, and do as he says, my hands planted on the counter, my breasts thrust into the air. I have no control. He has all of the control and

I am oddly, intensely aroused at this idea. His gaze rakes over my breasts. His cock drives into me. His powerful upper body flexes with every pump of his hips. I want to watch him. I want to devour every angle of his handsome, hard features, lost in pleasure, lost in what he feels, rather than schooled in that robot expression. But pleasure overtakes me with a sudden, fierce jerk of my body and I fade into my own panted breaths and barely hear the low, guttural moan that slides from Jacob's lips.

He leans over me, hands beside mine, and shakes with his release, while I tremble with my own. At some point, his hand has settled between my shoulder blades, and my hands have found his neck, my chest pressed to his chest. "Holy fuck, woman," he murmurs, pulling back.

"I'm not sure how to decipher the meaning of 'holy fuck, woman.'"

"Me either, but I'm damn sure going to enjoy figuring it out."

He grabs a roll of paper towels and tears one off, before offering it to me. He pulls out and I stuff it between my legs, because at moments like this, there is no beautiful. There is just wet stuff and oh shit, is that my bra, on the light above the island? Jacob pulls up his pants, and settles me on the ground. "I need something," I say.

"Anything."

"Anything?"

"Almost anything."

"I liked the first answer better, but actually." I point up and behind him and my reward is a low, deep rumble of laughter from his chest. He backs up and grabs the bra, and hands it to me.

"I really do like it when you laugh."

He sobers instantly. "Then stick around and keep me laughing."

"I'm not pushing you away."

"And I'm not going to let you." He kisses me. "I need to update Royce."

I nod and he pulls his phone from his pocket, perching on a barstool, and holding a short, barely-there conversation with Royce, before saying, "I told him we are leaving here in fifteen."

"That works," I say, tugging on my boots and then pulling a plastic bag from a cabinet before walking to the fridge to retrieve the note. I reach for it and then hesitate, my mind starting to let go of tonight's crime scene, to focus on the bigger picture. Jacob steps to my side. "What is it?"

"This saying is too close to what my uncle always said to me, and others, for that matter."

"You said yourself that if the slayer knew you, he would know about your uncle."

"Yes, or maybe he actually knew my uncle."

"Your uncle doesn't strike me as a man who would repeat butterfly stories."

"No, but maybe the slayer wants to prove that he's as good of a detective as my uncle. And that I am not."

"You're suggesting it really was Rodriquez."

"No. Rodriquez got in the way. This person doesn't want to die. This person wants to win the game. Or maybe he just wants the high of playing the game. He can't do either dead." I turn to face him. "Think about it, Jacob. This note on my refrigerator that said I wasn't ready. Then two years later, it begins. The butterfly is my friend. The umbrella is my mother. The card to take me back to the note that uses words my uncle used often. My friend. My mother. My uncle. The path started and ends with my uncle."

"No, sweetheart. Your uncle is dead. The path might begin with him, but it ends with you. And that means me."

Chapter Twenty-Nine

Jewel

When Jacob and I exit to the street outside my building, I don't feel the slayer nearby. Jacob is another story. No matter what the circumstances, when you have a man as big and intense as Jacob King beside you, you're aware of his presence, and not just because the man wears his jeans and black leather jacket like sin and satisfaction. Or, in my case, the fact that he's recently had his hands all over my naked body. Because he's a force of nature. You just feel it. You know it. He's the reason I feel comfortable wearing the Burberry trench my father gave me for Christmas, despite my service weapon being buried beneath it. He's here. He's fast. He's lethal. And he's a healthier eater than me, which is most definitely the reason I'm stuffing my face with a protein bar as we walk, not a candy bar. And why I now have six different flavors of protein bars in my pantry.

We're almost to the subway entrance, as I finish off a bar that is supposed to be as good as cookie dough, but it's not. A short ride later, we arrive at the Walker building. The lights inside the offices are on but the door is locked, which is to be expected at the nearly ten o'clock hour. Jacob uses a key to open the door, and then presses his finger to a sensor. "You weren't kidding about the fortress," I say.

"And we're always improving," he says, shifting my overnight bag to one shoulder. "Just one reason why, aside from you in my bed, of course, that you belong here now."

My stomach flutters with that statement, *you belong here now*, that suggests, at least in my mind, that we're headed toward more than fucking on my kitchen counter. I can't do more. I won't let myself get emotionally invested in anyone ever again.

As if proving that won't be an easy task where he's concerned, Jacob snags my hand, pulls me to him, and kisses me soundly on the lips. "Welcome to Walker Security, and my home, Detective Carpenter," he says, releasing me to open the door.

I hesitate with this crazy sensation that once I walk into that building, I will never be the same. We will never be the same. I shove the crazy thought aside, and enter what is a pretty normal-looking office space with a reception desk, seating area, and a row of offices lining the left wall. "They're waiting on us in the conference room," he says, his hand settling almost possessively on my lower back, guiding me down a hallway and indicating a doorway.

Jacob drops my bag at the entrance, and then together, we enter a large conference room, the centerpiece of the space is a long, rectangular mahogany table, and it's far from empty. I quickly count, seven people sitting at various spots around it. The display of manpower suddenly driving home Royce's urgency to get us here.

"Detective Carpenter," Royce greets from the far side of the table, motioning to two empty seats across from him. "Join us."

I don't even think about sitting. I turn to Jacob instead. "What is this?"

"Teamwork," he says softly. "All of these people have been involved from day one. You're just getting to see them firsthand now."

"You'll learn that we do everything big around here," Royce comments.

"Only I don't like to do things big. Not when big means lots of people to make mistakes."

Jacobs leans closer, lowering his voice, for my ears only. "They don't come together without a good reason."

And since that reason involves the slayer, I decide that I need to get over my phobia of group mistakes and listen to what Royce has to say. I offer Jacob a quick nod, and in unison, we move to the seats that Royce indicated, where we sit down. Jacob directly across from Royce. Me across from another man who resembles Royce, but has softer features, while a big, burly man sits to my right. There are two women I don't know. In fact, the only other familiar person in the room, other than Jacob and Royce, is Adam, who gives me a two-finger wave from the end of the table.

"We'll start by making the introduction rounds," Royce says, motioning to his right. "This is—"

"Blake Walker," Blake supplies, a smile on his lips and in his brown eyes. "Ex-ATF agent, and of course, the good-looking Walker brother."

"I'm his wife, Kara," the pretty brunette next to him greets. "The one who keeps his ego in check."

"I don't have an ego," Blake says. "She's joking."

"Kara's ex-FBI like myself," Royce interjects, and apparently eager to get things moving, takes over the introductions. "Next to Kara is Asher," he adds, indicating the tatted-up dude next to her. "He, like Adam is an ex-SEAL. In between Asher and Adam is Sierra." He glances at me. "As you already know, she has a forensic psychology background."

I glance at Sierra, a pretty blonde with soft features, and a sweet voice. "I hope you can help me."

"I hope I can too," she replies.

"And I'm Savage," the big burly dude next to me offers. I blanch and turn to him. "You're Savage?"

"Yes ma'am."

"Who's with my father?"

"I left him in good hands."

"I know the men with your father," Jacob offers, squeezing my leg. "He's safe."

My hand comes down on his hand, acknowledging that I heard him, but I focus on Savage, with his dark hair, hard features, and a deep scar down his face. "You look and feel like a killer."

"Do you want a Boy Scout guarding your father?" he asks. "Or a killer?"

"A killer," I approve. "But you aren't with him."

"I need to know what is going on," he says, "or I won't know who to kill on your father's behalf."

"I'll vouch for Savage," Asher says. "He's fucked in the head but good at his job."

Scowling deeply, Savage's head jerks to Asher. "Shut the fuck up."

"And welcome to the Walker Family," Kara says. "Where love is shared with the frequent use of the F-word."

"Okay then," Blake says. "Moving on to why we're really here. Asher and I found something on a camera near the murder scene that you need to see." He hits a remote that lowers a television from a high spot of the wall just behind Adam. "Before I show you the footage," Blake continues, "a few points of interest. The cameras in the building where the crime took place tonight were turned off an hour before the incident, and turned back on right before you arrived."

"Which we know," Asher adds, "because we identified you and Jacob on the footage, entering the building. Which means your Butterfly Slayer is a tech guy, or has a tech guy who helped him turn off and manage the cameras."

"You're suggesting Rodriquez wasn't working alone," Jacob assumes.

"I'm suggesting Rodriquez isn't the slayer," Blake replies. "I don't doubt he was dirty. I found proof that he was working with Gerome for all of the six months he was in the city."

"What proof?" I ask.

"Payoffs in the form of deposits into his bank account," Blake says. "And communications with Gerome he thought he'd erased, but I found."

"You found out all of this tonight?" I ask.

"Yes," Blake says. "We did."

"And if I might add," Sierra interjects. "Rodriquez really doesn't fit the profile of someone capable of the tedious planning involved in this person's actions. Blake pulled his records for me, and looking back at his performance reports, he was dogmatic. He attacked things in a very now, now, now mode."

I look at Jacob. "This explains the card being on Rodriquez's desk, don't you think? He put it on my desk and then took it back."

"I do think," he says. "And now would be a good time to give Royce those writing samples."

I reach in my bag and pull out a baggie filled with the notes, sliding them across the table toward Royce. "I took photos of writing samples as well," I say. "I'll have to email those to you."

"I'll get them to the lab first thing in the morning," he promises, grabbing them. "Though I make no promises a handwriting analysis will help. I've found they tend to be less than reliable."

"Back to the camera footage, boys and girls," Blake says. "Because it's not of small importance."

"There was nothing on the cameras at the crime scene," I say. "Our forensic team checked."

"I know that," Blake says. "But we don't give up. Which is exactly why Asher and I looked beyond the building itself."

"We found a camera a half block from the building at a corner store," Asher chimes in.

"That camera," Blake adds, "caught the side entrance of the building where Rodriquez died." He hits play on the remote.

Security footage begins to roll, and he shows us Rodriquez entering the building. He fast-forwards to fifteen minutes later and pauses. "Here is the important part." He hits play again and a man in a leather hooded jacket enters the building, an uneasy, familiar feeling washing over me as I watch the familiar way he moves.

"Do we know who that is?" I ask.

"We do not," Blake says, pausing the footage, "but that clip was taken three minutes after the cameras in the building turned off."

Jacob leans in close to me, lowering his voice for my ears only. "Any gut feeling about him and trench-coat guy?"

"I only saw him twice two years ago," I reply, glancing over at him.

"But what's your gut feeling?" he presses.

"That it's him."

"There's more," Blake says, drawing our attention back to the television as he fast-forwards the footage, then pauses it again. "This next clip took place three minutes before the cameras were turned back on." He hits play and the man in the leather jacket, hood still in place covering his face, exits the building and takes off down a side street.

"I assume," Jacob says, "that since you told Jewel that we don't know who this guy is, that we didn't get facial recognition?"

"You assume right," Blake replies. "The jerk-off covered his face and *kept* it covered."

"We even checked cameras on his path to the subway," Asher adds. "We found him in several screenshots, but he never uncovered his face. We even caught him in the subway, going through one of the gates."

Blake grimaces. "Yeah. The gate. Let's talk about the gate. We were certain that we could pull prints off the one he entered the terminal through, but look at what he does." He turns on the feed again and we all watch as this man pulls his jacket over his hands and never touches anything.

"He obviously knows what he's doing," Blake says, turning off the feed.

"What happened at his destination stop?" Jacob asks. "He had to exit the train."

"He disappeared inside Grand Central," Asher replies, "and we assume that means a clothing change took place, but we didn't find the jacket." He motions to Adam. "He's a master of disguise, and disappearing, that's his thing, if you don't know it yet. He walked the terminal the way he would walk it if he was disappearing, and we found nothing."

"We can assume that he had help," Adam offers. "Someone who took his jacket and hid it in a bag or something that was carried out of the terminal."

"He's smart," Blake says. "He isn't working alone. In fact, he appears to have a team of people working for him, though we have no way of knowing if they know their actions connect any dots. And now we know that he's not only willing to kill, but he's focused on you, Jewel."

Jacob looks at me. "One might even say he's obsessed with you," he says, and while I knew that was where he was headed, and I'm ready to fight and win, a chill of foreboding still runs down my spine.

Chapter Thirty

Jewel

This, of course, isn't the first time I've considered that the slayer might be obsessed with me. It's been in the back of my mind, nagging at me since the beginning. It's simply the first time that I've known that he's capable of murder. Which means that I can choose to run and hide, or I can face this thing. I choose to face it. I choose to end it.

"He's obviously a member of law enforcement," I say. "He knows how to cover his tracks and that's the connection between myself, Rodriquez, and my uncle."

"Not necessarily," Royce argues. "Gerome has been connected to an ex-FBI hacker named Darius Long. He's good. Really damn good. He knows law enforcement and he damn sure knows how to turn off a camera."

"Are you suggesting Gerome was the slayer?" Jacob asks.

"I'm suggesting," Royce replies, "that they all have a connection, and a role in what has, and is, taking place."

"How do those people connect to my uncle?" I ask. "Because the first note references one of his common sayings and I got it the day of my uncle's funeral. It said I wasn't ready. The last note says it's time."

"Like he was obsessed with your uncle, playing cat and mouse with him," Sierra says. "And wants you to be the mouse."

"Yes," I confirm. "Exactly where my mind is on this."

"But he didn't think you were ready," she adds. "He told you that in the note."

"Darius is ex-law enforcement," Jacob says, jumping in and looking for answers. "Have we looked for his connection to her uncle?"

"We didn't even know about Gerome until tonight to tie him back to Darius," Royce replies. "His FBI service is far from honorable. We need time to look into him with concentrated attention."

"Royce is right," Blake says. "He and Kara have FBI contacts that could be useful, but they take time to work. And there are places Asher and I can hack for information related to Darius, but that will take more skill than a five-minute search and retrieve, even for me."

"I get it," I say. "I know what working leads means and how much work it can be." I look at Sierra. "I know you aren't a profiler, but I assume you do some degree of profiling on anyone you study. Do you have input you can offer?"

"At this point," she says, "I can only offer vague assumptions, based on what I've been told now and before this meeting. That said, statistically he's mid-thirties to mid-forties. White. Highly intelligent, but I wouldn't call that an indication of a higher education, though most likely, he has one. It would be easy for him. For some people, intelligence is natural, higher level, and school is data feeding the machine. I believe that is this man. He gets bored easily. He likes, and needs, a challenge that stimulates his mind."

"Which could support my theory that he was playing a game with my uncle," I say. "And now me."

"The answers we need have to be in your uncle's case files," Jacob says, looking at Blake who takes the silent prompt.

"We've pulled reports," he says. "But we'll dig deeper."

"Have you reviewed Darius's history?" I ask, pulling Sierra back into the conversation. "Does Darius fit the slayer's profile as you see it?"

"I have reviewed his file," she says. "And no. He doesn't fit the profile of the slayer. Not in my opinion."

"Based on what?" Jacob asks.

"He worked for Gerome rather than himself," she says. "In my opinion, your slayer, as you call him, is a control freak. He needs power. He needs to be right in all things. Darius is challenged by his hacking. He doesn't look beyond that."

"We aren't ready to rule him out," Royce intervenes quickly. "Not until we know more about his troubles at the FBI. And if he's not the slayer, he was clearly plucked from Gerome's grip and turned into a slayer operative."

The idea that the slayer has an army of help does not sit well, and a key question drives my attention back to Sierra. "How will the slayer react to be me being here, well-guarded, and untouchable?"

"He needs that challenge I mentioned. You become more of a challenge when you're well-insulated. Getting to you as he did at the police station will bring him pride. And defeating the Walker clan to get to you will simply feed his ego."

"Wait," Jacob says. "Stop there. Are we talking about him trying to get past us to kill her?"

"I don't think he wants to kill her," she says.

"That would end the game that he wants to play, but I can't be sure. I can't know that I'm right about any of this."

I inhale and let it out, concerned not for myself, but for the other people the slayer's attention on me might cause to get hurt. "Assume you're right, Sierra. He won't kill me, but what about my father?"

Her expression tightens. "I can only make vague—"

"That's a yes," I say. "He'll kill my father." I look between Jacob and Royce. "Savage needs to get back to my father."

"Not yet," Royce says. "This is where we pool our expertise, and we all talk through how to protect him."

Adam leans forward, suddenly more engaged in the discussion. Actually, it's not just Adam. The entire table, I realize, has leaned in, as if huddling for a play. That's how much of a team they are together. That's how different they are from any group I've ever worked around or with.

"Your father just got back from Paris," Asher says, taking the ball first. "One of our men, Kyle, is there now. We have allies in Europe. Get him out of here, for now."

"He has a merger going on," I say. "He's not going to leave."

"Guess again," Blake says, shaking his hands out over his keyboard, as if warming them up. "Watch and learn." He starts keying and we all stare at him for a good three minutes before he shuts his computer. "By tomorrow morning there will be a lump sum of product missing in the European plant. Your father will be forced to do damage control and there's a requirement to report the financial loss to the involved parties."

I reject that idea. "No. We can't ruin his merger. That's not an option."

"Of course, we can't," Blake says. "That's why a miraculous recovery will follow the crisis, and make your father look like a hero. With my help, of course."

"How?" I ask. "I need details."

"The error will be found to be a hacker's attempt to steal from the company. We'll help your father catch the bastard's hacking fingerprint, and because he hired us, your father will be the hero. Leave it to me. It'll work."

"I'm not ready to leave it to you yet," I say. "Who's the hacker that goes down?"

"I can pick from hundreds of assholes that deserve to go down," Blake says. "I'll make sure it's a dirty one that needs to be done and over, anyway."

"But this doesn't ensure he's safe," I say. "We don't know how far the slayer can reach."

"We have resources in Europe," Royce says, "that reach well beyond our team."

"What resources?" I press. "This is my father's life. I *have* to know."

Jacob squeezes my leg again. "He's safer there than here. I promise."

His promise is what matters, I realize. It matters more than anything else anyone has said to me on this matter. And what option do I have here, but to go with this? "Then do it," I say. "Get him out of here."

"Pack a bag, Savage," Royce orders. "You're going with him." He eyes Adam. "Go or stay?"

"The slayer's a chameleon," he says. "I'm the most like him in that way. You need me here on this."

Royce gives him a nod, laces his fingers together on the table and looks at me. "What else do you need to hear from us?"

"I still need Savage to be with my father right now."

Royce motions to Savage and Savage starts to get up, but pauses, to look at me. "Take comfort, detective. There really is a savage killer protecting your father." With that, he stands and exits the room, and I've never reveled in a killer's confession as much as I do with his.

"We're going upstairs to my apartment," Jacob, says, taking my hand and guiding me to my feet, and in the process pretty much answering any question in the room about our relationship.

And I don't care. We *are* together. We start walking, heading to the door and about to exit, when Royce calls out, "We'll get him."

That stops me in my footsteps and I turn to face him, suddenly not sure he understands the magnitude of the challenge. "With all due respect, my uncle didn't get him. And my uncle was one of the best detectives who ever lived." I say nothing more. I ask for nothing more. I don't want lame guarantees. I don't want impossible promises. I just want to catch the slayer before he kills again. And before he catches me by catching someone I care about.

Chapter Thirty One

Jewel

Jacob grabs my bag from the hallway, and then leads me to a side door, where we're greeted by yet another security panel. I watch as he keys in a code and then uses his fingerprint again. The process is a welcome reminder that there are layers of protection here that I do not have at my place. Jacob clears the security requirements and the door pops open, after which, we enter a spacious foyer with a high ceiling, and head up a stairwell, with wide, marble steps. He doesn't speak. He doesn't push me to speak. He simply settles his arm over my shoulders and lets me know I'm not alone. Funny how until now, alone felt really damn good. I think I hate Jacob again. I think he's slowly taking away the peace that alone gave me in the past.

"I liked you better as an asshole," I whisper, thinking of how easily I could fall for him and how easily he can die on me. He glances over at me, his expression guarded, his only reply a slight tightening of his hand on mine, as if he's telling me he's not letting me go. As if he knows exactly where my head is right now, and it's out the door, in the other direction. I *know* he does when he pulls me just a little closer, and then in front of him at his door, when he knows

I don't really want to push him away, but I don't want to fall for him either.

His big arms reach around me as he keys in a code in his door, and repeats the numbers near my ear. An invitation to enter his apartment that feels as if it reaches beyond one open door. He's protecting me. I know this. But I don't know where that leave us when this is over.

Jacob pushes the door open and I realize now that this is the part of this visit that feels like it changes me forever. This is the part that changes *us* forever. I am about to see a part of Jacob, a window into his life, and by doing so, I become a part of that life. All the denial from the stairwell, disappear into my real feelings. I want to see in that window. I want whatever comes next. That desire, drives me forward and I walk through the doorway. Jacob flips on a light and what greets me is a stunningly crafted open concept space. A room that is divided in two halves by a see-through smoked glass strip of flooring with industrial pipes beneath; those two halves being a kitchen and a living area.

Jacob steps behind me then, and I let him ease my coat off my shoulders, as well as allowing him to take my bag. I glance over my shoulder as he walks them both to a coat rack that is steel and shaped like the Eiffel tower. This is no normal man's home and I have questions that he must expect, and that I really need answered.

He shrugs out of his own jacket. I walk to one of the barstools by the island, perching on the edge of its leather cushion, while taking in the living area. A space framed by massive windows, while those windows are framed by thin industrial piping, and heavy wood. The seating area in front of them is two couches facing each other, both framed by wood, with gray cushions.

Jacob joins me, resting an elbow on the island. "It's a beautiful apartment," I say, rotating the stool to face him. "It's also an outrageous expense, and it tells me I don't know everything I thought I knew about you."

"I bought it for a fraction of its market price from the Walker brothers. Myla, Kara's sister, is married to one of our men, and she's an up-and-coming fashion designer that does interior design on the side. She did all of this."

"And?" I press, aware that this is millions of dollars, even at a reduced price.

"Aside from inheriting a decent nest egg from every family member I lost?"

"That answer would be enough," I say, going with my gut, "if it was the whole story but it's not, is it?"

"When I got out of the army, I went home. I thought I needed out of the war, whatever the war might be. I took the security job I told you about, working at a large office complex."

"And met the Walkers through that job and a client."

"Yes," he confirms. "By that time, I was coming out of my skin, needing something, anything. I hated being 'home' when it wasn't home anymore without the people that made it home. And I hated not having a real purpose."

"And they offered you a job," I say, remembering what he'd told me.

"Yes. But they wanted me to do security work again. Bodyguard work. And I did and do, but on one condition. I am first on the high-risk, high-paying jobs."

"What does that mean, high-risk?" I ask, not liking where my mind is headed.

"The spectrum is broad. I rescued a Saudi princess. I hunted down a would-be assassin of a Turkish leader. I could go on. Each of those jobs was covert, and paid for in a lump sum that wasn't small."

I stand up with a rush of awareness and emotion I don't want to feel. That I never feel when I'm living my life alone. That's why alone is good. Alone helps me ensure that I'm good at my job. I see the scene, not the blood, not the death. Not the emotional side of the story. It's why I survive this damn life I live and suddenly, I need space. I need to breathe on my own, not with Jacob. "I need a shower," I say. "I need sleep."

Those gray eyes of his narrow. "What just happened?"

"I realized that you're the guy the girl falls for right before he gets killed. And I can't do that, Jacob. I *can't* do that. I don't even know how I could entertain doing that." I rotate and intend to escape this conversation, and him, but escape is never easy with Jacob. He catches my arm, turning me back around.

"Don't walk away. Talk to me." His phone chooses that moment to ring and judging from his murmured, "Fuck," he is not pleased. "I have to take it. There's too much going on for me not to take it."

"I know," I say. "Take it. I need that shower."

His lips firm and with obvious reluctance, but he releases me. "Upstairs," he says, motioning behind me. "I'll bring your bag to you."

"Thank you," I say, twisting away from him, and spying the carved wooden stairwell. "No," he says into the phone, as I move in that direction. "I know she'd like to talk to Sierra," he adds, "but we do not want to do dinner tonight. No. Yes. We do. We will."

The rest of the conversation is muffled, but the concept of a couples' night with me and Jacob as one of the couples, no matter what the reason, only rattles me all the more.

Proof that I'm hyped up emotionally and I'm never hyped up emotionally. I need to bring myself down a notch or ten.

I reach the top floor and enter a bedroom that is much like the lower level. Exposed beams. Gray and wood accents. A massive king-sized bed, with a gray headboard. Big comfy chairs in the corner. And bookshelves with books on them by those chairs. The man likes books, and I like a man who likes books, but the titles are elusive from the distance and I find that I really want to know every book he chose. I want to know too much about him, which is why I keep walking and enter the bathroom. I flip on the light and of course, it's gorgeous. An egg-shaped tub that is gray with a wood finish like the double sinks. The floors are gray. I walk to the gray stone-encased shower and turn on the water to as hot as I think I can tolerate, before grabbing a gray towel from a closet and setting it on the edge of the bathtub across from the shower. I strip and once I'm naked, I step under the water, exhaling as the warmth heats my cold body, but it does nothing to calm the cold inside. The cold that is the one fear I can't defeat: my fear of someone else I care about dying.

Suddenly, Jacob, in all his naked, impossible-to-resist perfection is stepping inside the shower, joining me. I decide I'm officially a mess right now because I want to tell him to leave while I also want him to pull me close, a moment before I'm wrapped in his arms, the hard lines of his body pressed to mine. "I hate you right now all over again," I say, my hand pressing to his chest.

He cups my face. "No, you don't. You never hated me."

"Yes," I say, unexpected anger sparking in me. "I did. I do. Because you're making me get emotional. Alone isn't emotional. I can't do my job if I'm emotional. I can't do my job if I—"

"Care?" he supplies.

"Yes. If I care."

"I took those high-risk jobs because I had nothing but those jobs."

"You don't have to say this or do this. We just met."

"We did just meet, but I know from my many warzones that those you fight with become more to you in less time. And we are fighting a war together."

"And what about when the war is over?"

"The bond still exists. And I've never met a woman that made me want more. You make me want more and I don't know what that means now, but I damn sure want to find out."

"I can't ask you to give up what you do. That's unfair to you but at the same time, I can't have you in my life while I wait for you to die on me."

"I don't need those jobs, sweetheart. I have plenty of money." He cups my face. "I *don't* need those jobs," he repeats. "I need *this*. And I'm not letting you go." He kisses me, and I don't resist. And when he presses me into the corner, and settles on one knee, his lips and tongue on my belly, I tremble, and he owns me like I've never been owned. All at once, his mouth takes me away, and pulls me back to him. He kisses my hip, scrapes it with his teeth, and then travels lower, and lower, until he's licking me in the most intimate of places, in the most intimate of ways, driving me over the edge. Until I'm shattering for him, and I can't stop it, or him, from happening to me.

Much later, I'm in his bed, pressed close to him, his heart thundering beneath my palm, I decide that even knowing how dangerously he lives, if I let myself, I could fall in love this man. I also decide that maybe the slayer is drawn to me because he's a sadist and as a masochist, not so unlike him.

Chapter Thirty-Two

JACOB

With moonlight beaming through the curtains of my bedroom window, I lay awake. In fact, the only reason I stay in the bed is that Jewel is in my arms, pressed to my side, her head on my chest, which is naked since she's in my T-shirt. My mind races with thoughts of the slayer and his game. With thoughts of me, her, *us*. I have never thought of anyone with me as an "us" before. But I am now. And while yes, Jewel is right, and we've just met, I was right as well. When you go to war together, you say things, do things, reveal things you would never consider any other time. It opens wounds, closes wounds, bypasses time, and closes space. It opens the door to discovering a connection that might begin with an understanding of death, but it doesn't end there. The slayer will not win and that takes me down the rabbit hole of my mind to analyze everything I know about him.

I've just noted the two a.m. hour when Jewel starts to murmur in her sleep. "No, no, no. Stop. Stop. Stop." She jerks to a sitting position.

"Easy, sweetheart," I say. "You had a nightmare."

She blinks, resting on her elbow, her hand on my stomach, realization seeping into her expression. "You're here."

"Yes," I say. "I *am* here. You had a nightmare."

She sits up, and presses her fingers to her temples. "All I know is that my head hurts again."

I reach into to the nightstand, grab her a dose of medication and offer it to her "Take this," I order.

She drops her hands and accepts the BC powder, a surprised look on her face. "You really do get headaches."

"All the damn time," I say, opening the packet for her and then reaching for the bottle of water I keep on the nightstand.

"And there really is no one that knows?" she asks, holding the powder in front of her.

"No one but you," I say, "not that I think the Walkers would care. I do my job and do it well. I just prefer to keep things to myself." I motion to the powder. "Down it."

She grimaces in anticipation and stuffs it in her mouth, before chugging the water. "Ugh," she says, handing me the bottle. "That's torture."

I set the water down and pull her back next to me, her head on my shoulder. "Do you have nightmares often?"

"Never actually and I'm not really having nightmares now. I just keep reliving my uncle's funeral. Like my mind wants me to see something I'm missing. I have no idea what. Nothing. I'm blank."

"And the headaches? Do either of your parents get them?"

"My mother," she says. "We were so alike and yet so different. She wouldn't have thought you were an asshole, by the way," she adds, peeking up at me. She settles her head back on my chest. "Because you're protecting her world. You'd be her hero."

She doesn't say anything else. Her body relaxes against mine and her breath turns steady, but her words linger in my mind. *You'd be her hero.* And I know right then that if I want this woman, *really* want her, I better hope she falls as hard as I'm falling and fast just in case she finds out that I'm no hero at all.

FALLING UNDER

Chapter Thirty-Three

JACOB

For the first time in my civilian life, I wake up and I'm not alone. Jewel is still pressed close to me, the sweet floral scent of her teasing my nostrils. Her long hair is draped over my chest, which stirs a few fantasies, like her mouth on my cock, her legs wrapped around my shoulders, and my mouth...

My phone buzzes with a text message, ending that perfect moment in my head, but fuck. I'd rather have the real thing anyway. I *do* have the real thing. Jewel, right here, in my arms, in my bed. Careful not to wake her up, I glance at the clock, reading the six a.m. hour, and then grab my phone. The message is from Blake and reads: *Operation Europe has begun. More soon.*

Much needed progress is in motion.

Soon Jewel's father will be out of the country, and out of the line of the slayer's fire, which I hope gives her some version of peace. Or at least some ability to breathe. Hell, if I could protect Jewel that easily, I'd already have her on a plane, but it's not that simple for her or us. Two years of her slayer watching her says he won't redirect his energy elsewhere. He won't play his game with someone else. Thinking back to last night's crime scene, realization hits me. She's a homicide detective. Did he kill Rodriquez and

263

Gerome to make himself more interesting to her? The idea doesn't sit well with me and not even Jewel laying all up close and personal next to me can keep me in this bed. Not when I could be up hunting this sick fuck myself.

I ease Jewel onto the pillow next to her and she rolls to her side and sinks deeper under the covers. Comfortable here with me, when she's usually a loner. Hell, I'm comfortable with her here, too, and I'm a loner. Or I was. I don't know what the fuck is happening to me. I don't invite women here. I didn't have to invite her here. She could have stayed in the spare bedroom or in the spare room of one of the brother's places. Ideas I never even entertained. She's here now. She's staying. And this damn fucking slayer isn't going to take her from me.

I round the bed and head into the bathroom, where I shower and dress in faded jeans and because it would amuse Jewel, I contemplate the T-shirt that I was gifted by Asher that reads "You Suck". But it also gains me attention that I don't like or want, so I settle on a plain black tee. Attention is the last thing myself or Jewel need right now. I pause on that thought. Maybe I'm wrong on that. Maybe attention is exactly what we need. If we hyper-focus the slayer where we want him focused, we hit him from behind. I want his focus on me, not Jewel. I take off the black shirt and put the "You Suck" shirt on.

Heading back into the bathroom, I have the razor in my hands to shave, and instead set it down, running a hand over my jaw, remembering Jewel's comment about the stubble humanizing me. Until now, human was the last thing I wanted to seem to anyone. There's a knock on the door and I quickly open the door to find Jewel in the doorway, my shirt covering her otherwise naked body. Her blonde hair is in a crazy, sexy disarray.

"Morning," I say, pulling her to me and right when I would kiss her, she covers my mouth with her hand.

"Morning breath. Don't even think about it."

I cover her hand with mine and pull it between us. "No kissing before teeth brushing. Got it." I kiss her hand. "How is your head?"

She contemplates a moment. "Good. The headache is gone. That's how it happens. I just forget about it and realize later that it's gone." She switches gears. "I know it's early, but any news on anything this morning?"

"Blake has the plan in motion to get your father out of the country. Other than that, nothing yet." I kiss her forehead. "I'll be at the coffee pot." I step around her and stop at the door, turning back to look at her as she does the same with me, and my need for this woman comes over me hard and fast.

"Unpack," I order. "Claim a sink and part of the closet. You're here. I'm not letting you go anywhere anytime soon." I turn to leave before she can argue, but she calls me back.

"Jacob."

I brace myself for whatever comes next, when I've never had to brace myself for anything a woman said to me. "Yes, sweetheart?" I say, looking back at her.

"Why does your shirt say, 'You Suck'?"

"It's a message to the slayer. He sucks and I'm coming for him."

Her lips curve. "I really like the shirt."

"Yeah?"

"Yeah. And the stubble."

Now, I actually smile, because fuck, she's here. "See you downstairs." I start to turn again.

"One last thing," she says, and when I look at her, she continues, "I don't want to go anywhere anytime soon." And she doesn't stop there. "That's the funny thing about waking up here with you this morning. I liked it."

I close the space between us, pull her to me, and press my lips to hers, before setting her away from me. I leave the room. I walk past the bed that she shared with me last night, and I know that I don't want to go to bed without her again.

It's insanity. It's total fucking insanity.

I don't want to need anyone. She doesn't want to need anyone, and yet, here we are. Here I am and holy hell, I can't stop it from happening. I reach the kitchen and stop beside the island, pressing my hands to the granite surface. This just got personal for me in a big way and as I once told Jewel, when things get personal for me my enemies find out just how cold, hard, and ugly my anger is.

I start a cup of coffee brewing and walk to the coat-rack where I'd hung Jewel's bag, which holds my MacBook and hers, last night. I retrieve it and return to the kitchen, bringing my Mac to life, while pouring straight liquid creamer into my cup, along with four Splendas. Once I sit down at the island, cup beside me, I pull up my email and download the mass of reports Blake and Asher have sent me. I print them all out, and by the time they're clipped and organized on the island, I'm on coffee number three.

My cellphone rings as Jewel, dressed in black jeans and a black sweater and boots, which contrast with her hair, heads down the stairs. I glance at the caller ID, when I'd rather keep my eyes on her, but the instant I spy Savage's number, I answer the line. "What's happening?"

"Holy fuck. Carpenter is in complete freak-out mode. If that man wasn't so fit, I'd be afraid he was going to stroke out on me. If I stop responding to messages, I'm dead."

"What happened to the killer at his back?"

"He just met the CEO side of Jewel's father and I'm about to suck my thumb in a corner."

"Fuck, man. I want photos of that. What's his plan?"

"He's chartering a plane right now," he says.

Jewel steps to the other side of island and I glance at her while answering him. "Keep me posted," I say, and disconnect the line. "Your father is scaring Savage."

She laughs. "What happened to the killer?"

"Exactly what I said."

She reaches for my coffee cup and sips. "Hmmm. I like this. Thank you. I'll keep it." She smiles and takes another sip.

"You can share," I say, taking it from her and drinking. "I'll make another cup when it's gone."

"I'm not good at sharing," she says. "Although I did let you eat my peanut butter. That was big for me."

"I'm not good at sharing either." I lean on the counter. "I damn sure don't want to share you."

She leans on the counter as well, facing me. Moving into my words, not away from them. "Who said you have to?" she asks.

"No fireman. No anyone but me."

"The same goes in reverse."

"Sweetheart, if I wanted anyone else, you'd be in Blake and Kara's spare bedroom right now. And I damn sure wouldn't have told you to claim a sink and part of the closet."

"Well then, you can have the peanut butter. I'm okay with that."

I smile and reach up and touch her cheek. "You're beautiful. I know you try to hide it by braiding your hair more days than not and being touchy with everyone, but you don't."

She catches my hand. "Thank you. And you aren't actually an asshole, but you were easier to hate when I thought you were. The truth is, you don't suck."

I laugh. "You are a piece of work, woman."

"And you're laughing again. I'm kind of addicted to hearing you laugh."

"Is that right?"

"Oh yes. It's very right. And Jacob, I have to be honest—"

Her cellphone rings before her confession, and she grabs her phone where it sits on the island. "Speak of the devil, otherwise known as my CEO father." She hits the answer button. "Hey Dad. How are you?" She listens a moment and gives me a look. "That sounds bad. Yes. Of course. I'm fine. I have this big-ass army dude following me around. I'm safe, but I can't promise the same of him." She smiles at me. "Okay. I promise to play nice. Not really. *Yes.* Okay. Just be safe. Love you, too." She disconnects. "He was his normal gentle self to me, but then, I'm his daughter, and Savage is Savage. And my dad is a CEO, who protects his company and his people like they're his family. Because that's all he allows in his life."

"Sounds familiar."

"Meaning me?"

"Meaning both of us. Two sides—"

"—of the same coin," she supplies, and the air thickens between us.

"Yeah, sweetheart," I say. "We are, which is why we're going to work together and get your slayer. I pulled all the reports Blake and Asher sent for us to go through today. He's hiding somewhere in here and we're going to find him."

"As much as I want to catch him, I have to deal with my case headed to trial. That's the reason I was going to meet

Gerome last night and I can't push it aside. A man killed his wife and unborn child, Jacob, and the only way to ensure he goes to jail is finding the bodies."

I study her a moment with the understanding that she has a need for control right now. She's shutting out the slayer as she tried to shut me out, only in this case, she gets to win. I understand what it's like to bury yourself in one war to shut out the one raging in your mind. I understand how defeating one enemy makes you feel strong enough to defeat the next. Which is exactly why I'll help her now. I'll protect her. I'll keep her head on straight. "I'm all in on putting this guy away, but we can multi-task and home in on Gerome, but you know, I'm sure that Rodriquez set you up, even if he didn't know he was setting you up. Gerome may never have had anything to do with this case."

"I do know," she says, sitting down on a barstool, "but really, truly, I'm desperate. This man is guilty. I can't let him get away with it."

"Why did they charge him if they weren't sure they could win?"

"Political pressure. I wanted them to wait, but I lost that battle."

I grab a stack of papers. "This one is everything we know about Gerome. I don't have anything on Darius other than a bio."

She grabs the Gerome stack and starts looking through it. "He has no connections to my uncle, which makes sense. He's only been here for six months. Interestingly though, he arrived in the city right about the time the murder took place. Right about the time the defendant killed his wife and child."

"That certainly supports Gerome as a suspect," I say, "but it feels too tidy. You're on this case. Rodriquez has a

connection to the slayer—we know this because of the card—
and he has financial ties to Gerome. Yet he leads you to
Gerome and they both end up dead. What does the slayer
have to do with the CEO billionaire that killed his wife and
baby?"

"Well," she says thoughtfully. "What if Rodriquez found
out about Gerome hiding the bodies and he wanted Gerome
to go down? But the slayer felt Gerome could lead me to him
and he was pissed that Rodriquez jeopardized his game."

"Maybe, but I am not big on coincidences as
explanations. And it feels too coincidental to me that the
slayer would be involved with a man who hid bodies for
someone you arrested and charged."

"Whatever the case, Jacob. I just need to find those
bodies. Do we have phone records on Gerome? I need to
know if he communicated with the defendant."

There's a knock on the door. "And that would be some
version of a Walker," I say. "No one else can get to us here."
I stand up and walk to the door to find Asher and Sierra
waiting there, both in sweats, and briefcases on their
shoulders.

"*You Suck*," Asher says, reading my shirt. "Did you wear
that for me, or what?"

"I expected you. It's my mental chant when you're
around."

Asher laughs. "Back at ya, Tin Man."

"We want to talk about the slayer," Sierra says, anxiety
in her tone, obviously ready to push past our bullshit.

"Did something happen that I don't know about?" I ask.

"No," Asher replies. "Sierra just wants to talk about how
to make something happen our way."

"Making something happen our way works for me," I
say, stepping back into the apartment and waving them

onward. "Jewel is in the kitchen," I say, shutting the door behind them and following. Of course, all the normal, expected chitchat I really don't care for ensues before we finally gather around the island, them on one side and Jewel and I on the other, focused on the slayer problem.

"I have a suggestion to deal with the slayer," Sierra says again, this time, for Jewel's ears. "And before I share it, I want you to know that I called a few experts and asked advice. None of us can say what is the right or wrong move, but the general consensus agreed with me."

"Tell us," I say, impatient for any plan that might end this hell.

"Yes, tell us," Jewel says, her energy just as impatient as mine.

"He needs control," Sierra says. "If you stay locked up in this building for long enough, he'll feel he no longer has it. He'll do something to drive you out, and that something will have to be big. He'll expose himself and we'll catch him."

I answer before Jewel gets the chance. "As much as I'm down with the idea of locking Jewel up and keeping her safe, to me, that's giving him control. That says he has the power to make her hide."

"He's proven to be patient," Jewel adds, "and I have to live my life and do my job. He'll know that. He'll try to wait me out."

"He's set the game in action," Sierra argues. "He left you three gifts in a row. He's hungry to keep going. I don't think it would take long to push his buttons."

"Even if that's true," I say. "I don't want him to come for her. We need a plan that makes him come for me."

"No," Jewel says, looking at me. "You aren't getting killed to get rid of someone who doesn't want me dead in the first place. The end. Do you understand me?"

"Jewel—"

"Do not do this," she says. "I will leave. I will shut you out of this if you start playing hero. And no matter what, we aren't doing this right now. I *have* to find a dead pregnant woman in time to put her scumbag husband in prison for the rest of his life." She turns away from me and looks at Asher. "I need to find out if the scumbag husband in this case ever communicated with Gerome. I was led to him by Rodriquez. If Gerome connects to the husband, then Gerome is the key to finding the bodies."

Asher smartly goes along for the ride. He pulls his MacBook from his briefcase. "I can get you those answers. I already know the case." He glances at her. "I watched the hearing on TV. Bastard tried to seduce you with all his money and you arrest him instead. I fucking love it."

So do I, I think. Holy hell, I fucking love everything there is to know about Jewel, aside from the heartache and pain that just set her off. She's afraid of me dying. I get it. I'm just as fucking afraid of her dying. It's a curse of our pasts we're going to have to deal with. Right after I deal with her slayer. Because she might not be able to do this now, but I damn sure can.

"There's no digital link between the dirt-bag killer and Gerome," Asher says, "But Gerome operated off the radar aside from a few clients that contract him for private investigative work. Of course, that's a cover up. For his real clients, he'd take a referral and meet the client in person. He operated in cash. He didn't keep records."

"What about Darius?" I ask, looking for a target I can take out.

"The FBI has eyes on Darius," Asher says, "He's in Germany, which doesn't mean he isn't working for the slayer. It just means he's doing it from a distance."

"And he's not the slayer," Jewel assumes.

I shake my head. "I disagree. He could be using hired help to leave the gifts and even watch you. I don't think we rule out Darius."

"It's not Darius," Sierra says. "He doesn't fit. Whoever this is, is close. He's watching. He's ready."

Jewel holds up a hand. "Okay. We're off track. Unless Darius hid the bodies I'm looking for, I don't care. I have to focus on finding those bodies." She grabs her phone off the counter. "I need to call my boss and get out of time-out." She heads toward the living room. Shutting out the slayer. Looking for control anywhere she can get it.

I eye Asher. He stands up. "We're going," he says, "and we'll look for those bodies." He shoves his computer back into his bag, and Sierra stands up.

"Can I talk to you?" she asks.

I nod, and I follow them to the doorway, stepping into the hall with them. "I'm sorry," Sierra says.

"What are you sorry for?" I ask. "You were trying to help."

"I didn't consider that my suggestion would make a control freak that already feels out of control, feel like a prisoner when she's already one, and make her fear even more for her father and everyone around her than she already does."

"She's a strong person," I say. "She'll ultimately do whatever she has to do to win. I don't want to stay out here and have her think I'm on Team Walker, not Team Jewel. I need to go back inside." I turn away, intending to go inside the apartment.

"Jacob," Sierra says.

I glance back at her. "Yes?"

"She's lost a lot of people. If you go against her wishes and risk your life without talking to her about it first, there will be personal consequences."

She turns and walks away, and Asher gives me a nod before following. Sierra means well. I get that, but she came here to ask Jewel to do what she will never do: hide. I'm going to do the opposite. I'm going to flaunt her on my arm. I'm going to claim her as mine. I'm going to be the distraction that doesn't leave room for the slayer. I'm going to make myself the one to kill next.

I just have to find a way to do this that saves Jewel without hurting her in the process. And I don't know if that's possible.

Chapter Thirty-Four

Jewel

I leave a message for my boss, after trying to catch him at his desk, by way of two calls through the switchboard. He's avoiding me. Just like Jacob is pissing me off. Really, really pissing me off. The front door shuts, and he comes walking into the room, all big and broad and good looking, and yep, I'm pissed, all right.

I charge toward him and poke his chest. "This shirt works for you because you suck."

"And why exactly is that?" he asks, zero emotion in his reaction.

"Because we both know that you're going to put yourself between me and this asshole stalking me, not because it's your job. Not because you want to protect me. Because you get a high off of it."

"That's not true, Jewel. I don't get high off trying to die."

"You've all but told me that's why you were a Beret."

"I never wanted to die. I just wanted to get lost in—"

"The high of living when you should have died," I supply. "Tell me right now that you don't plan to somehow turn yourself into the next target."

His hands come down on my hips and he pulls me to him. "I will protect you at all costs."

"Then we're done. I don't want someone who will die for me. I want someone who won't." I shove at his unmoving chest. "Let go, Jacob. We're done."

"We're so far from done, sweetheart, we've barely gotten started. You're in my bed now. You're in my life. And I'm in yours, and I'm not that easy to get rid of."

"I have to go to Rodriquez's funeral. I'm not going to yours. I'm not—"

He grips my wrists and walks me backward, pressing me against the wall beside the window. "You're not what?"

"Going to fall any deeper into this with you."

"Then I'll fall deep enough for both of us."

"Damn it," I murmur, lowering my chin to my chest. "You don't get it."

"I do get it," he says, tilting my face to his. "You're scared."

"I'm not scared."

"Remember when I said that it's okay to be human with me?"

"Yes, but—"

"I'm scared," he shocks me by saying, his hands coming down on the wall on either side of me. "I'm fucking terrified of how much I already need you. I'm terrified of how easily you could die, just like you are of me. But you have to know that it's not in my nature to stand back and watch you try to survive what I can end. My mistake here was even contemplating doing what I'm going to do to protect you without telling you." He pushes off the wall and tries to walk away.

I can't let him go. I catch his arm. "Please come back." He turns to look at me, his gray eyes hooded, expression unreadable but hard. "You don't suck. You don't even come close to sucking. You dying would suck. It would hurt." I press my hand to my face and shut my eyes before looking at him again. "I am scared," I dare to admit, before looking at him again. "I don't want anyone else to get hurt. And how long can my father stay in Europe before he's a target again? And I just can't seem to make it end."

He steps into me, hands returning to my waist. "Then let's set a trap. You and me together."

"I don't want you to be the bait, Jacob."

"We set him up or we sit and wait. Neither one of us are sit and wait kind of people. That's why we work. We get each other."

"Maybe I should do what Sierra said. Make him come for me. Make him make a mistake."

"And when he flushes you out by killing someone else? That's the flaw in Sierra's plan that I didn't want to point out with her here. She meant well, but we're back to every action has a reaction. He has proven he will kill. We have to pick the next victim and I am no average victim."

"Which means he'll get a high off beating you—killing you."

"He'll get a high off trying, but don't expect me to let you arrest him. I'm going to kill this bastard and if you want to cuff me and shoot me after the fact I'll kiss you before you pull the trigger."

"Maybe you should just kiss me now," I whisper, but I don't wait on him to do it. I push to my toes and press my lips to his lips. "Just so you know, every time I call you an asshole, it's because you're not an asshole at all. It's because you leave me exposed and—"

His hands come down on my cheeks, and he kisses me, God how he kisses me. Like he's drinking me in. Like he's inhaling me. Like he needs me just as much as need him.

Like he hates me just as much as I hate him and that is not all. "Jacob," I breathe. "I want to say—"

The doorbell rings. "Fuck," he breathes out. "Sometimes living in this building is like living with an open door. You want to say what?"

"Honestly, I don't know. Something. More than I have."

The doorbell rings again. "I want that more," he says, kissing me again. "Save it for me."

He releases me and walks away, while I sink against the wall, trying to catch my breath and yet, somehow breathing easier now just because I didn't hold any of that in. Because I talked to him then and there. Because even though he didn't say everything I wanted to hear, he was honest with me.

The sound of Royce's voice has me pushing off the wall and on edge. I head through the living room and join Jacob on one side of the island, while Royce claims the other. "My wife is having contractions. We think they're false alarms, but I wanted to share a few updates in case I'm out of the picture for a few days." He doesn't give us time to comment. "First, Detective Carpenter—"

"Jewel," I say, eying the writing samples I'd given him that are now on the island.

"Jewel," he amends.

"Did you already get the results on the samples back? Is that even possible?"

"My handwriting expert got called to Washington on a job. She's delayed a week. I took photos of everything and sent it to her. She prefers originals, but she'll make the alternative work. We also got the lab results back on the butterfly and the umbrella with nothing useful. I had a local lab run the card and notes. We got a cluster of fingerprints on both. Nothing helpful. All explainable, but we expected this. This guy is smart."

"But you did email me the reports?" I ask.

"I did," he confirms. "And I talked to your boss. He's now aware that Rodriquez was dirty. I provided him with the proof and suggested you return to the case. But, like all of us, he's still entertaining the idea that your stalker might have killed Rodriquez and Gerome. That means you're off duty, with pay, for the protection of those around you."

"Of course, I am," I say. "And he won't even take my calls today."

"One of the reasons I opened Walker Security was to get the hell out of the red tape and politics of the system," Royce says.

"Maybe you should hire her," Jacob replies.

I look at him, surprised. "What?"

"You'd be a damn good addition to the team," Jacob says.

"He's right," Royce agrees. "You would be, and you have a standing offer for double what you're making now, and a hell of a lot of freedom to choose the jobs you feel matter." He looks between us. "But you two need to be sure you're ready to work together." His phone buzzes with a text. He grabs his phone and glances at it. "Lauren wants me home." He shoves his phone back in the pocket of his jeans. "I'll let you know when I hear from the handwriting expert, but I'm of the opinion this guy has so many minions that he does nothing himself." He knocks on the counter. "You two be safe." He heads for the door and Jacob follows him, locking up after he leaves.

I pick up the bag of samples and battle with some niggling thought in the back of my mind. By the time Jacob has rejoined me, I'm sitting on a barstool and tabbing through the writing samples. "What's bothering you?" he asks, sitting down next to me. "Because the look on your face says something is."

"It's not about the job thing, if that's what you think," I say, "though you sideswiped me on that."

"Sorry, sweetheart. It came to me. I said it. You going to consider it?"

"A week ago I would have said no," I answer honestly. "The way I'm being treated right now though, it's hard to completely dismiss. At this moment, however, I am thinking about this." I show him the photo of the suicide note.

"Thinking what about it?"

"I don't know. Something is in the back of my mind." I read it out loud. "*I'm sorry, Jewel. He knew things you just weren't ready to know. If you were, you'd have seen what I already showed you.*" I look at Jacob. "If he had Rodriquez lead me to Gerome, why kill him before he can tell me whatever he knows? Especially if he'd already showed me, even if I have no clue what that means."

He considers that a moment. "It's a game to him. We know this. So, where does the game lead?"

"Right," I say, standing up. "A game." I start to pace and he turns to face me, leaning his back on the island. "A game." I stop walking. "He wasn't trying to keep me from finding whatever he's hiding. He was challenging me to find it. He was telling me I wasn't ready, and he wants me to prove I am."

"Ready for what?" Jacob asks.

"I don't know. I have no idea, but that's his constant theme." I look down at the photo on my phone again and murmur the words again, "*I'm sorry, Jewel. He knew things you just weren't ready to know. If you were, you'd have seen what I already showed you.*" I look at Jacob. "I've never met Gerome but the inference is that he showed me something about him before the murder." A sudden thought hits me. "On my God."

"What is it?"

"The note was lying on top of Rodriquez. We assume it referenced Gerome because it looked like Rodriquez had killed him to shut him up."

"But if it was written by someone else and it was laying on top of Rodriquez," Jacob says, following my lead, "then it could mean Rodriquez."

"Yes. I'll read the note again: I'm sorry, Jewel. He knew things you just weren't ready to know. If you were, you'd have seen what I already showed you. There is only one thing that connects Rodriquez with the slayer."

"The card," Jacob says, reaching for the bag on the counter.

"We still need gloves," I say. "Just in case there's something we've all missed." I dart to the coat rack, grab my bag and pull out a pair of gloves for each of us.

"Ready?" Jacob asks, unzipping the bag.

"Yes, and I swear I'm nervous, but pull it out."

He does just that and both of us study it. I read the note: "*Finally, it's our time.*" I look at Jacob. "Why is it finally our time? That is what I don't understand." I flip the card over. "I don't see anything. This was a long shot, but it felt right."

"We aren't done just yet," Jacob says, walking to a drawer and returning with a flashlight. He beams the small but powerful light on the bottom of the card and slowly climbs upward. He finishes one side and then flips it over and just when I'm ready to change directions, he murmurs, "Bingo."

"Bingo? What does bingo mean?"

"Each side of the card is basically two pieces of paper glued together. There's something inside the card." He pulls out a pocketknife and slices the end before holding up the card. A piece of paper falls out onto the counter.

Chapter Thirty-Five

Jewel

The untouched note lies on the counter. Jacob and I look at each other and then he flips it over. It's a plain notecard-sized piece of paper with typed words on it. I read it out loud:

Jewel—

You've proven yourself your uncle's niece. Your reward is justice for a pregnant woman and her unborn child. 4455 Chop Street, Brooklyn, New York. Look in the basement.

"Oh my God," I whisper. "Oh my God." I grab my phone. "I have to call my boss."

"I'll call Royce," Jacob says, and both of us stand up, pacing as we make our calls. From there it's a whirlwind of more calls, and in between it all, I bag the note and the card. In what feels like an hour but is only twenty minutes, we're rushing into the parking garage beneath the building to drive to Brooklyn. Jacob clicks the locks on a sleek black Mercedes and the minute we're inside, the scent, all perfectly spicy and him, tells me a story. It's his car. His very expensive car that he earned by doing very dangerous jobs.

He backs us up and in a few quick maneuvers we're on the road, on the way to Brooklyn. I sink down in the heated seat, and a full minute passes before he breaks the silence. "What do you want to say?"

That's all it takes. Words spill out of my mouth. "You really have made a lot of money trying to get killed, haven't you?" I cringe. "I'm sorry. I just—"

"You're on your way to pull two bodies out of rubble," he says. "Death is on your mind. I get it. I know what that means to you and to us. I've made a lot of money, Jewel. I've invested it well. I already told you. I don't need those jobs anymore."

"Is that how it was? Did you *need* them?"

"For the money, no. It was never the money." He stares straight ahead. "It was always about needing something that left no room for anything else."

"The way every case I work leaves no room for anything else."

"I guess that's where you're going to have to decide if you can leave room for me."

"You already made that decision for me," I say, without any hesitation.

He flicks me a look. "I don't want to make any decisions for you, Jewel. And that's not how I want to be in your life."

"But you did, by being so damn big and impossible to ignore," I tease, but quickly sober, reaching over the seat to press my hand to his leg. "I'm glad you're here, Jacob. Especially tonight."

He reaches down and covers my hand with his. "You're giving them justice. You're ensuring he never hurts anyone else."

"I know. I do. I want this, but I can walk into a gory crime scene and be fine. Watching someone who was shoved into the ground by a monster, get dug up, is another story. It's the finality of their lives that always hits me. I've never actually told anyone that."

"I'm glad you told me. That you know you really can be human with me."

"You be human now. What gets to you?"

"Children. I don't like to see children die." He glances over at me. "In other words, I'm not looking forward to this either. I vote we get drunk on tequila and each other when this is over."

"Because it's over or because it's not over? We still haven't found the slayer."

"But we will," he promises. "And when we do, I'll make sure he's gone for good. You have my word."

Four hours later, Jacob and I stand outside the broken-down building where the bodies of a pregnant woman and her unborn child have been found. And while there is much that isn't over, there is one thing that is: the lies of a billionaire CEO who will pay for his sins. My boss breaks from a cluster of forensics specialists and joins us. "You did good work, detective," he says, scrubbing the three-day old stubble on his jaw. "By next week, if the DA gets his way, the lead counsel on this case will have the monster who did this in front of a judge for sentencing. It will be a good day."

"Yes," I say. "It will be a good day."

He offers his hand to Jacob. "Thank you to you and your team for the support they've given Detective Carpenter. And to the department. Without you, we wouldn't know that Rodriquez was dirty." He refocuses on me. "Honestly, I knew he hated your uncle. I knew he was competitive with you—"

"Wait," Jacob says. "What? He had an issue with her uncle?"

He looks at me. "You didn't know?"

"No," I say. "I had no idea he had issues with my uncle."

"More like your uncle had issues with him. He didn't like him. Called him a snake in the grass to his face."

"My uncle hardly spoke to anyone. He certainly never spoke badly to anyone."

"Well he spoke to him and to me about him. Told me once over whiskey that Rodriquez had the same vibe as a serial killer he arrested a decade back."

I frown. "You knew all of this, and you actually accused me of sleeping with him?"

"He had a photo of you in his wallet."

I blanch. "What? He—what?"

"IA was going to question you as a suspect. I put them in check real quick when we found out Rodriquez was dirty. But there is much more to this story."

"What more?" Jacob asks, his hand settling protectively at my back.

"Rodriquez had newspaper clippings in his apartment from a half-dozen of her uncle's cases," he replies, looking from Jacob to me. "Bottom line, Little C. He won't be fucking with your head anymore. He won't be leaving you notes. And there won't even be a funeral or service for him. He's being cremated, and his will specified no service." Someone shouts for him, and he lifts a hand to hold them off, speaking to me as he does. "Go home. Rest. Deal with the DA tomorrow and then milk the Walkers for as many free hours as we can get to solve the next case. You'll go back in rotation after the sentencing hearing." He turns and walks away.

I face Jacob, but I say nothing. I honestly don't know what *to* say. "I know," he says, as if I've spoken my confusion out loud before he wraps his arm around my shoulder, and sets us in motion toward the car.

Once we're both inside, we sit there, in silence for several seconds. "It was Rodriquez?" I ask.

"Why was that a question?"

"Because it doesn't feel right. It doesn't feel done and yet, everything we were just told, says it was him. It just doesn't feel final."

"We'll make it final," he promises. "One way or the other. We both need to be at peace with how this ends."

A long time later, I lay in bed with Jacob, both of us on our sides, facing each other. For hours, we stay that way, talking about everything that happened today, and tonight. "Maybe I'll never be right with this ending," I say. "It doesn't feel like the right ending."

"Then I think we should take steps to ensure your safety." He brushes hair from my eyes. "Don't rush back to your apartment. You're safe here and I want you here."

"You think I need protection? For how long?"

He wraps his leg around mine. "What I think, is that you belong here with me. Stay, Jewel."

I could say no. I could leave and put space between us. I think about it, too, but the thing is, I don't want to leave. I don't want space. Tonight has reminded me that life is short and I don't want to waste one moment of his or mine. "Yes," I say. "Yes. I'll stay."

My reward is his smile, followed by his mouth on mine, his big body pressed close. His arms around me when I fall asleep, on a night when the finality of death would normally haunt me and keep me lying awake.

FALLING UNDER

Chapter Thirty-Six

Jewel

The very next morning my new life lessons begin: I'm no longer alone. There is no privacy in a building filled with the Walker clan. The slayer is no more. And I'm falling in love with Jacob.

Jacob and I are barely out of bed when the doorbell rings, and keeps ringing. Soon we have a living room filled with Adam, Blake, Kara, Asher and Sierra, all around the living room television watching the news with us, and talking about the billionaire baby killer as well as, the slayer, Rodriquez. At some point, I am aware that my hair is standing on end, I have on no makeup, well at least not on the parts of my face that it should be, and not one of them seems to notice. I forget makeup when my phone becomes community property and begins being passed around the room, as each person adds their favorite list of Walker numbers. I receive it back just in time to accept my father's incoming call.

"Hey Dad," I say, walking up the stairs to grab some privacy. "How's the merger?"

"Hell, I tell you, honey, but that Blake Walker is a real asset. He's going to get us to the other side of what looks like a hack but that isn't important. You are. I talked to Royce.

He said you guys found the note writer and all threats are neutralized."

"Yes," I say, not about to express any doubt about the threats, not to him, at least. "The note writer is neutralized. All is well. When will you be home?"

"Two weeks, at least. I'm going to stay and just get this merger done from here. I'm actually looking at a villa I might buy here in Italy. I'm thinking I might just buy it for you."

"Don't buy it for me."

"It gives you a getaway from the badge for a while. I'll buy it. You think about it."

"I'll think about it," I agree, when we both know I'm not going to Italy. I have a job to do. And I have Jacob, but I'm not ready to tell him that the man he hired to protect me is now the man I'm falling in love with. That thought sideswipes me and stays with me until the moment I hang up, and find Jacob standing in the doorway, looking as big and addictively handsome as ever.

Looking like the man I really am falling in love with.

"Maybe we should move to your apartment," he says, walking to the bed to sit down next to me. "The Walker clan won't follow us there. Most likely. They might. Fuck. They probably will.".

I laugh and the next thing I know he's carrying me to the shower. "What about all the people downstairs?" I ask, as he strips away my shirt and then his.

"If we're lucky, they'll take a hint and leave." He kisses me and it's not long before we're in the shower. It's a long time though when I'm finally dressed, and so is he, and we head downstairs to find everyone gone but Adam, who's asleep on the couch. We leave him there and head to the DA's office.

By that evening, the same crowd joins us to curse at the TV as the rich billionaire CEO Bruce Norton and his scumbag attorney Davis York hold a press conference, vowing to find the monster that killed his wife and child. It appears the victims' family will have to endure a trial.

Over the course of the next few days, I move many of my things to Jacob's place, and despite leaving my furniture behind, an army of the Walker clan help with the haul. It's on moving day, that I meet Luke Walker, the middle Walker brother and his wife Julie, as well as Royce's very pregnant, very sweet wife, Lauren.

Two weeks pass quickly. Two weeks that change my life. Two weeks in which Jacob and I create routines. We run together. We hit the gym together. Jacob even cooks healthy food for me while I shove cookies at him. At one point, over drinks that become more drinks, he tells me about his sister. About her dying in a car accident, while her abusive boyfriend was driving. This only two weeks after she'd left him a desperate message for help, that he didn't even get until after she was dead.

The next day, despite too much drinking, we start working a cold case together and in a matter of days, we solve a murder. Our success has my boss declaring me off rotation for good, calling me a part of a "special task force" that is me and the Walker clan. Two weeks and I am no longer *falling* in love with Jacob. I am in love with him. And I have *almost* forgotten the slayer ever existed. Until the nightmare. One morning I wake up shouting at the man in the trench coat, but the adrenaline of waking up that way fades into Jacob's kiss, and his warm body.

But it still doesn't feel like we've had the right ending. I know Jacob feels it. Sometimes I see it in his eyes. I always feel it in his touch. Rodriquez won. We're mind fucked.

It's day fourteen since the bodies were found when my father decides that he's staying in Italy for another week. It's also day fourteen when I get the news that the lab results are damning for the CEO billionaire Bruce Norton. He's going down for murder and the Walkers pop champagne with me. It's day fifteen when Norton agrees to a plea deal. And on day sixteen, Jacob joins me in court for the plea deal to be made final. I leave my jeans on the hanger and wear a black pantsuit and heels, while Jacob chooses black dress pants and a Walker Security T-shirt. We arrive at the courthouse to the chaos of press and picketers everywhere. "Holy mother," Jacob murmurs, leading me through the crowd, and earning my laughter. More and more, he isn't a robot, or the Tin Man. He's human and all hot, hard man.

Once we're inside the courtroom, we sit behind the DA's table and Evelyn is back in her lead spot as the woman who will take down Bruce Norton, and looking like a brunette babe as she does it. I love it and when Norton enters the courtroom, followed by Davis York, she turns around and uses sign language to say "I love you" to me. I return the love, all so readily and with that "I love you" still formed on my hand, Jacob closes his around mine, and looks at me. In the midst of the crazy courtroom, we have a moment, when no one else is there, when there is just two people, falling into each other, that only ends when the judge enters the room.

The proceedings are quick. Norton will do life, with a chance for parole in twenty years, which we all know he won't get. The family cries. The bystanders cheer. The crowd starts to disperse when Evelyn motions me forward. "The family wants a word with you," she says. "They just want to thank you. I have a private room."

"Of course," I say, quickly giving Jacob an update, before kissing him and following Evelyn toward the back room.

"My God," Evelyn whispers as we exit through the side of the courtroom into a private hallway. "Who's the hot guy you just kissed? And can I have him next?"

"No," I say. "You may not have him. I'm keeping him."

"Really?" she says, casting me an interested look. "Well now, there is a story I want to hear. We need to have drinks and celebrate your hot man and our victory." We stop at a doorway, and she sobers. "Be ready to cry."

I inhale and enter the room, and it's not long before a family of four—a mother and father as well as two siblings—take me on an emotional journey that feels so very personal. I know what they are living. I know what they feel. It's almost an hour later when I leave them with Evelyn. I hurry down a hallway and suddenly someone runs right into me. I jolt and pull back to find Davis York standing in front of me, his hands on my shoulders.

"Well, well. If it isn't Detective Carpenter. You okay there?"

"I'm fine," I say, stepping back from him, forcing his hands away.

"Good to hear it," he says, shoving his jacket back to rest his hands on his hips. "But then it's not a surprise. You must be very happy right now."

"Happy isn't a word I use when murder is involved."

"Pleased then with the outcome."

"I am," I say, and I can't help myself. I add, "You must be defeated."

His lips quirk. "Defeated. You enjoyed that word in that sentence, didn't you?"

"Yes," I say without hesitation. "You defended a monster."

"With good reason. Have coffee with me and I'll explain."

"No. I don't want to have coffee with you."

"Okay then. No coffee." His lips quirk again, amusement in his eyes. "Have a good day." He starts to step around me and stops. "By the way. I don't lose. Whatever the outcome, I always know it's coming and why. Consider this one a gift." This time, he steps around me and exits a side door. I swallow hard with the unease rushing through me. A gift. That's what the note from Rodriquez had said giving me the location of the bodies. A gift. He just used those words. He knows this case. He thinks he's so above the law, that he can taunt me and I can't prove anything.

I pant out a breath and start walking, pushing through a door and entering the hallway. I dial Jacob. "Where are you?"

"Coffee shop by the door, what's wrong?"

"Meet me at the hotdog stand at the bottom of the front steps." I hang up and I swear I feel him now. I feel Davis York watching me.

I exit the courthouse and quickly travel down the stairs, and the minute I spy Jacob, I calm a degree. The minute I stand in front of him, his hands are on my arms, in the exact spots Davis York's had been. "What happened?" Jacob asks. "You look like you saw a ghost."

"I was right. Rodriquez wasn't the slayer. That wasn't the right ending. Davis York is the slayer."

Chapter Thirty-Seven

JACOB

I don't question Jewel's reasoning on Davis York. She's a damn good detective and I haven't liked the man since that first day I saw him attempt to shake her hand. "Tell me what you need right now," I say instead.

"To prove it. To end him."

"I'll gather the team," I say, motioning her down the walkway, away from the courthouse, and toward the subway, and by the time we're on a train, it's done. "Blake and Asher will be at the apartment when we get there," I say, motioning to the seats at the end of the car.

"I'm trembling," she says, as we sit down. "I don't think it's fear. I think it's just adrenaline. I don't know. Maybe both."

My hand comes down on her leg. "Tell me what happened." I listen as she relays her encounter with York. The words "a gift" hit me hard. "That's—"

"The same words used in the note found inside the card," I say. "I know. If anyone would know where the body was, the defense counsel for the killer would certainly be the one."

"Maybe he even helped his client hide the bodies." She presses her hand to her face. "Rodriquez didn't kill himself. York killed him. I just need to prove it."

"Do you know of any connection he has to your uncle?"

"No, but there has to be something."

She's right, there is, and thirty minutes later, with Blake, Asher, and Sierra, sitting at the island with us, Blake finds the connection. "Holy mother of Jesus," he says, drawing all of our attention. "We've hit gold. Get this. The only case Davis York has lost, aside from the Norton case, was seventeen years ago and it's widely thought that the testimony of Detective Jonathan Carpenter sealed the deal for the prosecution."

"*I don't lose,*" Jewel repeats his words for the group. "*Whatever the outcome, I always know it's coming and why.* Did he lose to somehow stay off my uncle's radar?"

"You're suggesting York had a reason to appear ineffective to your uncle," Sierra assumes.

"Yes," Jewel says. "Yes I am. It's the only thing that makes sense. He led me back to my uncle. The case files have to be the answer. Somewhere in them, we'll find Davis York."

"Let's hit the case files then," I say. "Who's in?"

"Me," everyone chimes in and from there we divide them out and start dissecting them one by one.

Hours and several pizzas pass, and we have no answers. By the time it's early evening, everyone is frustrated. "He's here," Jewel insists. "I know he's in these files. And we know he's killed at least two people. We have to find him."

Blake's cellphone rings and his eyes go wide. "Oh fuck. Yeah. Yeah. Right." He stands up. "Lauren's in labor. Royce is flipping out. No one can reach Luke and—" he looks at Asher, "can you get the car pulled to the front door? Royce needs help getting Lauren downstairs."

"Yes," Asher says, shutting his computer. "Going now."

"I'll go help with Lauren," Sierra says.

The two of them head to the door and Blake sticks his Mac in his bag and looks at me. "Call me if you find anything. We'll be back." He doesn't wait for a reply. He's gone, rushing toward the door.

In another thirty seconds, Jewel and I are alone. "If you need to go, Jacob," Jewel begins. "I can—"

"No way in fuck am I leaving you alone." I kiss her. "We have some quiet time. The entire group will go to the hospital. Maybe the two of us alone will be the kind of focused magic we need."

She nods, and I make us a cup of coffee to share before I sit down next to her and grab Sierra's batch of files. The top six are rubber banded together and on closer inspection, not even murder cases. They're all... "Fuck," I murmur.

"What is it?" Jewel asks, turning to face me.

"Rodriquez officially killed himself."

"No," she says. "It was murder. You know that."

"That's my point. Right now, officially, he's assumed to have killed himself. Meanwhile, there are six suicides that your uncle had batched together."

"Suicides?" Her eyes go wide. "Why would he—Oh God. I see where you're going now. Like in Rodriquez's cases, they're not suicides at all. They were just made to look like suicides." She grabs my arms. "Wait. I have a thought. I need to get something." She rushes away and up the stairs.

I follow her, and locate her at the bookshelves in the bedroom, holding the memory book, she'd stored on one of them when moving here. "What did you piece together?"

"Give me a second," she says. "I need to read—oh wow. Wow." She looks at me. "You have to see this." She rushes to the bed and sits down, and I sit next to her. She sets the book in my lap and shows me the newspaper clipping of her mother with the umbrella. "What am I looking at?"

"The article published right next to it."

"Community rattled by local woman's suicide."

"Yes, and read the second paragraph."

"Husband suspects foul play, insists wife had strange events taking place. He's quoted as saying 'one day last week three people called her and said they were returning her message, but she didn't leave them a message.'"

"On the day of the bail hearing, I had several people call me, and tell me they were returning a message. One of those people was Davis York. And that day was the only day I ever felt the slayer's presence and Davis York was in the courtroom." She stands up. "I'm ending this." She tries to dart away.

I stand, catching her arm and turning her toward me. "What does that mean?"

"He wants to play a game. I'm ending the game. I'm going to tell him I know. I'm going to tell him I have him on camera at one of the suicide scenes. And I'm going to record it all."

"He's not dumb enough to buy that."

"He's not dumb enough to make a mistake we catch, or my uncle would have caught him. I need to shock him. I need to do this right now, tonight."

I could hold her back. I could stop her. But the truth is, I have plans for Davis York, and I've always said plans are better acted on now, rather than later. Now, when the Walkers are too tied up to stop me from doing what I need to do. "Study the files," I say. "Know what you're talking about and then let's go."

Chapter Thirty-Eight

Jewel

Thanks to Asher, who apparently didn't drive the car to the hospital after all, we discover by way of his hacking that Davis York is still in his office. And thanks to Asher as well, when we arrive, the security guard is distracted by an alarm and the elevator panel has been overridden to allow us to punch in the twentieth floor.

By the time we reach the lobby of his offices, it's eight o'clock and the place is empty, the halls dark, the light at the end of one hall guiding us toward our target. The second mini-lobby outside his door is lit up, but his door is shut. We pause there and while I'm not one to be nervous, I am now.

"I'll go in with you," Jacob offers.

"The game is between me and him. He will brag to me. I know he will."

Jacob doesn't look pleased. "Leave the door open. The minute I hear a hint of trouble, I'm coming in."

"I like that plan," I say, "but I have my gun and I know how to use it."

He kisses me. "Shoot first. Ask questions later."

"I will," I promise, turning the recorder on my phone on, as I stuff it in the blazer of my pantsuit.

I head across the small space between me and that door, and I decide not to knock. I need to be confident. I need to be bold. I move my badge to the front of my pants, in plain sight. I then inhale and open the door, shoving it to the wall.

He's standing at his window, his jacket gone, and he rotates to face me, a smile curving his lips. "And here I thought you weren't interested."

I walk right to his desk and press my hands on the surface. "I know. And I assure you, I'm ready."

Surprise flickers in his blue eyes. "I don't think you're ready at all."

"A stack of murders that were made to look like suicides say I am. The footage I managed to get from the home of one of the victims says you're not."

"There is no footage, detective. We both know that."

"I'll show you. At the station."

"Arrest me or I'm going nowhere."

"I'd rather talk, just you and me. It's our game, right?"

He arches a brow. "Is it?"

"Now it is. But it wasn't always that way, was it? I want to know about you and my uncle."

"There's nothing to know. I met him once at a trial. That's it. Nothing more. Nothing less."

"How did you find out about the butterflies?"

"I have no idea what you're talking about, but as a general rule, if you fuck the right people, they give you what you want. Get them naked or simply become the holder of a secret they don't want revealed, and they will do anything for you." He leans on the desk, close to me, so close I want to hit him or move away, but I do neither. "You have nothing on me," he says. "You want to play though. I like that. So, let's do it. Let's play the game. That's the only way this ends."

"My uncle was better than you and you hated him for it."

"I didn't hate your uncle."

"Did you send him gifts?"

He laughs. "Your uncle didn't need gifts to get his job done. He got right there," he holds up two fingers, "so close, always close, on *his own*."

"Did Rodriquez get close?"

"Rodriquez was useful but pathetic."

"You're pathetic."

"That's not nice."

"It's not meant as an insult," I say. "Simply a statement of fact."

"I have an idea. Let's play a game right now." He straightens and rounds the desk.

I rotate and my hand goes to my gun, but just as I would pull it, he offers me his hands.

"Cuff me. Like you cuffed that asshole you've been fucking. It'll be fun."

FALLING UNDER

Chapter Thirty-Nine

JACOB

I'm standing at the edge of the doorway when I see that little bitch round the desk, and that's the trigger I'm looking for. "How about we skip the cuffs," I say, drawing my weapon and entering the room. I don't dither. I charge at him, grab his shirt and shove him in the corner against the glass window. "You killed them all, didn't you?" I demand.

"Sure. I did it." Davis laughs. "Of course, that confession is under duress."

"How did you kill them?"

"I can't tell you what I don't know," he says. "But I think I will enjoy the lawsuit coming your way."

"You don't want to do that," I say. "And I really don't want to have this conversation. I just want you dead."

"Jacob, what are you doing?" Jewel demands softly.

"What I promised you I'd do. Killing your slayer."

"You won't kill me," he says. "There are fingerprints, ballistics, registered weapons and we both know yours is registered. There are cameras. And there's me making her life hell because you went macho on me."

"The cameras are off," I say. "And here's why everything else you said is shit I don't give an extra shit about. I'm not just an ex-Green Beret. I was an assassin for the government. I did dirty work for a lot of important people.

303

They don't want my trouble to be their trouble. So, if I say: 'clean it up and make it go away,' they clean it up. That means I can kill you, make a phone call, and walk the fuck away." I cock the weapon.

"Jacob!" Jewel calls out. "Do *not* kill him."

"You heard the lady," he taunts.

"She'll thank me when you're gone," I promise him. "And damn man. I haven't killed anyone in six fucking months. You know how that feels, right? How you want to kill, how you *need to* kill."

"Jacob! Put your weapon down." Jewel's gun cocks.

"She won't kill me," I promise him. "The only reason you're alive is that she's a better person than me and she's feeling guilty about wanting you dead." I move him, shove him hard and flat against the glass, and point my gun at his head. "You decide. Her way or my way." I look him in the eye and let him see how much I want to kill him. How willing I am to kill him.

"I did it. I killed them. Are you happy?"

"No," I say. "I want proof. The kind that puts you away for life."

His lips tremble, anger burning in his eyes. "National lockers, number 2899."

"Call Adam, Jewel."

"I'm calling."

I back up and motion to the corner. "Stand in the corner, hands on the wall."

"Adam," Jewel says behind me. "Go to this address now. And wear gloves."

Ass-twat glowers at me but walks toward the corner. I shove him into it and check him for weapons. "Cuffs," I call out to Jewel, who is quickly there to hand them to me.

I cuff the little prick and then lean in close, for his ears only. "You come at any of us from prison, or anywhere else, I'll make sure you die in your cell after you put some pretty smiles on some of the lonely guys in there with you. The idea of that is so enjoyable that it's all that is keeping you alive right now."

I shove away from him and I turn to face Jewel. She stares at me and there is judgment in her eyes that I don't want to see. I look away and grab a chair, setting it behind Davis in the corner before shoving him to his knees. Once he's there, I sit down behind him, and the little bitch sobs.

It's a full twenty minutes before Jewel's phone rings. "Adam?" she asks. "Yes. Okay. I'm sending a team." She hangs up. "We have what we need," she says, appearing beside me and then kneels next to jerk off. "You're under arrest Davis York," she states, going through the formality of reading him his rights before she stands back up, but she doesn't look at me when she does. I feel that punch of anger in her, between us, but I leave it alone.

I stay focused on Davis who is still a danger until he's dead as far as I'm concerned. I want to kill him. I should kill the bastard, but some part of me knows that's what I can live with. Jewel cannot. A reality I will soon face, and I know it.

Ten minutes later, the place is swarming with officials and Davis is hauled away. When I stand up and look for Jewel, she's not there. My gut knots with her absence, and I fight anger and other emotions I don't want to feel. I exit the office and end up cornered for questioning. I don't locate Jewel again until I'm finally on the street a good hour later. She's standing with a uniformed police officer and the minute her eyes find me, the look on her face punches me in the heart. She breaks away from the officer and walks toward me.

"Is it true?" she asks, when we meet in the center of the sidewalk. "Were you, are you, an assassin?"

"Was," I say, "as in past tense."

"How many people did you kill?"

"As many as I was told to kill."

Her blue eyes flicker, her ivory cheeks heating. She doesn't like that answer. "Did you ask questions?"

"Does it matter?" I challenge.

"Did you kill Jesse Marks?"

"Yes. Now go ahead and ask me if I killed his family."

"I wasn't going to ask you that." Her voice is a low, emotion laden rasp.

"But you wanted to," I say. "I see that and a whole lot more in your eyes."

"I'm just trying to understand." Someone shouts her name and she leans closer to me. "What happens when he tells them you're an assassin?"

"He's not that stupid, but if he does, just call me a sniper. That's what the government will claim as well."

"But you were more."

"Yes, and I should never have gotten close to you. I won't come home tonight." I turn and walk away. I leave her behind like I should have left her behind the day I met her. Because my past was always going to be the end for us.

Chapter Forty

Jewel

I can't follow Jacob when he walks away. I'm immediately pulled into the legality of the scene I'm working. When I finally end up in a car on the way to the precinct, I sink into the back seat of the unmarked vehicle and process what I know: Jacob is an assassin. That realization stunned me at first, it still does, but it changes nothing. I love him. And I hate that he thought I would question him about Marks' family. I didn't. I don't.

I grab my phone and dial his number. It goes to voice mail. I try three times before I have to refocus on my duty. I feel every minute of the hours I'm at the precinct after that, and when I stand behind the glass and listen to Davis detail his evil storyboard, I want Jacob to be right here listening with me. Davis is proud of his work. He wants to talk about it. He wants to brag, especially about leading my uncle on for years. How he'd killed people and made it look like a suicide but it had gotten too easy. He needed a challenge. My uncle was that challenge. I was that challenge. He confesses killing Rodriquez and Gerome for no reason other than to fuck with my head. To test me.

The breadth of his web, proves wide. I discover just how he's used people, just as he'd told me he did in his office.

He'd fucked my neighbor quite literally, and convinced her the gifts by the door were a joke. He'd blackmailed Rodriquez to help him and then threatened his daughter to get him to swallow the pill that killed him. He'd paid off Gerome. The list went on and on.

It's almost three in the morning when I finally leave, and I try to call Jacob on the way. I still get his voice mail. I arrive at the apartment and the instant I walk in, I know he's not here. I turn right back around and exit, heading to the hospital.

I arrive on the maternity floor to find an entire waiting room filled to the brim with Walkers and extended family. Sierra hops to her feet when she sees me and gives me a huge hug. "How are you?"

"I'm okay. How is Lauren?"

"Still in labor. It's apparently going to be an all-nighter. I heard about the slayer. Thank God you're okay. I'm so glad you got him."

"Jacob got him," I say. "He's the reason he was arrested. Is he here?"

Asher joins us and motions me down the hall. "I'm not going to like what you have to say, am I?" I say when we step around a corner and stop.

"I don't know what happened between you two, but he was not good when he left."

"When he left? What does that mean?"

"One of our other guys was headed out on a mission. Jacob agreed to split the money with him and do the job himself. It paid five hundred grand. He gave up two hundred and fifty thousand just to leave."

"Where? Where did he go?"

"Saudi."

"Saudi," I breathe out. "One of those missions you don't know if you'll come back from."

"He's good. He'll be back."

"This can't be happening. He told me something about his past. I blinked. I can't believe I blinked, but I was rattled. I had the slayer I'd just faced. Help me, Asher. Can I catch him? When did he leave?"

"Sorry, sweetheart. He left hours ago on a private jet, but he'll be back."

I cover my face with my hands. "I want him to be back right now." I fight the tears trying to overtake me and look at him. "Can I call him? Can I get a message to him?"

"He's dark until it's over."

"How long?"

"Uncertain. A week. Maybe two."

"Two weeks?!" I inhale and let it out. "Okay. Okay I—I need to leave now before I melt down in public."

I turn and start walking. "Jewel!" he calls out, but I don't stop. I'm not good right now. I'm so not good. I exit the hospital and I don't get on the subway. I walk.

It's almost an hour later when I walk into the apartment I'd started to call home with Jacob. But I don't belong here. He's made that clear. He left. He told me we were done. I box up all of my things and set them by the door, aside from my suitcase, which I fill with essentials. I'll have a service pick up the boxes. I barely remember taking the suitcase and going to my apartment. My lonely, cold apartment. I turn on the heat and I sit down on the couch, where I proceed to do what I haven't done since my uncle died.

I cry.

Chapter FortyOne

Jewel

With coffee in hand, I sit down at my desk, planning a late night at the office after a long day. I set my bag on the floor beside me, staring down at the envelope that reads *"Detective Carpenter"* sitting beside my phone. Adrenaline spikes inside me, and it pisses me off. It's been eleven days. The slayer is in jail. He does not get to mind-fuck me over and over.

I grab the envelope and open the damn thing to find the final stamped toxicology report for Rodriquez, with nothing new to report. We had the preliminary a good week ago. We have the confession from his killer. I toss it to the side of my desk and stare down at the X's marked on my calendar that I tell myself are the days since the slayer was captured. But they're really the days Jacob has been gone and silent.

I change my mind. I am not staying late. I grab my bag and I decide I want pizza. A huge pizza, and I'm going to eat the whole damn thing. In my pajamas. That pizza occupies my mind with surprising effectiveness and when I walk in my door, I lock up and head to the bedroom with the intent of undressing for a quick shower, when my phone rings.

My heart races, as it always does, with the hope it's
Jacob, before I glance at the ID. I frown at the central
records number. "Detective Carpenter."

"Detective," a man says. "It's Joe Welch."

Joe's my go-to guy for research, but I have nothing
outstanding. "Hi Joe. What's up?"

"I've been digging on that case you called me about. It
intrigued me and—"

"What case?" I ask, a bad feeling in my gut.

"Jesse Marks."

I go cold inside.

"There is a rumor that he was part of some covert team
reporting to some senator. I talked to a guy at the state
department and—"

"Stop right now," I say, my heart racing. "Covert.
Government. You do not speak of this again. Ever."

"But I—"

"Ever," I say. "EVER. Do you understand?"

"Yes. I ah—yes. I'm sorry—"

"I have to go. Do not—"

"I won't."

I hang up and I dial Jacob. I get his voice mail. Of course.
I pull up the first Walker number in my phone and it's
Adam. I punch in his number. "Jewel? Everything okay?"

"No. I don't know. I need Jacob. I have to talk to him."

"Talk to me."

"No. No, I need to talk to him. You find a way. The end.
Non-negotiable." I hang up and start to pace. Assassin.
Covert team. Jacob killed Jesse Marks. Did I just get Joe
killed? I try to call Jacob again. He doesn't answer. I call
back to central records. "I need Joe Welch."

"He's left for the day."

"I need his personal number"

"I'm sorry, but—"

"This is Detective Carpenter." I give the woman my badge number. "I need his contact information."

She gives it to me and I dial his line. He doesn't answer. I leave a message. "Joe, call me but don't go home. Go to a hotel. Don't use your credit card and wait on me." I hang up and there is a knock on the door. I pull my weapon and move cautiously to the side of the door, where I flatten.

"Who is it?"

"Adam. Let me in."

I breathe out and open the door. He looks at my gun. "What the fuck is going on?" he demands, crowding me to enter and lock up.

"I need you to find a man and protect him."

"Tell me what's going on."

"I need you to do this first."

He grabs his phone. "Who?"

"Joe Welch. He's in records for the department. I think I just put his life in danger and mine, too. Get him and his family to safety. Please."

He punches a line on his phone, "Royce. Problem." He relays the information and hangs up. "We're handling it."

"Jacob—"

"I called him."

"And you talked to him."

"Yes. I talked to him."

Because Jacob could always get my messages. He just didn't want to talk to me. "Okay. Tell him he'll have to endure a conversation with me. I'm not talking to you." I turn and walk into the bedroom and shut the door. I lean against it and try to think. I'll have to leave. God. I may have ensured I have to go into witness protection. And my father.

Oh no. I turn to open the door and suddenly it opens, and Jacob is standing there, just as big and intense as ever.

He steps forward and I back up, giving him room to enter. He shuts us inside and I hold my breath, not even sure what I expect. "My father—"

"I already sent someone to stay with him in Italy," he says, his voice as hard as his eyes. "Tell me what you did."

Anger sparks, right along with a lot of everything else. "What *I* did? I didn't do anything. When I first found out about Jesse Marks, I made calls. I forgot about them. I never touched the case after I told you I wouldn't. But a records guy took interest. He called someone at the state department. He—"

"The state department," he says, his tone sharp as a whip.

"Yes. I had Adam put his family into protection."

His lashes lower and he pulls his phone from his pocket, dialing a number. He listens to the line and then gives them a series of codes. For five minutes I wait until he finally says. "Code black message. Stand down. The problem is neutralized." His jaw sets harder. "I need confirmation." He listens. "I need fucking confirmation or I will not stand down." He ends the connection, inhaling sharply and turning for the door, obviously about to leave. *Just leave.*

"Do not even think about walking out of that door without talking to me first."

Chapter Forty-Two

JACOB

Just seeing her, just being in the same room with her, is driving me crazy. I cannot be with her and not touch her. I cannot be with her and be me though.

"Jacob," she says again, my name a plea on her lips that I can't refuse.

I turn and look at her. "What?"

"What happens now?"

"We wait for me to get the confirmation that any action is called off."

"Here or at the Walker building?"

"Royce has a baby and a recovering wife at the Walker building. I'm not putting them through that hell."

"No. Of course not. I shouldn't have suggested that." She wets her lips, and fuck me, I want to kiss her. I want to fuck her. I want to just hold her one last time.

"I really need you to talk to me," she says, and talking is exactly what I don't want to do.

A barely contained eruption is rising to my surface and I close the space between us, stopping just in front of her. "You want answers? You want to know what door to hell you opened?"

"I want to know about you."

"If I tell you my story, I'll have to kill you. Do you still want to know me?"

"Very much," she says. "So very much."

I should walk away. I should tell her nothing, but I still stand there. I fucking stand there and words come out of my mouth. "I was pulled into a special task force that was off the books. I became the go-to guy to take out hard-to-reach targets. I felt like I made a difference. I kept wars from happening. I kept villages from burning. Until I discovered one of my superiors, and a portion of my team, were running an illegal arms operation and I could tie back some of my kills to the support of that operation."

"What did you do?"

"Myself and Jesse Marks went to a high-level member of government who helped us take down the team. Some of them ended up dead. Others in prison. We both exited the army, but we were both told that if we ever talked, we were dead, and so was everyone close to us. Not long after I exited, I got a call to eliminate Jesse. His family was already dead. They said he killed them. I found him. He said they killed them. But I found his plans to blow up a government building. He was a rabid animal. He'd lost his mind and I put him down. Because that's what I do. I kill people. And the only reason I left your slayer alive was because I didn't want you to hate me more than him."

"I never believed—"

"That I killed that family? You say that, but I saw the look on your face."

"I had just faced that man and learned that you were—"

"A killer?"

"That you didn't trust me enough to tell me. It's like you wanted to shock me and push me away. I've thought about this a lot. You were so quick to leave. To ignore my calls."

"You damn sure packed your bag and got the hell out of my apartment quickly."

"Because you didn't want me there," she hisses. "I went looking for you at the hospital. I begged for a number to call you. They told me I couldn't reach you. The message was clear. I blinked for one moment and that was it. In other words, you didn't really mean it when you told me it was okay to be human when I'm with you. That was a lie."

"I guess it was all a lie, now wasn't it?"

I turn and cross the room, and this time when she calls my name, I don't stop. I get the hell out of that bedroom.

***

Jewel

I should have told him that I love him.

I am back to pacing, this time in my bedroom with male voices coming from the living room. Adam and Asher, if I'm correct. Actually, I think I hear Savage out there too. I now have two SEALs and two Green Berets guarding me, from what must be a massive threat. Or maybe they're here to guard him from me? It's obvious that he doesn't want to talk to me. He has to talk to me. I have to talk to him. I open the door and I find Jacob in the center of the couch, with Savage and Asher on either side of him. Adam on the floor. Some kind of sports is on a laptop they are all watching. A bottle of tequila is sitting on the table—no, make that two. Jacob is holding one of them. There are also two handguns on the table, though I doubt any of them are sober enough to use them.

I storm toward them, shut the laptop and step between the table and Jacob. "I guess the threat is over and you forgot to tell me?"

He gives me a hooded stare. "No news. I'll let you know."

"So bad guys might be coming to kill us and you're drinking tequila."

"Sweetheart, I've killed more men drunk than sober. I'm just that good at killing."

Now, he's just trying to push my buttons. I point at Asher and Savage. "Get up and leave." I glance at Adam. "That means you too."

"I don't think that's a good idea," Asher says.

"I have to agree," Savage says.

"What they said," Jacob adds.

I grab the two handguns and point them at Asher and Savage. "Get up and leave." I look at Asher. "Asher, yes I can shoot left-handed. Try me."

Asher looks at Jacob. "We'll be just outside."

"Yep," Savage says. "Just outside."

I wait for them to leave, and I let the guns lower to my sides. "Now what?" Jacob asks. "You gonna cuff me and then shoot me with those guns?"

I set them both on the cushions on either side of him, and shove his legs part, stepping between them. "No, you asshole. I love you. I loved you before I knew you were an assassin. I love you now. You're killing me. I hate us like this. I don't want to be like this."

"Do you know what they say about loving an assassin?"

"That he'll stab you in the heart and leave you to bleed? You're already killing me. I'm sorry. I obviously read us wrong." I start to leave, and he catches my hand.

"I don't want to hurt you. That's the point."

"The minute you let go of my hand, it will hurt. I don't know how else to explain how much you made me need you."

"Come here," he says, and right when he would pull me to his lap, there is a huge blast through the window. Jacob takes me down to the ground, sheltering me with his body. "Are you okay?" he whispers.

"Yes," I whisper. "Yes, I—"

The front door bursts open and bullets splatter the walls, the sound muffled by silencers.

"Go to the bathroom and lock yourself in," Jacob orders. "I'll come for you." He lifts off of me, and in a blink of an eye, he's firing. I grab my sidearm just in time to shoot the man in black who is jumping through the window. Everything is an adrenaline rush from there. Jacob is wrestling a guy on the island. Savage is on top of another man, shoving a blade in his chest. Another man is on top of Asher. I shoot him. Asher looks at me and gives me a nod, just in time to shoot another intruder as he enters the window. It feels like it will never end, until it does. Everyone on our side is alive. Bodies are clustered on the floor, and Jacob is kneeling next to a man who is bleeding out.

"Was it Emerson?" he asks and then leans down, speaking to the man in a tone I can't hear. The man murmurs, "Emer-son." Jacob stands up and shoots him, his gaze rocketing to me, as if he feels me watching him.

He studies me a moment and then eyes Savage. "Call the number I gave you."

Savage nods and heads for the door. Jacob closes the space between us and stops. "Everyone leave," he orders, and the room clears, the door shutting, leaving just me, Jacob, and a mess of dead men.

"You don't take orders well."

"Is that news to you?"

"No. No, it is not news to me."

Suddenly his fingers are diving into my hair and then he's kissing me like a starving man who can't survive without me. I sink into him, mold myself close and I don't want to let him go, but he pulls away. "I love you, too. It killed me not to be with you."

"Then why did you leave?"

"I can't have this conversation now. I have to go kill someone, because you know I'm good at that."

"Can you do it quickly, because I really need to finish this conversation?"

He strokes my cheek. "I'll be back soon. Savage is going to clean all of this up. Do what he tells you to do." He kisses me again and when it's over, his mouth lingers above mine, as if he can't bring himself to leave. But he does. He releases me and heads for the door.

"Do not die!" I shout after him.

He turns and looks at me. "I have too much to live for now, sweetheart. I'll come for you, soon."

And then he's gone.

And I'm alone.

Chapter Forty-Three

JACOB

I'm sitting in a chair in the dark bedroom of my target when he enters his house. The door opens. The door shuts. The locks flip into place. I sit, patiently waiting on him. Frank Emerson. Fifty-five. Five-star retired general. The man who helped me take down my own team. The man who ordered the hit on myself and Jewel, despite telling me on the phone, not an hour before the attack that he was cancelling any action against Jewel. After the fact, he'd had the balls to call his team rogue. He'd called them dirty. He'd let them die to protect his program. The one with so many dirty kills, too many that I made before I knew they were dirty at all.

Every single one of us involved in that program will go to hell. There's no saving any us but I'll be living longer than he will.

It's a good hour before he heads to the bed, and the clank of ice and glass tells a story. With three glasses of vodka down him, he enters and turns on the light and stops dead in his tracks. To his benefit, he doesn't show fear. Not even when he looks at the gun I have sitting on the bed, on top of a file. "What are you doing here, King?"

"I wanted to say goodbye in person."

"Where are you going?"

"I'm not. You are. See, your commander in the attack on myself and my woman didn't die right away. I promised to give his daughter half a million dollars if he told me how to take you down. It was a long shot, but David People had been with you since before me. And since I knew him, I thought he had to be loyal to you for you to send him after me. But he wasn't. He told me to go to an address."

"Where?"

I wait a few beats to let him suffer. "It was in Alaska," I finally say. "You know the place, right? That hidden spot in the mountains you keep. I took photos of everything. And then my tech, he's real good, he used that and found proof of every dollar you stole from some very nasty people. Iran? Did you really think you could survive stealing from Iranian royalty?"

He pales. "You win, then. No one will ever come after you or her again."

I cross the room to stand in front of him. "Not good enough. If I wake up tomorrow and you're alive, I'm sending everyone you stole from a gift with your name on it. Inside will be your confession and proof of what you stole." I step around him and start walking. He doesn't follow. I'd know.

I walk down the hallway and I stop at the front door. I stand there, giving him time to see how damning the information in that folder is. One second. Two. Ten. A gunshot sounds. Operation fuck-you-once-and-for-all is complete. I open the door and exit, heading into the woods where a motorcycle waits on me. I climb on it and rev the engine, and I know I should disappear. I should walk away from Jewel. Give her space to find another guy. But then I'd have to kill him.

Chapter Forty-Four

Jewel

It's been five long days since Jacob left and I've been staying in his apartment—our apartment again, I hope—without him. The only reason I'm not losing my mind is that Savage has assured me that Jacob is alive and well, and that radio silence is a necessity of mission safety. My survival is staying busy. I run. I run some more. I work a cold case. By ten p.m., I'm dreading the empty bed, so I have milk and Pop-Tarts. I'm about to pour chocolate into the milk when the door beeps. That means Jacob or one of the Walker clan, and none of them would just come right in.

My heart leaps and I set the chocolate down. I turn toward the entrance and stand there, waiting until it opens, and he appears. He steps inside and kicks the door shut, and just that easily he consumes the room and me. He stops when he sees me, and he looks good, so very good, in black jeans and a snug black tee. I'm in sweats, and potentially have Pop-Tart crumbs around my mouth, because apparently, I don't know how to do a sexy welcome home greeting. I just stand there, frozen, afraid to find out where we stand. And he does the same, like he feels the same. "Jewel," he says softly and that is all it takes to jolt me into action.

I move toward him and he does the same and we come together in a collision of bodies. "You're home," I say, because I'm brilliant like that.

"You're home," he says, the words telling me everything, while his mouth seals the deal. He kisses me, oh how he kisses me, a deep drugging, forever kind of kiss. I forget everything. I want everything. I think I say that and somehow my shirt is off, and I got one thing right. I'm not wearing a bra. I get another thing right when I get his shirt off.

He lifts me and carries me upstairs, and the minute we're on the bed, our bed, we're kissing again. Touching each other like we want to crawl under each other's skin. Somehow, some way, the rest of our clothes come off, and then we're on our sides, facing each other, and he's pressing inside me. "God, how I missed you," he whispers, settling in the deepest part of me.

"I missed you, too. Tell me it's over."

"It is," he promises. "But we aren't. You used your one chance to get away."

I open my mouth to tell him I don't want to get away, but he's kissing me again, and cupping my backside to mold us closer. Our bodies are swaying, slow and soft, and then wild and hard. I want to live in this bed, in this moment, forever, but I shatter anyway, and I smile when he shakes with his release. He holds me so hard I think I might break, but I want him to hold me tighter.

"I love you, woman," he whispers.

I pull back to look at him, my fingers curling on the stubble of his jaw. "I love you, too. But I don't understand why you shut me out."

"I'm no Royce Walker. I will never be the good guy who always does good. I need to know you can handle that."

"I'd tell you that you're one of the good guys, but you'd think I had on rose-colored glasses. So, okay. You're a killer. I know it. Now what?"

He seems to consider a moment, and then kisses me. "Get dressed. I want to take you somewhere."

I hurry to the closet and pull on jeans, a T-shirt and boots and join Jacob back in the bedroom. "Where to now?"

"To the airport. I have a private jet waiting on us."

"Where are we going?"

"To Italy so I can ask your father if I can marry his daughter."

I suck in air. "You want to marry me?"

"Yes. I do."

"The detective and the assassin, happily ever after?"

He goes down on one knee, and presents me with a box, which he opens. I suck in a breath at the stunning sapphire and diamond ring. "I wanted it to be unique, like you. Like us. Will you marry me, Jewel?"

"Yes. Yes. I will marry you."

He slides the ring on my finger and then stands up, and we end up back in bed, because the plane will wait, but the assassin will not.

THE END

Looking for more breathtaking suspense? Flip the page to check out MURDER NOTES, book one in my Lilah Love series coming in March!

FALLING UNDER

MURDER NOTES
(Lilah Love Book One)

March 27, 2018
PRE-ORDER NOW HERE:
http://lisareneejones.com/lilah

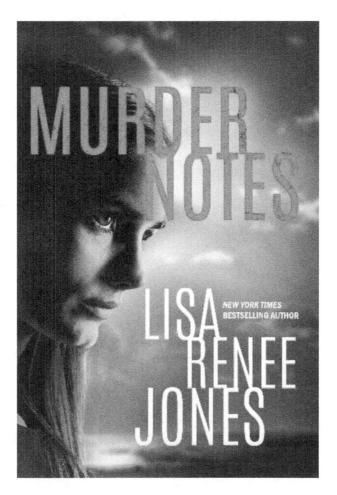

FALLING UNDER

About the Book

Deep in the heart of the night, there is always murder, passion, and lies, even when we don't see it. But FBI agent Lilah Love has seen more than most. Years ago, while at her family's home in the Hamptons, back in the days when she loved the wrong man and trusted the wrong people, she lived a nightmare she can never forget. That horrible night, some think that she saw a little more than she should have. It was a night that changed her life forever and made her abandon the man she's never gotten over, and a future a future in New York near her family, for a one in L.A. as an FBI profiler. But now, a series of brutal murders connect to her home, forcing her to return to the Hamptons, where her father is the mayor, her brother is the police chief, and her ex is now running an empire believed to be as corrupt as he is powerful.

Soon, she is certain she's dealing with an assassin, but more and more there seems to be a connection to a very secret part of her past, and to her ex, who is still a dominant force in the Hamptons, and it seems, her life. Alphabet letters begin appearing on her car, her door, in her house, along with clues that begin to paint a picture that has her questioning everything she knows of her past and threats to that long-kept secret. She calls them her "Murder Notes" and as they continue, they become darker, more threatening, and Lilah begins to worry that "M" is for murder. Lilah must find the sender, and the serial killer, who could be one and the same, before she's the one who ends up dead.

FALLING UNDER

Also by Lisa Renee Jones

The Inside Out Series
If I Were You
Being Me
Revealing Us
His Secrets*
Rebecca's Lost Journals
The Master Undone*
My Hunger*
No In Between
My Control*
I Belong to You
All of Me*

The Secret Life of Amy Bensen
Escaping Reality
Infinite Possibilities
Forsaken
Unbroken*

Careless Whispers
Denial
Demand
Surrender

Dirty Money
Hard Rules
Damage Control
Bad Deeds
End Game

331

FALLING UNDER

White Lies
Provocative
Shameless

Lilah Love
Murder Notes (March 2018)
Murder Girl (July 2018)

*eBook only

About the Author

New York Times and USA Today bestselling author Lisa Renee Jones is the author of the highly acclaimed INSIDE OUT series.

In addition to the success of Lisa's INSIDE OUT series, she has published many successful titles. The TALL, DARK AND DEADLY series and THE SECRET LIFE OF AMY BENSEN series, both spent several months on a combination of the New York Times and USA Today bestselling lists. Lisa is also the author of the bestselling the bestselling DIRTY MONEY and WHITE LIES series. And will be publishing the first book in her Lilah Love suspense series with Amazon Publishing in March 2018.

Prior to publishing Lisa owned multi-state staffing agency that was recognized many times by The Austin Business Journal and also praised by the Dallas Women's Magazine. In 1998 Lisa was listed as the #7 growing women owned business in Entrepreneur Magazine.

Lisa loves to hear from her readers. You can reach her at **www.lisareneejones.com** and she is active on Twitter and Facebook daily.

MAR 2018

CPSIA information can be obtained
at www.ICGtesting.com
Printed in the USA
BVOW11s1645180218
508416BV00001B/1/P